"It is my curse, to speak without thinking.

"Please, forgive me."

She gave him a smile that was both bitter and rueful. "If I had thought before speaking, too, and behaved as you yourself told me I should," she said, "I would not be in this predicament."

He regarded her quizzically. "Predicament?"

She nodded her head. "I fear Lord Cynvelin acted with undue haste."

"What are you saying?" he whispered, scarcely daring to believe what her words seemed to be indicating.

"I am saying that there has been a mistake."

She looked so sorrowful and distressed, he wanted to comfort her. "If you do not wish to stay…"

"I don't."

"You should ask Lord Cynvelin to escort you."

"I have and he will not…. Would you help me?" she asked softly, a pleading look in her eyes.

A trusting look. A look that made him feel an honorable man again.

Dear Reader,

Next month, Harlequin Historicals® turns ten years old! But we have such a terrific lineup this month, we thought we'd start celebrating early. To begin, the ever-popular Margaret Moore returns with her fifteenth book, *A Warrior's Honor,* the next Medieval in her WARRIOR SERIES. Dubbed a "master storyteller" by *Affaire de Coeur,* the versatile Moore brings us the sensational story of a knight who is tricked by a fellow nobleman into abducting a beautiful lady, but, guided by honor—and love—seeks to rescue her from the evil clutches of his former friend.

And in a rescue of a different sort, a rancher turned fugitive inadvertently becomes a bodyguard to the very visible Duchess of Malvern in *The Duchess and the Desperado,* a dynamite Western by award-winning author Laurie Grant. A beautiful young woman on a quest for vengeance unwittingly falls in love with the man she thinks may have harmed her sister in *The Shadowed Heart* by Nina Beaumont.

And don't miss Susan Mallery's latest historical, *Wild West Wife,* the final book in the MONTANA MAVERICKS: RETURN TO WHITEHORN series. This is the story of the very first Kincaid, who kidnaps his enemy's mail-order bride to get revenge but instead falls for his beautiful captive!

Whatever your tastes in reading, you'll be sure to find a romantic journey back to the past between the covers of a Harlequin Historical®.

Sincerely,

Tracy Farrell
Senior Editor

Please address questions and book requests to:
Harlequin Reader Service
U.S.: 3010 Walden Ave., P.O. Box 1325, Buffalo, NY 14269
Canadian: P.O. Box 609, Fort Erie, Ont. L2A 5X3

MARGARET MOORE

confesses that her first "crush" was Errol Flynn. The second was "Mr. Spock." She thinks that explains why her heroes tend to be either charming rogues or lean, inscrutable tough guys.

Margaret lives in Scarborough, Ontario, with her husband, two children and two cats. She used to sew and read for reasons other than research.

To Geoffrey Clayton, Ph.D,
coauthor of
"Starburst-Like Dust Extinction in the
Small Magellanic Cloud"
and
"Ultraviolet Observations of the Hot R Coronae Borealis
Type Star, V348 Sagittarii, During a Deep Minimum,"
among others;
and a friend who reads my books.

Chapter One

England, 1228

Bryce Frechette leaned back against the stone wall, a small, indulgent smile on his face as he watched the boisterous company enjoying the festivities after Lord Melevoir's tournament.

Their host was a genial man who believed in fine food and wine, good sport and loud music. His hall, while not as large as Bryce's father's had been, evinced the Norman nobleman's appreciation for the luxuries a wealthy life afforded. A blazing fire in the hearth dispelled the chill of the spring evening, and fine beeswax candles in a number of holders brightened the room, as did torches in sconces upon the walls.

After an excellent and bountiful meal, the long trestle tables had been taken down and now leaned against the thick stone walls, with the benches in front for those not dancing. Well-fed hounds prowled among the rushes, looking for scraps and somehow managing to avoid getting in the way of the energetic dancers, who whirled past like so many colorful children's tops in the center of the floor.

Bryce reflected it was a wonder some didn't fall and break their heads, especially the ones who were obviously drunk. As it was, the laughing and talking of the lords and ladies nearly drowned out the music of harp, tabor and drum.

His gaze strayed again toward a lovely young woman with dark hair and bright eyes who danced gracefully, and whose joyously merry laugh had nothing to do with too much wine. Sometimes he could see her face clearly when she passed near him in her bright blue gown under an overtunic of indigo and gold brocade, and with her gold jewelry flashing in the light of the candles.

The skin crinkled at the corners of her mirthful, shining green eyes beneath shapely dark brows. Wisps of black hair escaped her headdress and scarf to brush her smooth pink cheeks. He admired her straight and shapely nose, and her full, smiling ruby lips parted to reveal pearl-like teeth.

He wondered who she was and what her name might be. She was without doubt the most attractive woman he had ever seen, and he envied whatever man danced with her, including their portly, elderly host.

If he were titled still, Bryce thought, he would be dancing with her, too, looking into those expressive, vivacious eyes and, he had to admit, trying to get her into a shadowed corner to steal a kiss from those enticing lips.

But he was not titled, he reminded himself with a bitter scowl. He was not the Earl of Westborough, although by rights he should be; he had no estate.

And the beauty was probably a spoiled, pampered young woman who would want nothing to do with the likes of him.

He could not even afford an extra shirt. The only one he possessed had been torn in the tournament, so he had been forced to come to the feast wearing only his leather tunic. Acutely conscious of his less-than-well-dressed state, he nevertheless wanted to enjoy the banquet a little longer. It gave him a taste of the life he used to know, when his father was alive.

Therefore, he told himself, it didn't matter who she was or what her name might be, any more than it mattered that these noblemen and their ladies ignored him.

As if to refute that rankling thought, a darkly handsome man with a silver goblet in his hand came to sit next to Bryce on the bench. Bryce knew he was a Welshman, and the black-haired beauty had been talking and laughing with him before joining in the dance with Lord Melevoir.

"Seen happier faces on a tomb, I have," the stranger remarked casually. "And you winning the purse, too! A pity it is ten silver pieces don't make you happy. I'll gladly take them from you if that would please you."

"You could try," Bryce answered in a calm yet warning tone.

"Ust, man, no need to sound so fierce." The

Welshman grinned, his eyes dancing with merriment. "You deserved to win. There aren't many who can beat me, but glad I am to say that I do not bear a grudge. Look you, you were the finest with the lance on the field, and it would be a fool who would say otherwise. I am not a fool."

Bryce relaxed, pleased by the fellow's manner as much as his words. It had been a long time since a nobleman had treated him as an equal. "Forgive my lack of courtesy, sir," he said with an answering smile. "I would that every man I bested spoke with such generosity." He bent his head in welcome. "I am Bryce Frechette."

"Generosity, is it?" the dark-haired man replied. "Good sense, I call it, and of course I know who you are."

Bryce mentally braced himself for the inevitable questions.

Which did not come. "I am Lord Cynvelin ap Hywell of Caer Coch, the finest estate in Wales," his companion announced jovially. He ran another appraising glance over the Norman. "I've made it my business to hire the best men for my company. I hope you will consider joining my retinue."

Bryce's first impulse was to refuse. He was not born to be any man's hireling.

"Since we are gentlemen, we will not barter terms like merchants. If you agree, you shall have whatever you require in arms, clothing, food and lodging, and if, after a year or so, we are both well pleased with one another, I see no reason I should not reward you further."

Bryce knew he could always make a living fighting in tournaments. If worse came to worst, he could go to his sister and find a home in her castle.

Yet he had been traveling and fighting for years, and no one else had ever offered him such a chance. As for going to his sister…he would feel like a beggar at their gate.

Bryce's pride gave way to practicality. His family had lost title and estate, and all the money he had was the ten coins in his purse. If he didn't accept this nobleman's offer, eventually he would be reduced to fighting in yet another tournament and hoping to win a prize, as if he were a trained bear fighting for his food.

Besides, this fellow was not just friendly, but respectful, too. Both were rare reactions to him these days. And, he reasoned, how difficult could service in such a man's retinue be? He could always leave it if he chose to, and his alternatives were few indeed.

"My lord, I shall be delighted to accept," he answered with another bow of his head.

Lord Cynvelin clapped his hand on Bryce's shoulder and smiled warmly. "Excellent, my friend!"

Bryce took a deep breath. "You can rely on me, my lord," he said, the words almost a challenge.

Lord Cynvelin became serious. "If I thought it would be otherwise, I would not have made the offer. Many of us were foolish and headstrong youths. Besides, man, think what it will do for my glory when others hear that Bryce Frechette, champion of Lord Melevoir's tournament, is in my company."

Bryce nodded, pleased and relieved and flattered all at once.

"We leave for Wales after mass tomorrow. I trust you can be ready?"

"Wales?"

"Aye. Where else would a Welshman live?"

Bryce nodded. "Of course."

"That is not a trouble to you, is it?"

"No, my lord," Bryce replied, stifling any reluctance to travel into the wilderness inhabited by the Celts.

"Good." Lord Cynvelin sighed and took a drink of his wine. "A fine feast, this. I have never seen so many pretty ladies in one place."

"Pretty, rich and titled ladies," Bryce amended, giving his newfound friend a sardonic glance. "That puts them out of my reach."

Lord Cynvelin chuckled and looked at Bryce appraisingly. "You're as good-looking a man as I've ever seen, except for myself, of course. I would find it difficult to believe you would have to sleep alone tonight."

Bryce's smile had a tinge of bitterness. "Given my lack of title, none of these ladies would look at me twice."

The remarkably handsome Cynvelin laughed, a deep, rich bass laugh that caused several people to look their way questioningly, including the beautiful unknown.

"Look you at all the women watching us," Cynvelin said when he quieted. "What more proof do you need?"

Bryce slid a surreptitious glance around the hall. "It's you they're watching, my lord."

"Well and why not?" Lord Cynvelin observed with another chuckle. "But you, too. I noticed when I was at the dancing. And you it was took the finest prize in the joust when you got your lance through the ring five times. I tell you, man, you have but to crook your finger and you could have your choice to share your bed tonight."

"I think I would do better to prepare for the journey tomorrow."

Lord Cynvelin smiled. "If you would rather. I can only admire such dedication to duty. As for me, I'm off to speak to the woman I'm going to marry, if she'll have me. There she is, dancing with Lord Melevoir. Have you ever seen a more graceful, lovely creature than Rhiannon DeLanyea?"

"She is very beautiful," Bryce observed, watching the no-longer-unknown beauty step lightly to the music and deftly avoid their host's awkward and large feet.

"I warn you, Bryce Frechette, she belongs to me," Cynvelin chided, his eyes full of laughter. "Besides, her father is half-Welsh, and a baron, and a very fierce fellow. The man who would win his daughter's love will have to deal with him."

"I assure you, my lord, I have no interest in her beyond the admiration all men must accord her."

Cynvelin chuckled again. "You speak like a Norman nobleman right enough," he said as he rose. He straightened his black tunic and adjusted the gold-embossed belt at his waist. "Now then, I will go to her rescue. We shall meet at the stables in the morning, Frechette.''

Bryce nodded his farewell, then watched Lord Cynvelin stroll across Lord Melevoir's hall and approach the beauteous Rhiannon DeLanyea.

Lady Rhiannon DeLanyea, Bryce silently corrected, who was his new overlord's intended bride.

Well, so be it, he thought as he once again leaned against the wall, smiling to himself. He had come to believe that no nobleman would ever offer friendship or treat him as an equal again. That he would forever be the dishonored, disgraced son of the Earl of Westborough.

Now it seemed there was hope that this could change and he might yet gain title on his own merits. If that, what else could he not hope for?

After all, there would be other laughing, beautiful young noblewomen who would not be beyond the reach of a knighted Bryce Frechette.

Rhiannon sat upon the nearest bench and tried to catch her breath. Lord Melevoir bowed his graying head and she reciprocated before the elderly nobleman tottered away, looking for somebody else with whom to dance.

At least she had managed to stay on her feet, she reflected as she fanned herself with her hand. Lord Melevoir had been rather zealous in the round dance, and at one point, Rhiannon had feared she was going to be sent spinning into the musicians.

''Some wine, please,'' she panted when a maidservant appeared at her elbow.

"Allow me, my lady," a masculine voice said in Welsh, and slender, familiar fingers held out a goblet.

She accepted the drink gratefully and looked up into the smiling face of Lord Cynvelin ap Hywell.

"Lord Cynvelin!" she said happily. "How good of you! Thirsty, I am, and worn my feet to my anklebones, I think."

"There is not a more lovely, delightful dancer here, so all the men want to take a turn with you," he answered, sitting beside her.

Rhiannon smiled in response, then took another drink, nearly choking. *"O'r annwyl!"* she spluttered as Cynvelin quickly moved to take the goblet from her. "If I am not careful, I will be reeling about like a sot. Lord Melevoir is a most excellent man and so is his wine. I am not used to such full-bodied drink."

"Whereas I am getting drunk only on your beauty," Cynvelin replied in a low voice.

Pleasantly flattered, Rhiannon blushed. "I thought you didn't like me anymore. You might have rescued me sooner from the round dance instead of talking to that Saxon. Imagine coming to a feast without a shirt on!"

She nodded at the man seated across the hall. His brown hair fell to his broad shoulders, and he wore only a plain leather tunic laced up the front, open at the neck with no shirt beneath, so that his bare, muscular arms and chest were exposed. There was something almost savage or untamed about him, and the unnerving way his gaze darted about made her feel he was containing a vigorous energy that he could release at will.

"A Norman he is, my lady," Lord Cynvelin revealed. "And don't your father and brothers wear their hair in such a fashion? I have heard that they do."

Rhiannon laughed gaily. "Indeed, you are right. They claim it makes their helmets sit better, although in the case of my brothers, I think it is only vanity. Perhaps it is so with that fellow."

"Have you never heard of Bryce Frechette, the Earl of Westborough's son?"

Rhiannon regarded Lord Cynvelin with genuine surprise. "Of course! Everyone knows about him, and how he argued with his father and left home, and never came back even when his father lay dying. I wonder what he's doing here? I'm surprised he dares to show his face among noble folk."

She glanced at the disgraced Norman again, to see him rise and saunter toward the opposite end of the hall. His walk had all the grace of a large cat, and once more she had that sense of a contained power waiting for release.

"And to think you had never heard of me until we met three days ago, whereas you know all about that fellow," Lord Cynvelin said with a wounded air. "You are breaking my heart."

She smiled at her countryman. "I am sorry to be breaking your heart, but I'm sure there are plenty of other ladies here who would like to help you mend it."

"There is only one lady who can do that," he replied with unmistakable significance.

"Oh, I think not, my lord," she said with a laugh,

suddenly rather uncomfortable. To be sure, she liked the Welsh nobleman and found his attention flattering, but there was a new, searching quality to his gaze she found disconcerting. "Lady Valmont would surely gladly give away her estate and count it well lost if she thought she could win your heart."

"Perhaps if I am rejected by a better lady, I might have to console myself with a woman obviously inferior and take an estate as a consolation prize." He leaned closer, so that his breath was hot on her cheeks and she could smell the wine on it, too. "But I would rather not. Besides, I think you overestimate my ability to attract a Norman lady. Lady Valmont has no use for Welshmen. Look you how she's staring at Frechette."

"Only because he is a dishonorable rogue, I'm sure," she said soothingly. "Lady Valmont has made no secret of her fondness for scoundrels."

"Are you saying, my lady, that *I* am a scoundrel?" he asked worriedly, placing his palm against his cheek in a gesture of dismay.

"Oh, most certainly not!"

Her companion gave her another smile. "Then I forgive Frechette his notoriety," he said magnanimously. "I hope you will not question my judgment when I tell you I have asked him to join my retinue when I leave for Wales tomorrow."

Rhiannon paid little attention to the first part of Lord Cynvelin's announcement. "You are leaving tomorrow?"

"After mass."

"My father comes tomorrow," she reminded him. "I was hoping you would be able to meet him."

Lord Cynvelin's expression was all contrition and regret. "Alas, my lady, I cannot linger here, as much as I would like to. I have business that requires my immediate attention."

"Oh."

"Perhaps I might be permitted to visit you at Craig Fawr when my business is concluded," he suggested.

She could think of no reason he should not, beyond a certain discomfort in his suddenly proprietary manner. "We shall be pleased to welcome you."

"I shall count the hours until I see you again," Lord Cynvelin whispered, gazing at her with eyes full of meaning.

She blushed again and looked away, taken aback by the possessive expression in his dark eyes. Did he want to meet her father because he wanted to ask for her hand?

She liked Lord Cynvelin. She admired him and she was pleased that he apparently admired her. She respected him. He was Welsh. For those reasons she had sought out his company during Lord Melevoir's tournament and invited him to Craig Fawr.

But she had only known him three days. That was hardly enough time to know him well, and certainly not enough to fall in love or commit herself to marriage.

Her mother often cautioned her to be more circumspect, and right now Rhiannon wished she had heeded that advice. Obviously she had inadvertently given him cause to believe she cared more for him than she did.

"If you will excuse me, my lady," he said, standing, to her undeniable relief, "I must speak with Lord Melevoir before I leave and thank him for his hospitality. Then I should retire to my quarters."

"Yes, certainly, my lord," she stammered, flushing even more as he lifted her hand and pressed a kiss upon it, looking at her with an expectant expression.

"Until later, my lady."

He bowed low and strolled away, and for the first time since she had made his acquaintance, she was happy to see him go.

Until later? What had he meant?

She almost groaned aloud. Did he think she was willing to join him in his quarters?

What *had* she made him believe?

She watched him pause to speak with Lady Valmont, who gave her a speculative look. Did she wonder, too, at the nature of the relationship between Rhiannon and Lord Cynvelin?

Looking away, Rhiannon's gaze encountered a group of Norman noblewomen whispering and smiling as they glanced at her.

What did all these people assume?

Suddenly the hall seemed too crowded and far too hot. She rose and hurried out into the cooler air of the courtyard. It was a huge open area, surrounded by the high inner walls. Beyond that lay another ward encircled by thicker outer walls, and the most imposing gatehouse Rhiannon had ever seen.

She slowed her pace to a more sedate walk, as befitted a gentlewoman.

Then she halted. His back to her, a man stood in the shadows near some carts outside the barracks where the visiting knights and their retinues were housed. He seemed to be rummaging among the goods on the back of one of the wagons, yet it was too late and too dark for any of the castle servants to be preparing for a journey.

"You, there! What are you doing?" she called out, moving closer, prepared to summon the guards if need be.

She realized the man had shoulder-length hair only a moment before Bryce Frechette turned to face her. "I am looking for my baggage, which isn't in the barracks. I was told one of the servants put it here by mistake."

As he spoke, Rhiannon saw that he did resemble a Saxon more than a Norman, with his hair to his broad shoulders, angular face and an aloof, slightly disgruntled expression.

He also stood in an interesting manner, as if he were in a relaxed battle stance. She knew only one other man who stood that way when not actually engaged in combat. Urien Fitzroy, a friend of her father's, was credited with being the finest trainer of fighting men in England.

Bryce Frechette was a most imposing warrior, too, and yet, now that she was close to him, she did not find him frightening. She found him rather intriguing and wished she could see his face more clearly, particularly his shadowed eyes. "I'm sorry. I made a mistake."

"Did you think I was trying to steal something?" he charged.

"Yes...no..." she began, then she straightened her shoulders defensively. "You must appreciate that your activity did look questionable."

"Especially when I am not a nobleman?" he queried, his tone ostensibly polite, but with an undercurrent of hostility.

Why should he have cause to be angry at her? she wondered, her own ire rising when she recalled what she knew of him. "If you are no longer a nobleman, you have only yourself to blame, Bryce Frechette," she retorted.

"I am honored to think you know my name, Lady Rhiannon," he replied sarcastically, and with a mockery of a bow.

He was pleased to see her surprise that he knew her name, too, and some of the haughtiness fled her face. He reached out and grabbed her hand, bending low as if he would kiss the back of it.

She snatched it away. "Obviously I know more than just your name," she said.

"Perhaps you do not know as much as you think you do, my lady," he said quietly, stepping closer.

He noted that she didn't move away and remembered how she had behaved in the hall, especially when she was with Lord Cynvelin. Perhaps she was not nearly as virtuous as she seemed. "Would you care to learn more?"

"I might. But this is hardly the time or place for such a conversation," she finished firmly.

Her forthright answer took him aback, but he recovered quickly. "That is a great pity," he replied, his deep voice seductively low. "I would like to know more about you."

Rhiannon cleared her throat. She had been complimented and flattered much these past few days, but no other man's words seemed to stir her as his did. "Yes, well, another time," she prevaricated.

"Why in so much of a hurry, my lady? Are you going to meet someone?" he said, advancing toward her.

"No!" She retreated into a shadowed alcove, then raised her chin in defiance of his insolence.

He cocked his head to one side and ran an admiring gaze from the top of her silk scarf to the hem of her gown.

"Please don't look at me in that impertinent manner, sir!" she said, her whole body warming as he continued to regard her steadily.

"Sir? I see I am rising in your estimation. Let me assure you, my lady, I do not mean to be rude. Far from it." He took another step closer and smiled.

Not as Lord Cynvelin smiled, as if it were nothing more than a habit. She suddenly felt such a smile from this man was a rare thing, and very much to be prized.

She wished she could see his face better, but it was too dark here in the shadows.

She suddenly realized he had backed her nearly

into a corner, and they were quite shielded from the view of the men on the wall walk above.

"From the way you were acting in the hall," he continued in a husky whisper, "I thought you enjoyed being the object of men's admiration."

"Some men's perhaps," she answered, crossing her arms over her chest defensively, feeling far too vulnerable. "However, I have no wish to be noticed by a man who would abandon his family and leave his sister in such a perilous situation. Indeed, I was surprised to learn that Lord Cynvelin would want such a person in his company."

He froze, staring at her. Then his brows lowered ominously and she remembered the sense of controlled power that had seemed to emanate from him. "That is what you think of me?"

"Yes," she retorted.

He stepped back. "You surprise me, my lady. I thought you had more intelligence than to believe rumors and gossip."

"So what I have heard is not true? You did not quarrel with your father and leave in a huff like a spoiled child? You did not stay away, even when your father lay dying? Are you telling me that contrary to everything I have heard, you returned to help your sister, who was left impoverished and had to become a servant in her own castle?"

"Have you not heard more?" he charged. "That I am a rogue and wastrel? That my sister cast me out? That her husband, the mighty Baron DeGuerre, detests me? That I lie and cheat and steal?" He came close again. "That I have sold my soul to the devil?"

She gasped, her eyes wide, until he chuckled scornfully.

"Have you so little sense that you will believe everything you hear?" he said.

"How dare you!" she cried, shocked by his criticism. "You dishonorable—"

"No, my lady, how dare *you?*" he demanded quietly, his voice as cold as ice. "You know me not, yet you dare to chastise me for my past actions. You do not know why my father and I quarreled, or why I left as I did. You do not know why I stayed away, or how I felt when I learned what had happened." His voice dropped. "You do not know how I have suffered, knowing that I was not with Gabriella when she needed me most."

Rhiannon flushed with guilt when she heard the remorse in his voice. She had been wrong to judge him so quickly, she thought contritely, yet before she could speak, he was suddenly directly in front of her, his face no more than a hand span from hers.

"Who are you to stand in judgment of me?" he demanded. "I could believe, from the way you danced and smiled and laughed with more than one man in Lord Melevoir's hall, that if I am lacking in scruples, I am not the only one. So how dare you, my lovely hypocrite? How dare *you* act as you have, and then upbraid me?"

He looked at her so intently it was as if his gaze rooted her to the ground. She couldn't speak. She couldn't make an answer to his charges, or utter one word to excuse her own behavior.

He came even closer, so that his body was within

a hairbreadth of hers, and when he spoke again, his voice was a low, husky growl. "How dare you stand there in the shadows looking as desirable as any woman I have ever seen, yet if I were to so much as touch you, you would probably call out for the guard and denounce me for a disgraceful villain?"

She swallowed hard, unable to take her eyes from his face. "I wouldn't," she said softly.

His expression seemed to change. "You would not do that, my lady?" he whispered, shifting closer. "You would not call out the guard and condemn me for acting on my desire?"

He reached out and gently ran his hand up her arm, his touch sending thrilling tremors of excitement through her.

"I am glad to hear it, for you are the most tempting woman I have ever seen."

He put his hands on her shoulders and pulled her into his warm embrace.

She knew she should pull away, and yet the moment his mouth touched hers, kissing him did not seem wrong, or immoral, or disgraceful. It felt absolutely, perfectly right.

She had been kissed before, by shy boys who pecked her cheek or lips. Never like this, with power and passion and a desire that seemed to call forth an equally strong reaction from deep within her.

Never had a man's tongue pressed urgently to enter her mouth.

That did not seem wrong, either, but absolutely, perfectly right, and so she opened her lips to him.

His arms tightened about her. Slowly, languorously, she began to caress the smooth leather of his tunic. As his mouth continued to work its seductive magic, his tense muscles relaxed beneath her fingers.

He gently pushed her back so that she was against the wall. Then his knee thrust between her legs, and her body began to throb with an unfamiliar, primitive anticipation.

Suddenly the door to the hall opened and light spilled into the courtyard. A raucous voice called out a good-night.

At the boisterous interruption, Lady Rhiannon DeLanyea gasped, then a horrified expression passed over her face before she pushed Bryce away from her, lifted her skirts and fled.

Chapter Two

Bryce Frechette muttered an oath as he watched Lady Rhiannon run away. What had just happened here?

What more might have happened if that door had not opened?

Then another curse sprang to his lips as he just as suddenly recalled that Lord Cynvelin ap Hywell wanted to marry her.

God's wounds, he was a fool. If she told *him* of their confrontation…

Was he never going to learn to curb his impulses? What did it matter that she was a beautiful, intriguing woman who spoke to him frankly, as an equal. Why hadn't he left her after he had explained what he was doing at the baggage carts?

He had already caused no end of trouble and shame because he followed his desires first and thought afterward. Had he learned nothing in all the years since he had left home?

Bryce slumped against the wall. It would serve him right if he had lost the opportunity Lord Cynvelin had kindly offered, and he would have only himself to blame.

No, not only himself. Not this time. She was just as culpable as he for what had occurred in the shadows. Lady Rhiannon had not uttered so much as a murmur of protest when he had taken her in his arms. Indeed, she had responded as fervently to his kiss as any man could ever hope.

Surely she would say nothing to Lord Cynvelin, not unless she was willing to lie.

Which she might very well do.

Scowling, Bryce pushed off from the wall. If questioned, he would not lie, he decided. He would tell Lord Cynvelin exactly what has passed, and let the Welshman believe what he would.

The next morning, Rhiannon scanned the gathering in the chapel. She easily spotted Lord Cynvelin, dressed for traveling in a short black tunic, brown breeches and with a black cloak of light wool thrown over his broad shoulders. He stood beside Lady Valmont, so close that their shoulders touched, and he seemed to be whispering in the lady's ear almost constantly.

Good. He might not notice *her*, then, and hopefully she could get to the hall to break the fast without having to speak to him. After last night, she thought avoiding him would save her any awkward moments or explanations.

She had even considered avoiding the rest of Lord Melevoir's guests, too. Then she had decided she couldn't stay hidden in her chamber like a terrified mouse. She had to know if she had been seen in the arms of Bryce Frechette, or if he had told anyone that she had acted little better than a wanton bawd last night.

That kind of gossip was too scandalous not to fly about the castle like a feather in a stiff breeze, and this morning, she could sympathize with Bryce's denunciation of hearsay.

Fortunately, no one seemed to be taking any special notice of her. Nobody stared or darted pointed glances her way. Everyone who caught her eye gave her a friendly smile, not a smirk of derision.

She sighed with relief.

Nevertheless, she was glad the Norman was not at mass. She didn't know what she would do if she had to speak to him.

Perhaps he, too, regretted what had happened between them. After all, he had not treated her as befitted her station.

Just as she had not behaved as befitted her station, or she would have gone on her way the moment she had realized he was not a thief rifling through a baggage cart.

It had to be because he was not what she had expected that she had lingered. He was not a wastrel, for he had behaved with all due decorum at the feast, even holding himself rather aloof from the other celebrants. He was not a bully and a hothead…or rather, not until he was provoked, perhaps.

She had obviously provoked him—but then, he had not been right to criticize her behavior. That was for her parents.

As for what her father would make of her behavior in the courtyard last night, letting herself be guided into the shadows, out of sight of the guards, alone with a young, virile, misunderstood, exciting man....

She shuddered—and she was not thinking of her father's reaction.

One of Lord Melevoir's guests, who was standing beside her, gave her a quizzical look that reminded her she was in company. Besides, she chided herself, she shouldn't be having such thoughts, not in a chapel. Not of a dispossessed nobleman, who had kissed her with such fervent passion.

She could only hope that Bryce Frechette never saw fit to brag of his easy conquest.

And she would never, *ever,* allow herself to be put in such a confusing, overwhelming situation again.

The mass ended at last, and she quickly went outside into the chill of a spring morning. She walked briskly toward the hall, her only concern getting inside before Lord Cynvelin saw her.

Outside the stable she passed Lord Cynvelin's black horse, saddled and waiting. His men and his baggage carts were all ready to leave, too, apparently, for several of his guards loitered nearby, some leaning against the stable walls.

"Wonder if she's a moaner or a screamer?" a rough Welsh voice muttered just loudly enough for her to hear.

Rhiannon halted and slowly swiveled on her heel to look at the lout who dared to make such a rude remark in her hearing. She thought it was the brawny

fellow who ran a bold gaze over her, for he grinned
when she looked at him.

"What did you say?" she demanded in Welsh,
putting her hands on her hips.

"Nothing, my lady," he answered with wide-
eyed—and quite false—innocence.

"Is there some trouble here?" a familiar deep
voice said in Norman French.

Her whole body warmed as Bryce Frechette came
to stand beside her, as if he had materialized out of
thin air.

As before, he was simply attired in leather jerkin
and breeches, his sword belt slung low on his narrow
hips. Despite his lack of mail or other armor, he
seemed far more imposing than the chain-mailed
brawny fellow, perhaps because of his regal bearing
and the sense of self-confidence that seemed as much
a part of him as his deep brown eyes or sensuous
mouth.

What on earth was she doing, thinking about his
mouth? She was supposed to be quite properly indignant.

He looked at the man, then her, his expression
inscrutable. "Is anything wrong?"

Rhiannon lifted her chin slightly. "He said something rude to me."

"Is that so?" Bryce asked before walking toward
the soldier. His tone had been calm and noncommittal, but she saw the tension in his shoulders and
guessed that he was angry. "Did you say something
rude to the lady?"

The man gave him a blank look and answered in Welsh.

"He says he doesn't understand you," Rhiannon explained.

Bryce glanced at her over his shoulder. "But you understood him, did you not, my lady?"

"Unfortunately, I did."

In the next moment, Bryce had the man pinned against the wall, his hands on the man's shoulders. "Apologize to the lady," he muttered between clenched teeth. "You understand that, don't you?"

The man looked at Rhiannon with fear in his eyes. "I don't understand him!" he cried in Welsh. "What did I do?"

Rhiannon ran forward and grabbed Bryce's arm, his muscles hard beneath her fingers. "He doesn't understand you! Let him go."

Bryce didn't move. "Then you tell him he should apologize to you, or by God, he will be sorry."

Rhiannon quickly told the man what the Norman had said, and just as quickly the Welsh soldier stammered out an apology.

Bryce let go and the man slumped to the ground. The rest of the men gathered round him, a few casting wary glances at the Norman.

"As grateful as I am for your championship of my honor, I fear you've made some enemies," Rhiannon said when Bryce turned to face her. She tried to keep an icy demeanor, even though she felt as hot as if she were in the deserts of the east, and if the trickle of perspiration made her feel as if the ice was melting, that had to be because of her physical activity moments before.

He didn't look at all concerned. "I should thank you, my lady, for the opportunity to show my soon-to-be companions-in-arms that I am not to be trifled with," he remarked grimly. "Otherwise, I might have been forced to create a situation myself."

Her eyes widened. "Do you often have to create situations, sir? Or is it more usual for you to wait until a lady is insulted, and then you rush to her defense to prove your manliness?"

"I never thought my manliness was in question," he replied.

Her cheeks grew warm with a blush as he continued to regard her. "Your effort to make him apologize seemed rather extreme," she noted.

"I know."

She knew she should leave, yet courtesy decreed she say more. "You were most effective," she admitted. "You have my thanks, Frechette."

He bowed stiffly. "It was my honor."

She glanced around and noted that the soldiers had moved off, away from them, and that no one else was near. "Frechette?" she began, her tone conspiratorial.

His gaze likewise grew serious. "Yes, my lady?"

"You...you will not tell anyone about last night, in the courtyard?"

His expression personified frigid offense. "Did you think I would?"

She was dismayed to think she had insulted him, yet she had to be certain he would continue to be silent. "As you said, and rightly, I do not know you."

She thought he looked a little surprised, but she could not be sure.

"Then know that I will keep what happened a secret between us," he replied, "and I trust you will not disparage me to Lord Cynvelin."

"No!" she cried, startled. "We will just pretend it never happened."

He nodded, but there was a look in his eyes that made her flush again. She knew he would not forget, and neither would she.

She would not forget the passion he had aroused within her, or his harsh condemnation of her apparent hypocrisy. She would always remember the bitter remorse beneath his ostensible anger when he spoke of his sister. She would never forget him, no matter how much she thought she should.

Then, out of the corner of her eye, she caught a most unwelcome sight.

Lord Cynvelin was striding toward them, concern on every feature. "My lady! What's amiss?"

Rhiannon had no choice but to acknowledge the speaker, so she turned away from Bryce, who immediately moved toward his horse.

She also noticed that Lord Melevoir and the other guests were making a more leisurely progress toward the hall, and they were watching.

Very aware that many people could hear them, Rhiannon spoke in Welsh when her countryman drew near. "All is well in hand, my lord," she replied lightly.

"I am glad to hear it, and I am very glad to see you. I knew you would not let me leave without bidding me farewell." He took her hand and kissed the back of it. "I thought to see you last night, but you had disappeared."

"I decided to retire."

"I missed you," he said softly.

She swallowed hard. "Yes, well, the hall was hot and I was tired."

He glanced up at the sky, and she did likewise. "We intend to make an early start and break our fast upon the road," he told her. "The weather threatens to change."

He was quite right. Gray clouds were moving in from the west. She also noted with relief that his manner was as open and friendly and distant as it had been when she had first met him, with none of that sense of hidden meaning of moments ago.

They looked at each other and she, happy that he was leaving, smiled. "A good journey to you, my lord."

"Is that all you have to say to me, my beautiful Rhiannon?" he whispered, regarding her with the significant look in his dark eyes that had been there last night. He moved closer as if unaware that they were in the full view of so many people. Including Bryce Frechette.

She felt helpless. She knew she should try to correct whatever false impression she might have given him—but here, where everyone could see?

"All for now," she prevaricated, not meeting his gaze.

"Until I see you again?"

"If you wish."

"If you only knew what I wish!" he murmured.

She blushed even more, feeling that this situation was unbearably awkward.

Then she began to get angry. Could he not see her reluctance? Did he not realize how embarrassing this was?

"Farewell, my lord," she said, a hint of challenging defiance in her voice as she began to turn away.

Without warning, Lord Cynvelin suddenly pulled her into his embrace and pressed a hot, fierce kiss upon her mouth.

She was too stunned to move.

Then he stopped and stepped away, giving her a triumphant smile. She glanced swiftly at Bryce Frechette. What must he be thinking?

His expression was enigmatic, yet that seemed a condemnation, nonetheless.

"My lord," she said sternly, keeping her voice low by great effort. She had no desire to make more of a spectacle than they already had. "Perhaps it would be better if you were to wait for my father to issue you an invitation to Craig Fawr before visiting there."

"I...I beg your pardon?" he said, obviously as surprised by her words and tone as she had been by his kiss.

"I believe you heard me. Do not come to Craig Fawr until my father invites you. Good day, my lord."

She turned on her heel and walked toward the hall.

* * *

From his place beside his horse as he waited to mount, Bryce watched Lady Rhiannon leave Lord Cynvelin and enter the hall.

They must be as good as formally betrothed for the Welshman to kiss her in such a way and in so public a place, he thought, even if last night, with him, she had not acted as if she belonged to another man.

What kind of woman was Rhiannon DeLanyea?

Perhaps she was the type of woman whose affections changed almost every hour. Her passion had certainly seemed sincere when he had kissed her.

Or perhaps she was the kind he had originally accused her of being, a woman who enjoyed men's attention—many men, and many kinds of attention, including the most intimate?

If so, Lord Cynvelin was more to be pitied than envied.

The Welshman bowed to the people who were still gathered in the courtyard. "Alas, she is sorry to see me leave!" he announced mournfully.

Bryce supposed that would explain her abrupt departure as well as anything else.

After his remark, Lord Cynvelin was rewarded with sympathetic looks from the women, and knowing chuckles from the men as he turned toward Bryce.

"Excellent morning, Frechette, is it not?" the nobleman demanded cheerfully as he strolled toward Bryce and his men. "A good day for a journey, eh?"

"Yes, my lord."

For a moment, Bryce contemplated telling the nobleman about the lady's behavior.

Then he checked himself. He had only just met Lord Cynvelin, and the lady, too. Even if Bryce was trying to warn him, it could be that Lord Cynvelin would condemn the messenger without heeding the message. Besides, how would he explain what he had been doing in the shadowed corner of the courtyard with her?

And if Lady Rhiannon was a minx, Bryce told himself, she would surely take up with another man before they were five miles down the road, and Lord Cynvelin would find out the truth on his own.

When Lord Cynvelin reached Bryce, the nobleman gave him a curious look. "What happened here before I came?"

"Nothing of consequence, my lord. Your lady felt insulted by one of your men and I insured the fellow apologized."

Lord Cynvelin ran a scrutinizing gaze over his men, who all wore full chain mail beneath their black tunics. Bryce had also noted that their weapons were very fine, and their accoutrements the best. It seemed his new overlord spared no expense on his troops, even if some of them were lacking the proper respect due their lord's bride. "Which of them upset her?"

"I'm certain he will not do so again, my lord," Bryce answered, somewhat surprised. The man made it sound as if he were a child, expected to tell tales on another.

He thought he saw a flash of disapproval in the Welshman's eyes, but must have been mistaken, for

Lord Cynvelin laughed. "If you chastised him, I'm satisfied."

"The lady needed little help."

"She has her father's pride, no doubt."

Surprised by the slightly hostile tone in the man's voice, Bryce gave him a curious sidelong glance. "It was my pleasure to defend her honor."

"Rhiannon was grateful, of course."

"I gather you have reached an understanding with the lady," Bryce remarked, leaving aside all talk of gratitude as Cynvelin checked his saddle before mounting.

"Obviously."

"I offer you my congratulations, my lord."

"Thank you." Cynvelin surveyed his men and baggage carts. "Well, then, we are all ready to leave. Come, let us away," he ordered, moving his horse to the front of the cortege.

Yes, let us away, Bryce seconded inwardly, telling himself he was pleased to be taking his leave of confusing, flirtatious beauties who lured men into the shadows when they were as good as betrothed to another.

Bryce glanced back at the guest apartments, expecting to see the teasing Lady Rhiannon watching her beloved depart, a handkerchief poised to catch her sorrowful tears.

If she was there, he did not see her.

That afternoon, Rhiannon rushed toward the merry company of knights and soldiers who rode into Lord Melevoir's courtyard.

For the moment, her joy at her father's arrival took precedence over any dread she might be feeling about certain events becoming known to him. Although she no longer feared her encounter with Bryce Frechette would become common knowledge, she could not entertain any similar hope that Lord Cynvelin's kiss would be forgotten by those who had witnessed it, or that they would have realized she was not a willing participant.

Certain looks and whispers had already passed between some of the other ladies since the incident, which made her certain that what had happened this morning was the talk of the castle.

She told herself not to worry. Her father would understand. Her anxiety would have been much worse if there was a chance he might hear about her impulsive response to Bryce Frechette.

There were only twenty men in her father's party, but it seemed like more as their Welsh banter echoed off the stone walls surrounding the courtyard. Then her father caught sight of her and waved.

She was so proud to be Baron DeLanyea's daughter! How commanding he looked, sitting upon his horse with all the majesty of a king, even though his clothing and accoutrements were plain and without ornamentation. He could be fierce, she knew. She had heard the stories of his battles.

But he had always been the doting father to her. She chewed her lip and hoped he would continue to be so, despite what he heard. Then she smiled and returned his gesture.

She looked beyond him, her smile growing as she

saw that her foster brother, the roguishly handsome Dylan, was behaving in typical fashion. He was paying more attention to the female servants than anything else.

In contrast to Dylan, her elder brother, the grave, gray-eyed Griffydd, was not bantering or gawking at women. Instead, he surveyed his surroundings with deliberate care. She knew that should she ask him later, he would be able to tell her the exact number of men-at-arms at the gate and on the wall walks, the number of buildings within the castle walls and probably even the count of the windows in each.

Her younger brother, Trystan, who resembled her so much they could have been taken for twins save for the difference in their ages, was not among the company. He had been fostered to Sir Urien Fitzroy to complete his training.

The baron dismounted and she ran happily into his warm embrace. He kept his arms about her as he drew back to look at her with his remaining eye. The other had been destroyed in the Holy Land long ago when he had joined King Richard on crusade.

"So, daughter, did you enjoy yourself?" he asked.

"Lord Melevoir is an excellent man and a fine host," she answered honestly.

"I knew I should have offered to be your escort!" Dylan declared, easily slipping off his horse. "Who knows what I've missed—and for nothing, too."

"You had other, more important duties," Griffydd reminded him.

"Supervising a wall being repaired?" Dylan replied scornfully. "I hardly think—"

Her father laughed, the sound deep and rich. "No, you hardly think. Besides, Mamaeth said only Rhiannon and no brothers. I think she had great plans of this visit, didn't she, my daughter?"

Rhiannon tried to smile as she thought of her father's old nurse, who had made it very clear that she expected Rhiannon to return either with a husband, or a betrothal, at the very least.

Instead, Rhiannon had made a mess of things. "How is Mamaeth? And Mother?" she asked, deciding to get away from this prickly subject.

"Well enough, but missing you," her father replied. Suddenly he sniffed and looked up at the darkening clouds overhead, and she realized it did indeed smell much like rain. "Getting inside, us, or we'll be drenched."

Griffydd nodded, then began issuing commands to their men while the baron took Rhiannon's arm to escort her inside. Dylan handed his reins to a groom before sauntering toward the kitchen. He always claimed to admire the arms of the women who kneaded bread and Griffydd always retorted that he simply liked all his appetites satisfied simultaneously.

"I'm going to have to put a leash on that fellow," the baron muttered sardonically.

Despite his good-humored acceptance of Dylan's foibles, Rhiannon guessed he would not find hers so laughable. She tried to stay calm, and the thought that Lord Cynvelin was far away was very comforting.

She tried not to notice that she didn't feel quite

the same way about Bryce Frechette although she should, and more so, given what had happened in the courtyard.

The baron smiled at his daughter. "We have all been missing you. Craig Fawr seemed half-empty without you. I think even Mamaeth was reconsidering the notion of having you wed and away by the time we left to fetch you back again."

"I assure you, Father, I am in no hurry to be married," Rhiannon answered truthfully.

When her father paused and looked at her with a serious expression, she feared she had betrayed too much.

Fortunately, at that precipitous moment, a puffing and beaming Lord Melevoir appeared at the entrance to his hall.

"Always a delight, Baron!" the older man cried as the baron and Rhiannon hurried toward him. "Forgive my tardiness. It's this cursed damp. It gets into my bones and makes them ache like the very devil."

"Then please go back to your place at the hearth, my lord," the baron said.

"If you will join me," their host replied.

"Indeed, my bones are not so young anymore, either," the baron admitted ruefully as they followed Lord Melevoir to some oak chairs that were near the large hearth. A small yet comfortable blaze warmed the air.

As they sat on the age-darkened furniture, they could hear the rain begin to pelt against the stone walls. Lord Melevoir smiled and said, "I am glad you didn't get caught on the road in such weather."

"What is rain to a Welshman, my lord?" Baron DeLanyea asked cheerfully. "Nevertheless, I am happy to stay and enjoy your hospitality a day or two."

When her father looked at her, Rhiannon forced a smile onto her face. She had known that her father's visit would be more than a night; still, that meant more chances for him to hear about Lord Cynvelin's kiss. For a moment she considered broaching the subject herself, to put it in the proper light, but before she could, her father spoke.

"Who won the prizes?" he asked their host.

"Bryce Frechette took the largest purse," Lord Melevoir replied. "He has the truest aim with a lance I ever beheld."

"Frechette?" the baron asked, giving Lord Melevoir a surprised look. "The Earl of Westborough's son?"

"The same. I confess I had my doubts about allowing him to participate, but I tell you, Emryss, I've never seen a more improved young man," Lord Melevoir replied.

Rhiannon tried not to betray any overt interest in the lancer, especially after what had happened between them. Indeed, he could well be a fine warrior. That didn't mean he was a gentleman.

Unexpectedly her father fastened his shrewd gaze on Rhiannon. "What did you think of him?" he asked coolly.

She struggled to keep her expression bland as she

shrugged her shoulders. "Lord Melevoir wouldn't let us watch the competitions."

"Of course not!" the nobleman declared. "It is not fitting for young ladies to see such things."

"Frechette acquitted himself well, eh?" her father noted, facing the older man again. "A pity, then, his family lost their estate and titles. We can always use a fine knight."

"His family lost their estate and titles?" Rhiannon asked innocently.

"His father spent too freely—a warning to us all and I should have used him for an example before I let you go to the fair last spring." The baron's expression was severe, but the hint of laughter in his voice betrayed him.

"I had to have new dresses," Rhiannon reminded him sweetly. "Mamaeth said so."

"If you were to catch a husband, she said. Did you?"

Lord Melevoir started to laugh, or rather, wheeze with merriment as he looked from one to the other, his eyes twinkling mischievously.

"I told you, Father, I am in no hurry to wed."

"Then not wanting to be in your shoes when we get home, me, when Mamaeth hears that all this visiting and spending of money has not brought you a husband," he answered gravely.

Lord Melevoir took a great, deep, recuperative breath. "She was greatly admired, Baron. *Greatly* admired."

"Ah, her father's daughter, then," the baron said smugly, and he winked his good eye at her.

"One young man seemed particularly smitten. A countryman of yours, too. Indeed, the infatuation seemed quite mutual."

Rhiannon squirmed uncomfortably as her father regarded her steadily and with no hint of a smile. "Indeed? Who might this Welshman be?"

Rhiannon looked down at her hands, knotting them in her lap.

"Ah, *now* she will be coy," Lord Melevoir replied and Rhiannon heartlessly wished he would fall into a swoon or fit. Anything to make him be quiet.

"There was nothing—" she began desperately.

"Nothing?" Lord Melevoir declared indignantly. "Nothing to be kissed in my courtyard?"

Rhiannon wanted to shrink until she was invisible.

"This man kissed you out in the open of the courtyard for all to see?" the baron asked, his tone making Rhiannon cringe.

"Father, I—"

"Now, now, Baron, I fear you are showing your age! A young man does impetuous things when he has been struck by Cupid's dart. Don't be cross with your pretty daughter. She made it very plain that she felt he had acted improperly."

"I am glad to hear it."

"Oh, tut, now, man! Lord Cynvelin—"

"Who?"

The single word was softly spoken, but never had Rhiannon heard such cold menace in her father's voice.

Chapter Three

Rhiannon stared at her father as he turned a searching gaze onto her before once again looking at their host.

Lord Melevoir cleared his throat. "Lord Cynvelin ap Hywell. A Welsh nobleman," he concluded rather hopefully.

"A Welshman born he may be," the baron said, "but he is a disgrace to us all."

Rhiannon had never seen her father react with such instant antipathy—and she had not even known that her father was familiar with the man! What on earth had Cynvelin ap Hywell done to so enrage her father?

He regarded her with that same forbidding expression. "Did he speak to you?" he demanded.

She nodded.

"Did he know who you were?"

"Yes," she answered softly. "Cynvelin ap Hywell said that he knew of you when he introduced himself, but he never implied, either in word or look, that there was anything between you. He was very nice to me, although rather forward.''

"I daresay he was," the baron growled. "Not waiting for Lord Melevoir to make the introduction, you?"

She shook her head remorsefully, for he was quite right. It would have been proper for Lord Melevoir to make the introduction, and she should have realized that at the time.

"Baron, if I had known there was anything—" Lord Melevoir said haltingly.

Rhiannon's father took a deep breath. "Forgive me, Lord Melevoir. None of this is your fault. Or yours, either, daughter." He looked at Rhiannon ruefully. "I should have guessed he might be here and I should have warned you about him."

He stared straight ahead and she wasn't sure if he was speaking to her, or only to himself. "But never did I think he would have the gall to speak to any member of my family."

Despite his hushed voice, Rhiannon got the distinct feeling that her father was still trying very hard to control his rage.

"What has he done to make you hate him so?" she asked wonderingly.

"Indeed, yes," Lord Melevoir seconded. "If he is such a blackguard, I will not have him back again."

"He *was* a blackguard. If Bryce Frechette can be so changed, perhaps Cynvelin can, as well." The baron smiled, but not with his eyes, which made Rhiannon believe he was saying this only to reassure their host that he had not made a terrible blunder.

"He had the makings of a fine knight when I first admitted him into our household."

"He was at Craig Fawr?" Rhiannon asked, taken aback. "I don't remember him."

"You were visiting Lord Trevelyan at the time and, not wanting to admit I had made a mistake, I never mentioned his name after I sent him away."

"What made you do that?" Lord Melevoir inquired.

"First, it was only cheating at games. Then he started making trouble among all the young men, spreading lies and rumors until they were nearly at each other's throats. Not that any blame would ever attach to him. Oh, no, he was too clever for that. I finally realized what was going on when Griffydd blackened Dylan's eye, and I made him tell me why he had done it. When they understood what Cynvelin was about, Dylan was all for killing him on the spot." The baron grinned wryly. "Cynvelin will never know how close he came to going to God that day. I thought a good talking-to would be sufficient, but I was wrong. Shortly after, somebody cut the cinch on Dylan's horse's saddle, so that it snapped when he was galloping during a practice with the lance. He fell and could have been killed. Of course I guessed who had done it."

"And you sent him away," Lord Melevoir said, nodding his head in agreement.

Her father hesitated, lost in his thoughts, while Rhiannon waited tensely for him to continue. "Yes," he said after a long moment of silence.

There was more to it than that, she felt certain, but ask anything more, she dared not.

Lord Melevoir sank back in his chair. "Well, by all the saints and cherubim, Baron DeLanyea. If ever there was a wolf in sheep's clothing! Next thing you'll be telling me he's one of those damned rebels, too."

"A rebel? God's wounds, no, not that one. Although not surprised, me, if he were to claim to be when it suited him among the Welsh," her father continued grimly. "But the only person he thinks about is himself. If he ever starts spouting rebellion, you can be sure there'll be a prize in it for him."

At that moment, Dylan and Griffydd marched into the hall, followed by their men.

"Do you know who Rhiannon's been kissing?" Dylan declared angrily, glaring at Rhiannon in a way that made her more angry than mortified.

After all, however shamefully she may have conducted herself, Dylan was hardly a saint. Many a night he sneaked out of Craig Fawr for trysts with village girls. He had already fathered three children by three different women. To be sure, to the Welsh an illegitimate child was nothing to be remorseful about, but such behavior hardly gave him the right to act so indignant.

Griffydd's expression, however, only made her feel humiliated, and she was very glad neither one of them knew about that other unforgettable kiss in the courtyard.

Nevertheless, she rose swiftly and glared at them,

because they were making accusations without knowing her side of things.

As she had accused Bryce Frechette without knowing his side of things.

Which was completely immaterial at the moment.

"I don't think—" she began angrily.

"Sit down!" her father commanded Rhiannon. "Dylan, lower your voice."

Lord Melevoir stood slowly. "I believe I will leave you to discuss your family business in private," he said before tottering away as fast as his legs would take him.

The baron gestured for Dylan and Griffydd to come closer. "We will deal with this once and for all, and then there will be no more said about Cynvelin ap Hywell."

Dylan glared angrily at Rhiannon. "Do you know what they're saying about you? That you threw yourself at that cur."

"I never did!" Rhiannon protested, almost sick to realize that was how her behavior in the hall had been interpreted by some people. Bryce Frechette had certainly been of that opinion. No doubt that explained why he felt free to embrace her. What must he think of her now?

She suddenly wished with all her heart that she had never come here!

The baron glanced at the rest of his men who were coming into the hall, calling out for drinks from the serving wenches. "Lower your voices," he repeated firmly.

"That is what they are saying," Griffydd confirmed, his steady gaze far more unnerving to Rhiannon than Dylan's words.

She flushed hotly, her stance still defiant, even though inwardly she wanted to flee from their accusations. "Who?" she demanded. "Who dares to say such things? I spoke to Cynvelin ap Hywell and danced with him, too!" she declared defensively. "I didn't know anything wrong of him, and I think you have no right to condemn me." *Not for that.*

Her father spoke, his voice calm and firm. "She did not know anything about him. I never told her." He fastened a steely gaze onto Dylan. "You are hardly worthy to chastise her behavior."

"But she is a woman and—"

"And I am her father, so I will speak to her about her behavior, not you, although I gather she was not pleased by what he did any more than you."

Dylan frowned. Rhiannon knew he would sulk a while, yet she didn't care, not as long as her father realized she deeply regretted what had happened, even if he did not know all that she regretted.

"No fights need be fought over whatever men with too little time on their hands might say, either," her father warned. "The Normans have never understood the Welsh. They are often as gloomy as hermits in a cold cave, so I would not pay them much heed when they criticize your spritely sister.

"Dylan, Griffydd, this conversation is finished. Your sister may have acted with less decorum than I might have hoped, but even you have done so on occasion, Griffydd—and you often, Dylan. Go, now, and make certain that the men understand they are not to quarrel with Lord Melevoir's guests or his men over any perceived insults.''

Dylan looked far from pleased; however, he, like Griffydd, heard the baron's tone of finality and knew it would be useless to object.

They went to the join the others.

"Father, I—" Rhiannon began, even though she was not quite sure what she was going to say, whether to defend herself or beg for forgiveness.

Her father held up his hand to silence her, and when he spoke, his tone was gentle and understanding. "Rhiannon, I know how likable Cynvelin can be, and I blame myself that I did not warn you about him. Do you care for him at all in the way Lord Melevoir implied?"

"I think I did, Father, a little," she answered honestly. "But when he kissed me in the courtyard and embarrassed me in front of everyone..."

Once again the memory of Bryce Frechette intruded into her thoughts, but she pushed it away.

Her father nodded thoughtfully. "Cynvelin can be very charming," he said with a sigh. "That's what makes him dangerous. Tricks people with his manners, that one. Courtesy can be nothing but a costume, daughter, and a title no more than a cloak to hide dishonor. Remember that."

"Yet clearly he thinks I care for him very much," Rhiannon said. "On the strength of that belief, he may come to Craig Fawr."

She expected her father to curse, at the very least. Instead, and to her great relief, he smiled. "He would never dare come there, Rhiannon. Not if he values his life. He knows that well enough." He reached out and patted her hand tenderly. "There has been no real harm done here, daughter, and I daresay you have learned a lesson."

"Yes, I have," she confirmed. "I promise you, Father, the next time I am at a tournament or visiting, I shall be the most modest, decorous young lady alive."

Her father smiled and his eye twinkled with merriment. "Then you would not be my lively, spirited daughter, and I would be an unhappy man. Griffydd is serious enough for all of us.

"But look you," her father continued, his tone once again serious as he rose and regarded her steadily, "I may be tempted to send Mamaeth to watch over you, and then there would be no getting into mischief!"

Rhiannon rose swiftly, the prospect of her father's elderly and loquacious nurse as caretaker far from heartening. "I'm sorry if I embarrassed our family. I will be more careful in future. I give you my word."

The baron hugged her gently. "I know, Rhiannon. I was young and impetuous once myself. I have not forgotten, and so of course I forgive you."

Rhiannon held her father tight, loving him with all her heart, and pleased to think no lasting harm had been done by her careless behavior.

A steady drizzle soaked the valley. Beyond, high, rounded hills seemed to enclose Cynvelin ap Hywell's entourage, so it was like being in the mouth of a large animal. Bryce didn't think he had seen the sun once since they had reached the Marches, the borderlands between England and Wales, nor had he been completely dry in what seemed an age.

They were making for what Lord Cynvelin described as one of his minor holdings, a fortress named Annedd Bach, and hoped to reach it today.

However, the journey itself had not been long or much of a hardship, for Cynvelin ap Hywell was a generous man who clearly believed his Welshmen worthy of fine food, ale and accommodation. Obviously they believed it, too, for they were all rather arrogant. The fellow Bryce had made apologize, whose name was Madoc, continued to regard the Norman with barely disguised loathing, but that didn't trouble Bryce overmuch. He was used to being alone after months traveling in Europe trying to earn money for his family, only to find it was too little too late, and then making his way in the world as a dispossessed, disgraced warrior.

As for the others, not a one of them even so much as attempted to converse with Bryce, and after a few futile attempts, he gave up trying.

Lord Cynvelin didn't seem to care a whit about Bryce's past, and for that, he was truly grateful. He treated Bryce almost as an equal, just as he had at Lord Melevoir's feast. During their journey and as they rested, they talked of many things: the tournament; Lord Cynvelin's castle, Caer Coch, which sounded like the finest fortress in Wales; jousting; Bryce's experiences in Europe; women.

With one notable exception.

Neither of them mentioned Lady Rhiannon De-Lanyea.

Bryce was glad of it, for he wouldn't have known how to respond if Lord Cynvelin had spoken of her.

Perhaps when he had been with Lord Cynvelin longer, he might hazard a hint that Lady Rhiannon's deportment was not what it should be, for a lady. On the other hand, Bryce had heard that the Welsh were morally negligent. Judging by the frequency with which the Welshman bedded tavern wenches, that was apparently true. As astonishing as it seemed to Bryce, perhaps Welshwomen acted in a similar manner.

Thinking that was probably so, he told himself it was no wonder his fitful sleep was troubled by dreams of Lady Rhiannon in his arms, her hair loose about her beautiful face, her eyes shining, her lips parted invitingly. As he had told her, she was the most desirable woman he had ever seen.

And no matter how he tried to condemn her, he couldn't help admiring her valor. He could think of no other noblewoman who would dare to confront a potential thief, not even with guards close by, or one whose vibrant eyes would flash with such scornful anger at a big, brawny soldier who made a joke at her expense.

"There!" Lord Cynvelin suddenly called out, twisting in his saddle to look back at Bryce and the others, pulling him out of his reverie. "There is Annedd Bach."

Bryce strained to see past him, looking for anything that resembled a building through the dull gray mist.

Lord Cynvelin chuckled. "There, man," he repeated, "that thing that looks like a big rock. We have a ways to go yet, you see."

Bryce followed the lord's pointing finger and finally he could make out a large gray shape that looked more like a rock clinging to the hillside than a fortress.

"Now we will be getting dry!" Lord Cynvelin cried jovially. He spurred his horse to a gallop, sending clumps of mud flying backward.

As Bryce and the others galloped after him, the castle grew more discernible. It had what seemed to be a strong stone wall and inside, a round stone keep.

Soon enough they were nearly at the outer wall. When they approached, Bryce could see some hovels near the fortress. Not nearly enough to comprise a village, they seemed old and decrepit, as if the rain might wash them away entirely. No persons showed themselves, but that could be because of the weather.

The walls of Annedd Bach looked well made, and the wooden gates thick as they rode through the gatehouse, under the portcullis and into the courtyard. In addition to the keep, there was another rectangular stone building of rough, gray stone, which Bryce guessed was the hall. Other buildings in the enclosure were made of wattle and daub.

Lord Cynvelin called out something in Welsh, and a head appeared in the doorway of the hall. When the man saw who had called, he opened the door and hurried out, holding a ragged woolen shawl over his tattered clothing. His pale face was thin and Bryce thought he looked completely cowed.

Again Lord Cynvelin shouted something in Welsh, and a few more men appeared from one of the wattle and daub buildings, which Bryce took to be a barracks.

Like the first man, the other people's clothes were ragged and their bodies thin. Their manner was sullen and subdued; they certainly did not look happy to see their lord return.

Bryce recalled one of his father's favorite sayings, that a well-fed tenant was a contented tenant. For years Bryce had believed his father had taken that too far, allowing his villeins to keep too much of the produce of their farms. When Bryce had learned of the extent of his father's debts, he had been sure the earl had been far too generous to them and they had taken advantage of his goodness.

Nevertheless, as he watched the servants of Annedd Bach come forward, he thought that his father's opinion might have some merit after all.

Surprisingly, given Lord Cynvelin's generosity with his soldiers, he seemed to find nothing amiss in the appearance or the manner of Annedd Bach's servants.

Lord Cynvelin addressed his Welsh guards, who didn't seem to notice anything unusual, either. Then he dismounted and smiled at Bryce with his easy familiarity. "Come inside and get warm. Then something to eat, my friend. I do not know what kind of beds we'll find, but at least we'll be out of the wet."

Bryce nodded and handed the reins of his horse to

one of the waiting castle servants before following Lord Cynvelin into what was indeed a small, barren hall.

With a disgusted expression, Lord Cynvelin went to stand near the empty central hearth, his hands on his hips as he surveyed the room. A lone trestle table, unmade, leaned against the wall. Rain streaked the whitewash as it dripped from a series of narrow windows set high in the wall.

This place was nearly as dismal inside as out, Bryce reflected.

Lord Cynvelin shook his head and frowned darkly. "Away for a while, and what do I find? They've stripped the place!"

"Who, my lord?" Bryce inquired, wondering if this part of Wales was plagued with outlaws. That might explain the servants' unhappy expressions, although if that were the case, he quickly reasoned, they should be much more pleased by the arrival of Cynvelin and his men.

"The servants, of course!" the nobleman retorted with more anger than Bryce had ever seen him display. "Lazy dogs! I've a mind to have them all hanged and let the crows feed on their bones!"

"Would they risk your ire by doing that, my lord?" Bryce reasoned. "Surely they knew you would return. Perhaps they've moved things to a storehouse for safekeeping."

At that moment, they both heard a sound near the door leading to the kitchen. An old woman and some younger women watched them anxiously.

"Ah, this is better!" Lord Cynvelin muttered, and he called out jovially in Welsh.

Bryce glanced at him quickly. Lord Cynvelin's anger seemed to have dissipated like straw in a flame.

Cynvelin strolled toward the women, speaking to them as if nothing were amiss. The old woman nodded and tottered off while Cynvelin slowly turned on his heel and smiled at Bryce. "You were right. They put the furnishings away, not knowing when I would be coming. Regrettably, they tell me that they have little food. I gather the harvests were not good." He shrugged his shoulders. "No matter. We have enough provisions in my carts for a few days. And the hunting is good in the hills." He sighed and once again surveyed the hall. "Perhaps I do not come here as often as I should," he mused.

When the rest of the men came into the hall, Lord Cynvelin called out to Madoc. The soldier punched his friend on the shoulder and came forward.

The other man was Twedwr, smaller and more compact, but Bryce didn't doubt who was actually the stronger of the two. Like Madoc, Twedwr always had a glint of hatred in his eyes when he looked at Bryce, although whether it was because of what had happened with Madoc, Bryce's past or the fact that he was simply a Norman, Bryce didn't know.

After Lord Cynvelin talked to them, Madoc and Twedwr reluctantly went back out to the courtyard while the others broke into small groups, grumbling. Clearly they, too, had expected better accommodations. Lord Cynvelin sauntered toward them and made placating gestures as he spoke with them in their native tongue.

A serving wench, who looked about fifteen, appeared from the kitchen, carrying rushes which she proceeded to lay upon the stone floor. Every time she bent over, one or another of the men would make what had to be a lewd remark, to judge by the chortles and winks that passed between the men, and the blushes on the young woman's face. Smiling, Cynvelin made no effort to interfere.

Madoc and Twedwr returned, accompanied by servants carrying baskets and pouches that Bryce recognized from Cynvelin's carts. The servants continued on toward the kitchen, getting an occasional kick or shove from Madoc to speed them on their way. Again, Cynvelin made no effort to interfere, and Bryce began to wonder how the man customarily treated his servants. He did not like what he was seeing.

Bryce reminded himself that he knew nothing about the people here. Maybe the girl was simply shy, or perhaps even coy, so her seeming embarrassment was nothing more than a show for their benefit. And maybe the slow-moving men were habitually in need of prodding of some kind.

Besides, now he was a hireling, too. He no longer had the right to chastise or criticize anyone for their treatment of their servants and tenants, so he had to hold his tongue, no matter how that galled him.

Other servants began coming to the hall with furnishings, wood for the hearth, and ale. They worked quickly and silently, occasionally casting nervous glances at Lord Cynvelin, his soldiers and Bryce.

Bryce wasn't sure what he should do while they labored, so he strolled toward the door. It was still raining. Although every so often he had to move out of the doorway to let a servant or soldier pass, he surveyed the wall surrounding the small castle. It was well built and strong; outlaws wouldn't be able to make much headway against such defenses if they attacked.

Yet why should the servants look so hungry? Had the harvest been that bad? It hadn't been in the rest of England—but then, the rest of England wasn't this wet.

He turned, thinking he would ask Lord Cynvelin if poor harvests were a common occurrence, and he saw the Welshman talking to the girl who had laid the rushes.

She looked frightened and flustered, her face flushed. Perhaps she had done something wrong, although Bryce couldn't begin to guess what that might be.

The girl bowed slightly, then hurried off toward the kitchen corridor.

"Annedd Bach usually looks better than it does today," Lord Cynvelin said, sauntering toward Bryce and then clapping a hand on his shoulder. "It seems you were right. There were reports of outlaws, so they thought it best to hide everything of value."

"Is that why she looked so afraid?"

"Who?"

"The girl you were just talking with. Have out-laws stolen their food?"

"Ust, man, they have enough to eat. If they seem afraid, I suppose they assume I have come because I haven't received my rent and there might be repri-sals."

"Forgive the impertinence of my question, my lord," Bryce said, "but why *have* we come here?"

Lord Cynvelin's handsome face grew serious. "Because I haven't received my rent and there are going to be reprisals." Suddenly he grinned, then laughed out loud. "Not the kind you seem to be thinking of, Bryce. God's wounds, you should know me better than that! I have something else in mind for Annedd Bach. A new overlord."

"Ah!" Bryce hadn't wanted to believe that the man who had behaved with such kindness and gen-erosity to him would prove to be capable of the kind of cruelty in which some Norman lords indulged. "Who, my lord? Madoc?" he hypothesized, glancing at the glowering Welshman.

"No." Cynvelin's grin widened. "You."

Bryce stared at him. "Me?"

"Indeed, and why not? Madoc and Twedwr and the others are fine fighters, but they'll never be suit-able overlords. Too bloody-minded, for one thing, and I'm sure you've noticed they hate Normans like the pox. What would the king say if he knew I'd given command of a castle to men like that? A Nor-man would please him. Besides, you've grown up in a noble household, so you'll know how things ought to be done."

"My lord, I don't know what to say."

"'Thank you' will do for a start. I want you to take command of Annedd Bach at once. There will be the rents to collect, half of which you can keep, and the garrison to command." Cynvelin's grin grew rueful. "They'll probably have to be retrained. You can curse me for a lazy dog if you like, but I fear I've been a neglectful overlord when it comes to this estate."

Cynvelin gestured toward a hearth, where a fire now blazed brightly, and they walked toward it. "This is a fine castle, and with a properly trained garrison, could command the entire valley."

"Command for whom?" Bryce asked, suddenly mindful of the tales of Welsh rebels. Despite his friendly and open manner, Lord Cynvelin was a Welshman, when all was said and done.

If Lord Cynvelin thought to move against the Normans, Bryce would leave at once. A dishonored, dispossessed Norman he might be, but he was still loyal to his king.

"King Henry, of course!" Lord Cynvelin replied. "I have sworn my oath of loyalty to him, and unlike some Welshmen, I intend to abide by it."

Bryce relaxed and nodded. "I shall do my best to be worthy of this command, my lord."

"Good, Bryce, good." Lord Cynvelin looked at Bryce, his eyes twinkling merrily. "Then you will not mind living in Wales a while?"

"No, my lord." Not if he was to have a castle to command, and income for his own. No more making a living fighting in tournaments, traveling from place to place like some kind of tinker.

"Excellent. Is there nothing more you would ask as payment for taking on this task?"

Bryce gave him a puzzled look. "My lord?"

"The man who commands a castle should be a knight, at the very least, would you not agree?"

"My lord!" Bryce gasped. He had not expected this. Not at all.

"Not yet, Bryce," the Welshman said with what sounded like sincere regret. "As much as I would like to, first I must be sure you will be able to control this valley."

"My lord, I give you my word that I shall do everything in my power—!"

Lord Cynvelin gestured for silence. "I know that, or I would never have given you the command. However, I am afraid that the people here may make it very difficult for you because you are Norman."

Bryce nodded.

"But I do not think that much of a condition for you, my friend." Again Cynvelin laid his hand on Bryce's shoulder. "I am quite certain that in a year, you will be Sir Bryce Frechette."

"I cannot begin to thank you, my lord."

"Then let it wait!" Cynvelin pointed at the kitchen corridor. "Here comes the meal, and not a moment too soon. My stomach is flapping against my backbone. Come, sit beside me at table."

Pleased and honored by all that had happened since their arrival, Bryce joined the Welshman at the trestle table, which had been placed on the dais at the far end of the long hall. Other tables and benches had also been assembled, and the serving wenches began bringing in bread and meat, and pouring mugs of ale. The girl Cynvelin had been speaking with brought two goblets of wine to their table.

She might have been pretty, had she been clean and well fed. As it was, her skin was pale to the point of sickliness, her eyes had no luster, and her dark hair hung limp about her narrow, expressionless face.

Bryce could not help comparing her to her countrywoman, Rhiannon DeLanyea. They both had dark hair, yet beyond that, Rhiannon was like a full-bodied vision of beauty, whereas this girl represented want in the worst form.

"I've asked Ermin—the steward, the man who finally answered my summons when we arrived—to gather the rest of the garrison tomorrow. I take it most of the men have been living out of Annedd Bach on their farms. They should be here at dawn. Unfortunately, I fear they won't be of any real use for weeks yet."

Bryce nodded, dragging his thoughts away from the memory of Rhiannon DeLanyea.

"Your father was noted for his fine castle and hospitality. Tell me, Bryce, how long will it take to get Annedd Bach ready for guests?"

"I…I have no idea, my lord," Bryce stammered, completely taken aback by the change of subject. "I would have to see what the sleeping quarters are like, and what linens are in the stores, and the food supply, and fodder for animals."

"I'm afraid you will have little time for all that, my friend," Cynvelin replied regretfully. "Your first guest will be here tomorrow."

Bryce realized that he couldn't very well refuse the hospitality of Annedd Bach to a guest of Lord Cynvelin, who was still the true overlord. "Who might that be?"

"Lady Rhiannon DeLanyea. We are going to abduct her."

Chapter Four

"Abduct her?" Bryce repeated in disbelief. "Lady Rhiannon?"

Lord Cynvelin chuckled. "Do not be looking so horrified, Frechette," he chided, his tone as calm as if suggesting a stag hunt. "I am not talking of a crime."

"By what other name would you call such an act?" Bryce demanded.

"A Welsh custom," Cynvelin replied, smiling. "Especially when the groom's potential father-in-law is a stubborn fellow who fails to see the groom's merit."

"A custom?"

Lord Cynvelin's usual good humor momentarily disappeared. "Aye. An old one, or surely you know I would never propose such a thing."

"My lord, you'll forgive me for—"

"Doubting that I am an honorable man?" Cynvelin finished, a hint of a frown on his face. "If so, there is the door, and you are welcome to leave."

Bryce didn't respond at once. In truth, he didn't

like the sound of this. Kidnapping as nothing but a quaint custom? It didn't seem possible, but what did he know of Welsh customs?

Cynvelin's manner was open and sincere. Surely a man about to commit a serious crime could not behave so blithely.

His companion laughed ruefully. "Forgive my harsh words. I know how this must sound to your Norman ears, but I assure you, my friend, Rhiannon DeLanyea is quite prepared for her abduction, although she's not quite sure when it will be. Indeed, she's expecting such a thing and she'll be disappointed if I don't come for her."

Bryce stifled the surge of disappointment that seemed to hit him like an unexpected wave on a calm day at sea.

"And by taking her," Cynvelin continued, "her father will see how serious I am in my desire to have her for my wife. If I don't abduct her, her family might think I am a coward. I cannot have that, can I?"

"She will be disappointed if you don't cart her off unexpectedly?" Bryce asked dubiously, still too wary of the proposal to find it at all droll, as Lord Cynvelin obviously did. "You are contracted then?"

"No, not in the Norman way," the Welshman replied with a dismissive wave of his hand that told Bryce what he thought of Norman legalities.

As he had suspected, Lady Rhiannon DeLanyea was the most audacious hussy Bryce had ever encountered, kissing him with such apparent passion when she was as good as betrothed to another.

Now more than ever he wished he had abandoned the lady in the courtyard before she had enticed him into the shadows. Nor did he want to be anywhere near Lady Rhiannon ever again.

Nevertheless, Cynvelin was offering him a great opportunity, one that he would not abandon without serious cause. Surely he could manage to avoid the lady for the short time she was here, and she had obviously not wanted her immoral behavior revealed to her future husband. Probably she would avoid him just as studiously. "This expected kidnapping is to happen tomorrow?"

"Aye. We will meet her father's entourage on the road not far from here as they journey home. It is too far to go to Caer Coch on the same day, so we will stop at Annedd Bach for the night."

"What is it you expect me to do?"

"Ride with me as one of my groomsmen. We will not be a large party, because this is mostly for show, you see." Lord Cynvelin ran a cursory gaze over Bryce. "Better clothes you must be having. There isn't time to buy new, so you may have something of mine I no longer wear." He held up his hand to preempt Bryce's protest. "Not hearing a word about that. You must be well dressed, or you will bring me disgrace."

Clearly Cynvelin didn't consider his offer of his old clothes an insult to Bryce, and he knew the man meant well, but he was insulted, nonetheless. He detested charity when he was the recipient.

"You, I think, should be the one to bring Rhiannon back here," Cynvelin mused.

"Me?" he demanded, too surprised to be polite.

"Madoc and the others would probably be too rough. I know I can count on you to do it right."

"Too rough? Why would they be rough if she wants to come away with you?"

"She has to at least feign some maidenly, modest aversion," Cynvelin replied. "She might even weep and wail and protest, but you should just ignore it, because it will only be pretend. The moment we are together, she will be happy again."

"What if the baron refuses to let her go?" Bryce asked.

"Oh, he very well might. He may even look to put up a fight. You know how fathers can be about their daughters."

In truth, Bryce didn't know. He had not been home when his sister was of an age to think of marriage, and he had not been there when she had fallen in love.

"That's part of the tradition, too, you see," Cynvelin explained, "and that is why I want you to take Rhiannon away as soon as possible. I wouldn't want anything to happen to my bride by accident.

"Not that it should," he hastened to add. "Any fighting is just for show, too. And honor, you see, to make the woman think she's worth a fight. There might be a few knocked heads and scratches. Nothing worse than you might get in a tournament, I promise you. Still, it would be best if you were to get Rhiannon away as quickly as you can. I will give you the word, and you take hold of her horse and gallop away, simple as can be."

Bryce nodded, convinced of the truth of Cynvelin's words by his earnestness and the Welshman's honest demeanor, as much as his explanation. "Very well, my lord," he said with a slight bow. "I shall be honored to act as your groomsman."

And he would be the one to take charge of Lady Rhiannon, because like Lord Cynvelin, he didn't relish the idea of Madoc and his friend having responsibility for her.

"Here, you!" Cynvelin suddenly shouted at the pale serving wench. "More wine!" He turned back to Bryce and said wryly, "By the saints above, all this talking makes a man thirsty."

"Don't you get a dowry or exchange gifts, my lord?" Bryce asked.

"Ah, a wise man you are, Frechette," Cynvelin replied. "Of course. Not savages, the Welsh. I get the dowry later, and I have to pay the *amobr*."

"*Amobr*?"

Cynvelin leaned closer and gave him a conspiratorial wink as he whispered, "The price for her maidenhead."

The Welsh must be barbarians to put such a thing so crudely, Bryce thought with disgust.

"What's the matter with you?" Cynvelin asked. "It's an exchange of gifts, like you said, only more honest about it, us."

"I understand, my lord," Bryce answered, believing that he did.

The thin, dark-haired serving wench came to refill their goblets. Bryce cut off a piece of cold roast mutton, then glanced over and nearly choked when he realized that Cynvelin was fondling her breasts as she poured the wine.

The young woman's face betrayed nothing as she turned and walked away.

Cynvelin gave Bryce a devilish grin. "Ula's not very friendly yet, but that will change when she sees a coin. You can have her after me, if you like."

"My lord, I would rather sleep alone," Bryce said without hesitation, instinctively recoiling from the notion that the servants of the castle were creatures to be used at an overlord's whim.

"What?" Cynvelin eyed him dubiously.

"I'm sorry, my lord," Bryce replied, fearing he had offended the Welshman. After all, many noblemen considered the duties of the female servants of their households to automatically extend to carnal pleasures.

However, Bryce had been raised to consider them not as things to be exploited, but as hirelings worthy of some respect. He had not thought the Welshman the sort to use his own servants in such a way and was not pleased to find out he was wrong.

Nevertheless, he was beholden to Lord Cynvelin for the opportunity to regain something of his lost rank, to stand on the first step toward the restoration of his family's fortune, so he decided he would prevaricate. "I would rather pay, my lord."

"Pay? Are you mad?"

"She doesn't look clean."

"Are you that fastidious?" Lord Cynvelin asked with a laugh. "No women at Lord Melevoir's. No whores on the journey. I am beginning to think you ought to have been a monk.''

"I thought about it."

Cynvelin stared at him, incredulous, until Bryce grinned.

"I did contemplate the priesthood," he admitted, then smiled again, attempting to reclaim his own good humor as much as his overlord's. "To be sure, it was only for an instant."

"You gave me quite a turn there, man!" Cynvelin raised his goblet in a salute. "A fellow has needs, Bryce, has he not? But if you do not want her, I will give her to Madoc and the others."

Bryce clenched his jaw so hard it hurt. "I didn't say I didn't want her, my lord," he replied.

Better the girl come to him than be handed about like a bowl of wassail.

Not that he had any intention of sleeping with her. Indeed, he could believe she had fleas, at the very least. No, when she came to him, he would give her a penny and send her on her way. That way, he would not seem to be criticizing Cynvelin's behavior.

However, he silently vowed, when he was overlord here and a knight, when he again had rank and the power that went with it, he would never allow anyone in his household to be used in such a fashion.

He ate some of the bread, and as he watched the young serving wench, her lips compressed and her eyes full of fear, he wondered how Cynvelin could even think of bedding another woman and one so obviously unwilling when he was betrothed to the beautiful, graceful, spirited Rhiannon DeLanyea.

The beautiful, graceful, tempting Rhiannon De-Lanyea, who had lured him into the shadows only to feign indignation. Who had seemed so genuinely sympathetic. Who had looked at him the way she did when she was already as good as betrothed to another.

A scowl crossed Bryce's face. Perhaps Lady Rhiannon was getting the husband she deserved, after all.

In the dim light of the foggy morning, Bryce surveyed the motley gathering of men in the courtyard of Annedd Bach. He could feel their gazes on him like the prick of several daggers, but he ignored their enmity. Indeed, he was used to seeing scorn in men's eyes, and women's, too. Not respect. Not gratitude for championing their honor.

He focused his attention on the men before him.

Dressed in a variety of mail and bits of armor, their clothes simple homespun and much patched, they stood in a sullen, suspicious group, eyeing Bryce and each other. Only five had brought swords. A few had spears; Bryce saw one or two daggers.

Hardly a mighty fighting force, he thought, although they did look somewhat better fed than most of the servants of Annedd Bach. Somewhat. The harvest must have been abysmal in this part of the country.

Bryce wondered if they had other weapons concealed beneath their clothing. He rather hoped they did, despite their glowering faces.

Not that he would be afraid of them for that. He

doubted there was a properly trained fighter in their midst. In a battle, men like these would either be killed at once or run away.

No doubt if a Norman were to lead them against their countrymen, they would not run away; they would turn on their commander.

Unless he could earn their loyalty, and that was what Bryce planned to do, no matter how difficult. He would mold these men into a garrison any lord would be proud of, and by doing so, he would prove himself worthy of a knighthood and any other rewards Cynvelin ap Hywell might offer him.

The first thing he would have to do was see what they could do. One or two of them looked as if they could give Madoc or Twedwr a good fight, if that fight was only a brawl.

Bryce adjusted his belt and shifted his shoulders in the new black woolen tunic Lord Cynvelin had given him. It was longer than the leather jerkin Bryce was used to, and the wool sleeves made his arms itch.

Bryce glanced at Ermin, standing nervously to his left. He was supposed to act as interpreter until the men could learn enough French to understand their commander.

Ermin's gaze strayed to the barracks. Twedwr and some of the other men of Cynvelin's guard were standing outside, wearing full battle dress. Likely they were so attired because of the need to make an impressive show, and they were certainly doing that.

They were also, judging by the tone of their remarks, making several unflattering comments about the shabby, poorly armed garrison.

Bryce was pleased to note that his men seemed not so much cowed as disgusted by the behavior of Cynvelin's men. It was good to know they had some pride.

Before Bryce could address the garrison, however, Lord Cynvelin strolled over to join them. He wore his finest chain mail beneath a plain black surcoat, which reached below his knees and was slit up the sides, as well as helmet and gauntlets.

"My lord," Bryce said with a respectful bow. He gave a sharp and meaningful glance to the men of the garrison, who quickly bowed, too.

"A pity it is these are all the men you will have," Cynvelin said, his tone betraying no regret. "Still, I have faith that a man of your skills will soon have them capable of defending Annedd Bach."

"Thank you, my lord. If they can be as well armed as yours, that will help a great deal."

Cynvelin nodded and smiled. "You're right, and this estate should provide enough income for you to see to that. As for my men," he went on, jerking his thumb toward Madoc, "we must be wearing our mail and weapons to show how rich and powerful I am to the baron."

"I thought that must be another part of the custom, my lord."

"You learn quickly, Frechette. Now, come, it is time to fetch my bride." He gave Bryce a searching look. "What is it?"

Bryce tried to keep any expression from his face, but no matter how hard he tried to convince himself that Lady Rhiannon's future was no concern of his, he could not get used to hearing that she was going to be Lord Cynvelin's bride. "I am surprised we would set out so early, my lord."

"They will be on the closest part of the road soon, I should think," he replied lightly. "Baron De-Lanyea likes to get an early start."

"Very well, my lord."

"When we meet them, wait until I tell you, then take Rhiannon back to Annedd Bach. At the gallop. It can be like a race, too, you see, and they may give chase."

Bryce nodded his understanding.

Lord Cynvelin then said something cheerily to the garrison in Welsh before sauntering toward his guard.

The garrison didn't move, although all their eyes followed the Welsh nobleman.

"What did Lord Cynvelin say?" Bryce asked Ermin.

The thin man looked at him, then at the ground. "To do what you are saying," he replied haltingly, obviously not very familiar with Norman French. Probably he was the only man they could find who knew any at all.

"To obey my commands, you mean?"

"Aye, sir."

That seemed a short order for all that Lord Cynvelin had said, so Bryce asked, "What else?"

"Or else..." Ermin hesitated, still looking at the ground, and Bryce assumed he was struggling to find the right word.

By now, however, Lord Cynvelin and his men were mounted and ready to ride out. "Frechette!"

Bryce turned to leave, then glanced back at Ermin over his shoulder. "Tell the men to go to the kitchen and get something to eat."

Ermin's eyes widened slightly as he nodded, and Bryce heard a murmur pass through the garrison, although whether of approval or simple curiosity, he couldn't say.

As Bryce walked toward his horse, saddled and held by a lad from the stables, he noticed Ula hurrying toward the keep, a stool in her hands.

"She seems well rested," Cynvelin remarked when Bryce prepared to mount. "A slow learner, but I daresay she'll catch on soon enough."

Bryce made a noncommittal grunt. He had no wish to reveal that he had sent the girl away last night after she had come to him.

"I'm glad you didn't tire her overmuch," the Welshman continued. "She has to prepare the chamber in the keep for Rhiannon. And me."

Bryce couldn't help the swift glance he cast at his overlord.

Cynvelin chuckled companionably as he gestured for Bryce to join him at the head of the column of men. "Another Welsh custom, Bryce. *Caru yn y gwely.*"

Bryce didn't think he needed an interpreter to know what that meant. Obviously waiting for the actual blessing of a priest or even the signing of a marriage contract was of no import to these people.

Lord Cynvelin raised his hand again, and the gate opened to allow them to go to fetch the bride.

Water dripped slowly from the leaves of the trees surrounding the cortege as it made slow progress through the forest in the valley. At the head of the entourage rode Baron DeLanyea, followed by his son and foster son.

Rhiannon was behind them, mounted on her gentle mare and glad of it, for a feisty animal required too much effort on a long journey. The day was misty and damp, so she wore a light brown woolen cloak and hood over her gown. Since they were traveling, her hair was in two long, thick dark braids that hung over her shoulders.

The only sound to break the silence was the clip-clop of the horses' hooves, the slight jingling of the men's chain mail and the occasional plaintive cry of a curlew. She suspected many of the men were dozing in the saddle, for her father always preferred an early start. She herself had to stifle a yawn as she wondered how far they would get today. They were making their way home at a leisurely pace and still had some ways to go.

In truth, Rhiannon was rather eager for the journey to be finished, and not just because traveling meant the discomfort of long days riding and uncertain accommodation at inns and monasteries, although the monastery of St. David, where they had spent last night, had been quite comfortable. After that disastrous episode during her visit at Lord Melevoir's, she wanted nothing more than to be where she knew everyone, and they knew her. She would not encounter curious, gossiping women who would make much of an unexpected kiss in a courtyard, giggling and whispering behind her back.

As vexatious as that had been, she at least had the comfort of knowing that her father understood what had really happened the morning of Cynvelin's departure between herself and the Welshman, and that his words to Dylan and Griffydd insured that they would not be overly—and unnecessarily—critical. The rest of her father's party, being Welshmen, did not make much of a kiss, or at least, not that one.

What annoyed her most about Lord Cynvelin's act was that he had selfishly misconstrued her responses during their time together, and then forced her into an embarrassing situation with his self-indulgent action. He had not given much thought to how such an act would look to the Normans at all, she suspected, although he had been among the Normans enough to guess how they would interpret the kiss.

Lady Valmont had insured that she heard Lord Cynvelin's explanation for her less-than-delighted response, slyly hinting that she thought it clever of Rhiannon to feign indignation.

Rhiannon had known it was hopeless to try to correct that impression, at least with Lady Valmont.

She wondered what would have happened if Lady Valmont had been the one to come upon Bryce Frechette that night. Would she have confronted him as heedlessly? Would she have found herself in the shadows about to be seduced?

When Rhiannon recalled the sensation of Bryce

Frechette's caress and the intense expression in his eyes, she thought not. And when she remembered his words, that she was the most tempting woman he had ever seen, she felt sure of it. She also felt more flattered than by any flowery address Cynvelin had made.

For all his tournament prowess and attractiveness, Bryce Frechette had had no female companions at the feast, she recalled. He had never even spoken to the other noblewomen. He certainly didn't dance.

He kept himself apart and aloof, friendless, with no companion to talk to him until Lord Cynvelin had approached to ask him to join his company.

How sad and lonely it must be to have no one to speak with at such a pleasant gathering. No friend to laugh with. No brothers to tease. No father to confide in.

She glanced ahead at her father and watched as he made an unexpected gesture for Griffydd to ride forward, his bearing suddenly as alert as if an alarm had sounded.

She looked at the trees around them. This was an ideal place for an ambush, she realized, and the lingering mist seemed a gray, secretive cloak.

Her father held up his hand to signal a halt—and at the same time, Rhiannon saw two men riding abreast out of the trees ahead of them. One of them called out a greeting in Welsh, and she relaxed, until she got a better look at them.

What in the name of the saints was Bryce Frechette doing here, appearing like some spirit she had conjured with her ruminations? A scowl crossed her face when she recognized Cynvelin ap Hywell beside him.

Both warriors were attired in black, and armed. Frechette stared straight ahead, inscrutable, while Cynvelin ap Hywell smiled broadly, and as if they should be happy to see him.

What in the name of the saints was Lord Cynvelin doing here?

Another glance at her father made it very clear that he was wondering the same thing, and that he was not at all pleased by these visitors, any more than she was.

Then Lord Cynvelin caught sight of her and nodded a greeting. Her face flushed hotly and she pulled her hood around her face as if she would hide. It didn't help that Dylan flashed a condemning look at her, implying that this meeting was somehow all her fault.

She had not invited Lord Cynvelin to accost her on the road, any more than she had asked him to kiss her in public.

She dearly wished Lord Cynvelin had taken himself to London, or Paris, or even Rome, and forgotten all about her!

"Greetings, Baron!" Cynvelin cried jovially, halting his horse. "A good day to you."

"What do you want?" her father demanded harshly, also in Welsh.

"*O'r annwyl*, Baron DeLanyea, forgetting your manners, are you?" Cynvelin replied, apparently unconcerned. "Allow me to introduce my friend, Bryce Frechette."

"Take your knave," Dylan retorted, "and get out of our way!"

Rhiannon glanced at the impassive Norman, then quickly away. She was glad he couldn't understand her foster brother's rude command, and when she thought of the way Bryce Frechette had gone after the soldier who had insulted her, she thought Dylan should be glad of it, too.

"Dear me, Baron!" Cynvelin chided. "Haven't you learned to curb that fellow's tongue?"

Her father gave Dylan a warning look as the young man's hand went to his sword hilt.

As surprised as she was by Cynvelin's words, Rhiannon silently urged Dylan to be patient. A fight was not necessary. This was all due to a misunderstanding that would soon be set right. Clearly Cynvelin continued to believe she harbored enough affection for him that she would be eager to see him, under any circumstances. She would simply have to make it plain that she was not.

Even if that meant she wouldn't see more of Bryce Frechette, either.

"What do you want?" the baron repeated, his voice eerily calm.

"Your daughter's company."

"*What?*" Rhiannon gasped.

She cursed herself for having so much as looked at Cynvelin ap Hywell. No matter what had passed between them at Lord Melevoir's, there was nothing to warrant a belief that she would ride off into the countryside with him!

"Doing things in the Welsh way, is all, which I

should think you would respect," Cynvelin said, his tone nearly as calm as her father's had been. "I am not forgetting you kidnapped your own wife, Baron."

He was quite right about her parents, but there was far more to the story than that. And any abducting was done on the day of the wedding. Indeed, the ritual that had once been true abduction was now little more than a game, with willing participants.

But she didn't feel like playing.

"Lord Cynvelin," she began, determined to correct whatever false impression he harbored, "I'm afraid—"

"There is nothing to be afraid of," he interrupted, giving her one of his charming smiles.

"I will kill you before I let you take Rhiannon," her father announced, his voice still quite calm, but oh, so deadly cold!

She edged her horse farther back. What was this talk of killing? Although her father clearly hated the younger man, surely there was no need for such language.

"No, you will not," Cynvelin replied with equal steadiness. "You are surrounded by my men, excellent archers the lot of them." He jerked his head at his silent companion. "And I have the champion of Lord Melevoir's tournament beside me. If you wish a fight, so be it, but then people might get hurt."

"I don't want to go with you!" she objected.

The Welshman smiled at her as if to say he appreciated that she had to make some show of protest, however insincere.

"Order your men to move off," the baron commanded.

"No. Not unless Rhiannon comes with me."

"That is impossible."

"Proper, I wanted this to be, Baron," Cynvelin replied with a weary sigh, keeping his gaze on her father. "And I am telling you that an honorable courtship it will be." He looked at Rhiannon. "I can see from your face, my lovely Rhiannon, that your father has been filling your head with lies about me since we were last together. I feared it would be so. This is the only way I can correct whatever false impressions—"

"Are you calling my father a liar?" Griffydd charged, his stern voice ringing out.

Rhiannon held her breath. Griffydd was much slower to anger than Dylan, but she had seen him when he did anger, and if Cynvelin didn't retract his statement, he would regret it.

Cynvelin obviously realized this, too, for she saw the glimmer of fear in his eyes. "I am only wanting to have the pleasure of your sister's company. You pride yourself on being Welsh, Baron," he continued, turning his eyes toward her father. "Is that only for show, to impress our so-impressionable countrymen? Perhaps it is, if you are not willing to abide by a time-honored custom. Nevertheless, I remind you these woods are full of my men." He switched to the Norman's language. "Bryce, please be so good as to assist my Lady Rhiannon."

Bryce nudged his horse toward the cortege, very aware of the hostile glares of the one-eyed baron and the two younger men beside him who had to be related to him, judging by their bearing as much as their looks.

The baron's eye patch hid only a part of the scar that mottled his face. Although clearly past the prime of youth, Emryss DeLanyea was yet too muscular and imposing to be completely discounted as a fighter. It was a good thing this confrontation was a ritual, not a prelude to a battle.

Although Bryce would have liked to know what Lord Cynvelin and the obviously displeased baron had said to each other, the baron hadn't drawn his sword or ordered his men to stop him. Therefore, Bryce reasoned with some relief, Cynvelin must have been telling the truth.

Nevertheless, it was a good thing Cynvelin had warned him of the man's dislike; otherwise, Bryce would have felt compelled to draw his sword, just for safety's sake. The baron really did look as if he would gladly take the head off Lord Cynvelin, and him, too.

Bryce had to ride around the cortege, for not a one of them gave quarter as he rode toward the lady. She regarded him with an anger that seemed to match her father's. Rather extreme, perhaps, but given that Lord Cynvelin had warned him about her feigned reaction, too, he paid her no mind as he reached out to grab her mare's bridle.

"What are you doing?" she demanded.

"I am escorting you to my lord's castle," he replied, ignoring her haughty visage to lead her forward through the men, who now moved out of the way.

"Don't touch my horse."

"I have my orders, my lady."

"Let go!"

Bryce didn't respond. Welsh custom or not, this whole sham abduction suddenly struck him as the height of idiocy and a colossal waste of time, effort and manpower.

All he wanted was to get back to Annedd Bach, where he should have been spending the day seeing to the books of account, or the tenants' list, or even checking the stores, not riding about like some kind of merry brigand.

As he passed through the cortege, the other men's horses shifted nervously.

"Father?" Lady Rhiannon asked when they were abreast of the baron.

The man didn't look at his daughter. He kept his gaze on Lord Cynvelin ap Hywell, who smiled at Bryce and nodded his head.

Seeing that, Bryce obediently kicked his horse into a gallop and rode off down the road, taking Lady Rhiannon with him.

Chapter Five

"Have a care, Baron!" Cynvelin warned, his voice strong, but with the undercurrent of a coward's fear. "Attack me, and my men won't hesitate to kill her, as I see you've already realized!"

"Then we'll kill you all, too!" Dylan snarled, pulling his sword from its scabbard in one fluid motion.

"No!" Baron DeLanyea shouted, holding up his hand. "No," he repeated in a lower tone, yet one full of command that no man ever dared to disobey. He looked sorrowfully at his foster son, then Griffydd. "No. He will have her killed."

They all turned toward Cynvelin, who smiled triumphantly. "I see you have learned some wisdom, Baron. Truly, there is no need to fight, or for anyone to be hurt or killed. *Anyone*," he reiterated, the threat obvious. "I only ask a month, and if Rhiannon does not want to be my wife by then, I'll send her home to you, unharmed and in no way dishonored. Now order your *mabmaeth* to put away his weapon."

The baron nodded, and Dylan obeyed.

Cynvelin ignored everyone but the baron. "I understand that you have a grudge against me—"

"With good cause, as you well know," the baron interrupted.

Cynvelin eyed him scornfully. "So *you* say. Be that as it may, your daughter seems to find my company most acceptable. Or at least she did, until you saw fit to repeat certain accusations. No doubt you painted me the most vile of men."

He waited for the baron or one of the other DeLanyeas to confirm that. Instead they gazed at him in stony silence, even Dylan.

"That is unfortunate, but not an insurmountable obstacle. You see, Baron, I find your daughter very appealing, and nothing will give me greater pleasure than to have her for my wife."

"She will not want you," the baron said coldly.

"You think not? Well, perhaps you know best," Cynvelin replied lightly. "Nevertheless, I ask a month of her company at Caer Coch with no interference from you. If I have that, and she refuses me, I shall return her as I said I would. If you try to take her from me before that time...well, it might go hard on someone, and I assure you, Baron DeLanyea, it would not be me."

"Would you threaten her?" Dylan cried heatedly.

"Dylan!" the baron barked, glaring at his foster son. "Silence! Keep still!"

"I am glad to see you still rule your underlings. Soon enough, I'm sure, they will chafe at your orders, like I did. Like any man of spirit would."

The baron's mouth twisted into a grimace of a

smile. "They are honorable men," he said quietly. "They would never do the things you have done."

Cynvelin flushed. "Enough talk. I have Rhiannon, and I will keep her the month. I give you my word, Baron, that I will not harm her in that time, and if she does not wish to remain with me after that, I will send her home to you." He smiled very slowly. "You had better hope I am more honorable than you believe, my lord. And you had better not try to get her back, in case I am far more dishonorable than you believe."

With that, Cynvelin ap Hywell wheeled his horse around. "Farewell, Baron," he called jauntily. "Or should I call you 'Father'?"

Dylan emitted a harsh curse as Cynvelin rode off down the road. "You are going to let him go without a fight?" he demanded, gesturing at Cynvelin's retreating figure. "We could take him!"

"But Frechette and his men would still have Rhiannon," the baron replied, his tone full of scorn as well as worry. "You heard him. We have no choice. As long as he holds Rhiannon, we must do what he says."

"Then why did you let Frechette take her?"

"Would you rather have her lying dead, an arrow through her heart?" the baron retorted. "You heard what he said. He had his archers aiming at her."

"Surely he wouldn't—"

"Yes, he would, if we had tried to stop them." The baron took a deep breath to restore some measure of calm. "Dylan, take five men and ride for Hu Morgan, then go to Bridgeford Wells and tell Fitzroy what has happened. He will come, and Lord Gervais will also send some men with him. We shall return to the monastery at St. David. If we must wait, we will do so as close to Rhiannon as possible."

Dylan nodded eagerly. "Of course we are needing more men to attack Caer Coch. What of Trystan?"

"No." The baron gave his foster son a shrewd look. "One hothead is enough. Order the rest of the men to prepare to ride."

Dylan nodded and immediately began issuing orders, moving back through the line of soldiers.

The baron signaled for his eldest son to come closer. "Go, you, and follow their path. When you know where they have taken her, meet me at the monastery." His gaze faltered, and suddenly he wasn't the proud, mighty Baron DeLanyea. He was a father worried about his daughter. "Make sure they do not see you."

"Take me back!" Rhiannon ordered fiercely, trying to pull her mare to a halt and panting because the jogging motion of the galloping horse made it hard for her to draw breath. "Take me back to my father! He's a powerful man! You'll regret it if you don't! He has friends at court!"

Frechette didn't respond.

"What kind of dolt are you? Are you deaf? Let me go!"

Still they galloped.

Believing she had little choice but to take action, Rhiannon slipped her feet from the stirrups. She didn't want to jump; nevertheless, she did, rolling on the muddy verge of the road.

She couldn't draw breath or stand, so she started to crawl toward the underbrush. Her cloak caught on a branch, so she tore at the tie and left it behind.

Then two booted feet appeared in front of her. She raised her eyes to behold Frechette looming over her. Instead of looking fierce or angry, though, he looked worried.

"Are you hurt?" he asked with apparent sincere concern, reaching down and helping her to stand on wobbly legs.

"I...I don't know," she muttered sullenly. She was covered in mud, but at least she could breathe. She gave him a sidelong glance. "If I were, would you take me back?"

His expression hardened. "I see you are not hurt," he replied.

"This was a mistake."

"Yes, it is a mistake to jump from a galloping horse, unless you want your neck broken," he agreed. "I would rather you refrained from such feats while you are my responsibility."

"Then you shouldn't have taken me away from my father."

He looked at her quizzically. "Is this not one of your customs?"

"Yes, but—"

"Then I would take your complaints to your countryman."

"You don't—"

"My lady," he interrupted dispassionately, "I

don't know your ways, but what I am learning does not impress me. Indeed, I would say Welsh customs are for fools. However, I have no wish to insult you."

Rhiannon glared at him, then crossed her arms and regarded him defiantly. "You had better take me back at once, or it will be the worse for you."

"I regret my orders are otherwise." He held out his hand toward her. "Come."

She didn't move. "I tell you, Lord Cynvelin has made a mistake!"

"I think so, too," Bryce replied calmly.

"Then will you not return me to my party?"

"Gladly, if it were up to me. I would save Lord Cynvelin from such a marriage. Unfortunately, he wants you for his wife."

"Marriage—what is this talk of marriage?"

He frowned darkly. "Betrothal. Courting. I know not what you might call it."

"Abduction is what I call it."

Her response made no impression upon him. "My lady, please get on your horse."

"If you do not take me back to my father and he has to fetch me, he might kill you," she warned.

"If he will kill me, I don't think it would be wise to go near him, do you?" Bryce replied with an infuriating calm. He put a hand to his ear and said, "I hear no sound of pursuit."

Rhiannon realized he was quite right. "He must be trying to reason with Lord Cynvelin."

Bryce ignored her comment and glanced up at the sky. "We had best go before it starts to rain. Again," he finished sarcastically, as if she were somehow to blame for the weather.

Rhiannon wanted to scream with frustration, but what good would that do? Obviously he was not going to listen; she would have to speak with Cynvelin himself to clear up this misunderstanding. "I cannot."

His eyes narrowed.

"My horse has run off," she said, her tone one she might use with a dolt.

Bryce shrugged his shoulders. "Then you will have to share mine."

"No."

"If you want to make this difficult," he muttered.

With that, he yanked her close, picked her up and slung her over his shoulder, knocking the wind out of her again. As she struggled, he marched stoically toward his waiting horse. "Don't make such a commotion. Your efforts are wasted on me."

"There was no need to manhandle me!" Rhiannon cried as he set her on his horse.

"I thought there was."

"*You* thought!" she muttered caustically.

"Yes, I did," he growled.

She looked as if she were about to jump off, then, as he glared at her, she apparently thought better of it and fell into a sullen silence.

Maybe she had finally realized there was no need to keep up her loud protestations for his benefit, Bryce thought irritably as he mounted behind her. By now he was sure such exclamations were completely fraudulent.

If they were not, the baron would never have allowed him to ride off with her. No one had followed them, either.

Perhaps, he thought sourly, the baron wasn't so sorry to be rid of his spoiled, flirtatious daughter.

Bryce nudged his horse into a walk. Despite Lady Rhiannon's continued silence, he had some difficulty restoring his equanimity. This whole scheme seemed such a ludicrous business.

And she was still far too tempting.

He glanced at the back of Lady Rhiannon's neck, visible between her thick braids. The skin looked smooth and soft, and very, very kissable.

Only if he wanted to get himself slapped, or worse.

Then she shivered, just as she had that night in the courtyard when he had touched her. He realized her gown, muddy and damp, was clinging to her body, and her cloak was missing. She must have lost it when she had dramatically, and foolishly, jumped from her horse.

He frowned. Maybe that was customary, too.

Nevertheless, she really was shivering. His first instinct was to hold her tighter, only for the added warmth, of course, yet he could easily guess how that gesture would be received.

He halted his horse.

"What...what are you doing?" she demanded, albeit in a less hostile manner as he dismounted. Staring at him, she crossed her arms over her chest.

"You are cold," he said.

Her eyes widened as he stripped off his new tunic, so that he wore only his breeches and boots.

"No. No, I'm not," she stammered, looking away.

She seemed suddenly, and surprisingly, modest, far different from the temptress who had lured him into the shadows.

Which was she, and which would he prefer?

His gaze strayed to her lower leg, exposed because her skirts were riding up as she sat astride. He just as quickly looked away, because it did not and must not matter to him what she was like. She was to be Lord Cynvelin's bride, and that was all he needed to know about her.

"Your lips are blue and you're shivering. Here," he said, handing up the woolen garment. "Wrap that about you."

"It will get dirty."

"Take it!" he commanded, hurriedly mounting again behind her before she could say anything more.

She did as he ordered, and he adjusted the garment about her slender shoulders, trying not to touch her, or to remember the kiss they had shared.

"Thank you," she said grudgingly.

"You're most welcome, my lady."

He clucked his tongue and his horse began walking again.

Forcing himself to concentrate on the way back to Annedd Bach, Bryce anxiously scanned the undergrowth, more than half convinced they had gone the wrong way. When they had ridden yet more distance with no sign of a stream, he cursed softly.

"What's the matter?" Rhiannon asked. "Are you cold? Do you want your tunic back—or have you seen the error of your ways? Will you return me to my father?"

"No, I am not cold. No, I do not want my tunic back. And no, I cannot take you back. I have my orders."

"Then what is the matter?" She twisted to look back at him, her dark brows furrowed, her eyes puzzled, her lips half parted.

She quickly faced forward again. "I want to go home," she mumbled.

"Believe me, my lady," he growled, "nothing would make me happier."

This was a monstrous lie. Nothing would make him happier than to capture her lips with his own and press her enticing body against his.

"Unfortunately, I fear I have lost the way."

With an incredulous expression, Rhiannon turned to look at him. "You are lost?"

"Hardly surprising," he replied defensively. "I am completely unfamiliar with this territory. I have never been this way before. All the trees look the same, and the underbrush, too."

"Then turn around and go back. I have no desire to be benighted in the woods."

"Nor do I, my lady." He glanced upward, where the sun shone feebly through the leaves and clouds. Perhaps he should have gone down that first path a little way back. "I am sure we are headed in the right direction. We should get to Annedd Bach soon enough."

"Little house?"

"Is that what Annedd Bach means?"

"Yes."

He frowned at her contemptuous tone. "Have no fear, my lady. It is a castle."

"Oh."

"You are an honored guest."

She made a dismissive sniff. No doubt she was disappointed they were not going to Lord Cynvelin's stronghold.

Bryce suddenly heard the babble of rushing water and in another moment, to his great relief, he caught sight of a stream. "I know where we are now," he announced.

"What a clever fellow!"

He ignored her sarcastic response. She was wet and probably tired, so he would excuse her rudeness, especially when they reached the stream and he could see up its course. In the distance he could make out the wall of Annedd Bach.

He decided it would be wise to follow the course of the stream. "This is pretty country, when it's not covered in mist," he reflected.

"How kind of you to say so," she said, turning her head to the side. "We Welsh wouldn't know that unless you Normans told us, of course."

Bryce scowled even as he regarded the smooth line of her jaw and the perfect shape of her nose. "You're part Norman yourself, aren't you, my lady?"

"Yes," she answered reluctantly.

"You're not ashamed of that, surely?" he asked, wondering if she was.

She straightened her shoulders and faced forward

again. "No, of course not," she replied brusquely. "I am proud to be a DeLanyea."

"Judging by your fathers and brothers, you have every right to be," he said truthfully.

"My father is the finest lord in all of Britain," she declared.

When Bryce thought of the baron's demeanor, he could certainly believe her father was one of the greatest warrior barons in Britain. "Tell me, my lady, how did he lose his eye?"

"Fighting the infidel in the Holy Land."

"Ah!"

"King Richard and the others left him there. It took him many years to get home. Unlike some, *his* exile was not self-imposed and the result of a family squabble."

Bryce stiffened at her condemnation. "Exile is still exile," he remarked when he thought he could keep his tone civil.

She turned again to regard him with searching, green-eyed intensity. "You could have gone home. There was nothing to stop you."

"Except pride."

"What was that when your sister was left alone and unprotected, and in poverty, too?"

He had had his misdeeds cast up to him a hundred times and thought he was immune to condemnation, but without pausing to examine why, he wanted her to understand. "I went away because I argued with my father over money," he explained. "My father spent too freely and when I realized there might be trouble, I tried to make him use more caution. He treated me like a child, telling me I shouldn't worry. I got angry and told him what I thought of the path he was taking and what I thought of him for taking it. Then I left.''

"When he was dying, you did not come home," she noted, her tone gentler. She looked at him in a new way, too, as if she were trying to understand.

"I never knew that he was ill, or I would have come at once.''

The sympathetic expression fled her face, to be replaced by the disapproval that was more usually there. "Because nobody knew where you had gone," she said. "Surely it was your duty to—"

Just as suddenly, he was tired of her disapproval. Tired of trying to explain.

"My lady," he growled, "when you have known what it is to feel you cannot return to your home because of hurtful words said in haste and frustration, then you may criticize me. When you have tried to earn money for your family without them knowing by fighting in tournaments wherever they may be, then you may chastise me for keeping my whereabouts a secret. I am quite certain you have no comprehension of what it is to feel ashamed of anything you have done, even if you should, so perhaps it would be wise to keep your ignorant opinions to yourself.''

Rhiannon reached out and grabbed the reins, pulling his horse to a halt.

"What are you doing now?" Bryce demanded.

"Here," she declared, pulling his tunic off her shoulders and tossing it onto the muddy ground.

"Get dressed. I will not have people see me riding with a man who is half-naked. I would be too *ashamed.*"

He emitted a scoffing laugh. "You would rather have them see you covered in mud?" he asked sarcastically.

"Since the state of my gown is your fault, that will not shame me."

He slipped from the horse, grabbed Lord Cynvelin's garment and yanked it over his head. He glared at her, only to realize she was smiling and, he thought, trying not to laugh. "What amuses you so, my lady?" he demanded.

"Considering you apparently do not know your back from your front, I would not be calling the Welsh dolts, if I were you."

He glanced down at the tunic and realized she was right. With another scowl, he tried to get his arms out to turn it, only to discover that it was not as easy as it should be.

"Here, let me help." Rhiannon dismounted and took hold of the garment, tugging on it.

To Bryce's dismay, he heard a tearing noise. "God's wounds," he muttered.

"If you would stop moving and put your arm down," Rhiannon ordered. "There!"

She faced him boldly, this beautiful woman with the shining eyes and lovely face who had enticed him and tempted him and who he could not forget any more than he could ignore the overwhelming urge to kiss her. With fierce passion he pulled her into his arms and his mouth swooped down upon hers.

This time, though, there was no answering response. She stiffened, then struggled in his arms.

At once he let her go, to see her glaring at him. "You blackguard! I hope my father does kill you!"

Angry and ashamed at his own rash act, Bryce cursed himself for an impulsive fool. He had never kissed a woman against her will in his life; therefore, he reasoned defensively, his impetuous action had to be her fault for looking at him that way.

"And I hope you will make your husband happy," he declared. "Tell me, do you honestly think you will be content with one man for the rest of your life?"

"The rest of my life is none of your business."

"Thank God!"

She turned on her heel and marched toward his horse. Fearing that she would take it and desert him, he hurried after her and reached the beast before she did, grabbing hold of its bridle. When he looked back triumphantly, he was shocked to see that she was wiping away tears.

"My lady!" he cried remorsefully. No matter how she had regarded him, he knew, that was no excuse to act like an immoral beast.

She halted in front of him, defiant despite her damp cheeks. "I'm not crying," she asserted.

She did not want to look weak, he conjectured sympathetically. Then his heart filled with admiration at her strength, and her pride.

"Your tunic is torn," she noted scornfully. "Do I not recognize this garment? Is it not a cast-off of your master's?"

It occurred to him that some women had too much pride and strength of character. "I am well aware of the origin of my current attire," he replied coldly. "I gather my clothes were not fitting for a grooms-man on such a delightful mission."

Her mouth turned down in a disdainful frown.

"You could not be a groomsman."

"No, of course not," he replied sarcastically. "I am a dispossessed Norman who selfishly abandoned his family in a childish fit of pique, not worthy of anything except your contempt." He held out his hand to assist her onto his horse. "Shall we, my lady?"

"As long as you leave me alone," she grudgingly conceded.

They rode the rest of the way in silence. Soon they came to a path leading from the stream up onto the main road, and Bryce turned the horse to follow it.

"Is there no village here?" Rhiannon asked when they came to the road and they could see the gates of Annedd Bach.

"There are some houses near the entrance, but I would not say it was much of a village."

"Oh. No wonder. Annedd Bach is not much of a castle."

Bryce scowled all the rest of the way to the fortress. To be sure Annedd Bach was not much now, but he would do the best he could to improve it, just as he would obey Lord Cynvelin. Then he would be a nobleman again.

He noticed the knot of Cynvelin's men loitering in the courtyard near the stables, talking among themselves. Then he spotted Cynvelin, who had obviously been waiting for them.

Bryce slipped off his horse and held out his hand again to assist Rhiannon. Without seeming to be aware of his existence, she placed her hand in his as she dismounted.

Bryce let go at once and did not look at her face. He never wanted to touch her or be close to her again. She was far too temptingly dangerous.

Chapter Six

"Ah, here is my beautiful Rhiannon!" Cynvelin declared, approaching them.

He made a sweeping bow.

"What has happened?" he cried, concern on every feature as he ran his gaze over her, then Bryce Frechette. "Did your horse fall and run away? I hope you are not injured, my lady?"

"No, I'm not hurt, and yes, my horse ran away, so I will need to borrow one of yours," Rhiannon said firmly.

It was taking considerable effort for her to maintain some fortitude. In addition to the shock and anger at Cynvelin's presumptuous plan, she had to cope with the disturbing, equally presumptuous Bryce Frechette. How dare he kiss her again?

How could she find it so difficult to repel his advances?

Was it written on her face that she was some kind of weak-willed creature who would welcome such treatment? If so, she would try all the harder to dispel any such erroneous notions. Just as she would subdue her surely immoral yearning to be in Bryce Frechette's embrace.

Cynvelin's brow furrowed with puzzlement. "Of course, my lady, if you wish. I shall be only too happy to give you a horse."

"Not give," she said. "I will see that it is returned."

"Returned? No, it would be my gift."

Rhiannon stifled the urge to retort that she didn't want gifts of any kind from him. However, the knowledge that her previous indiscreet behavior at Lord Melevoir's might be partly responsible for her predicament made her hold her tongue.

"I was beginning to fear for your safety," Lord Cynvelin said.

"I got lost," Bryce admitted. "I missed the first path."

"Ah!" the Welshman exclaimed with a smile. "I should have thought of that. But you are here at last."

Rhiannon was anxious to set things right as soon as possible, yet she was all too aware that Cynvelin's soldiers and another motley group of men were present, as well as Bryce Frechette. This was uncomfortably like the last time she had been in a courtyard with Cynvelin, so she said, "May we not speak in private, my lord?"

"Of course!" He gestured toward the hall. "I wouldn't want you to catch cold, my lady. I promised your father I would take good care of you, so please come into the hall. There is a fire in the hearth to warm you."

He held out his arm to escort her. Seeing no help for it, she laid her hand upon his forearm.

"Bryce, would you be so good as to excuse us?" Cynvelin said as he placed his hot hand over Rhiannon's. "There is some problem with the accommodation for Lady Rhiannon. See to it."

"As you wish, my lord," the Norman said before making his obeisance and striding toward the keep.

Watching him leave, Rhiannon had to fight to subdue the urge to insist that he stay, which was, of course, ridiculous. He was rude, impertinent, thoroughly disconcerting and he had kissed her when he should not.

Nor did he ever defer to her...or speak down to her, as if she was a child.

She impatiently pulled her hand from Cynvelin's arm and marched toward the hall.

"Women!" she heard Cynvelin mutter, and then a burst of sympathetic male laughter.

Rhiannon scowled, once again displeased by his behavior. She was a noblewoman, from a fine family and deserving of respect. She should not be made the butt of jokes, or kissed in public, or anywhere! No wonder Bryce Frechette had felt free to do so. In his eyes, she surely looked a brazen wench.

While her opinion of him, although not the best, was getting better, especially when she thought of what he had said about his family as they had shared his horse—until he had kissed her again.

She strode into the hall of Annedd Bach and looked around. It was a cold, barren room, with no tapestries to brighten the walls, no linens in evidence, and a small fire smoking in the central hearth. There were no servants anywhere, and no sign of food or drink.

Was this Lord Cynvelin's idea of hospitality?

She went to one of the two chairs and flung herself into it. In another moment, Lord Cynvelin strolled into the hall, his hands behind his back and that stupid smile on his face. She barely looked at him when he sat in the chair next to her.

She took a deep breath and spoke bluntly. "Thank you for your welcome, Lord Cynvelin," she announced. "Unfortunately, I fear there has been a terrible mistake."

"Mistake, my lady?"

"Yes." She took another deep breath, reluctant to apologize in view of what Lord Cynvelin had done, but she was determined to be just. "I must ask your forgiveness for misleading you. It was never my intention to have you believe I wish to marry you."

"My lady, you quite break my heart!" he cried, obviously surprised. "I thought...rather, I had hoped—"

"Again, I apologize," she said. "I should have been more circumspect. I enjoyed your company—"

"As I enjoyed yours," Lord Cynvelin said in a low, seductive tone that only made her want to scowl, "so much that I have been longing to see you again. Desperate men do desperate things. I know your father has told you stories about me, but I will do my best to set right any misunderstanding you may have of me."

"*Misunderstanding* is not the word I would use,"

Rhiannon replied. "He told me you were a liar and a cheat, and that you were always making trouble among the men."

"I am surprised that is all he said," Cynvelin remarked, looking away as if embarrassed.

"Are those not serious enough defects?"

"I was intimidated by your family," he explained, turning submissive eyes to her. "I thought only to reveal what was going on in the barracks to your father. Men who harbor grudges cannot make an effective garrison. Naturally, those involved claimed that I was lying, and then sought to discredit me by saying I cheated at some harmless gambling. If I had been older and wiser, I would have proceeded with more care. Unfortunately, I was a heedless, impetuous youth determined to do the right thing. Your father did not understand my purpose, nor would he listen to me. He sent me away instead."

"What of the lies? You told me you had never met my father. You cannot tell me that was not a lie."

"A harmless ruse, my lady," he said with a wistful smile. "At first I was afraid to. I didn't want to talk about my time at Craig Fawr. I...I confess I was pleased when I realized he had not spoken of me, that I was not already a villain in your lovely eyes. I decided not to tell you about what had happened until you knew me better, and then...and then I hoped it would not matter. I hoped you would forgive me whatever indiscretion I was guilty of in my youth.

"And I knew I could never go to Craig Fawr," he

continued fervently. "That is why I brought you here."

"Whatever their cause, your actions today were not honorable, or welcome," she said in a more moderate tone.

"My lady!" he beseeched. He reached for her hand and kissed it gently.

She snatched it away from him, then crossed her arms over her breasts. "No harm has been done. I will take the responsibility for your misunderstanding. I am sorry to have misled you, but I have been frightened, taken away from my family and brought here against my will. Now I want to go back to my father."

"I thought there was no other way to get close to you, my lady." He pressed his hands together in a pleading gesture. "As I told your father, I only ask one month in your company. After a month, if you wish to leave, I will provide you with an escort."

"My father agreed to this?" she asked dubiously.

"Yes, my lady," he replied. "Not without some persuading, I will confess, but at last he conceded and gave me this chance, for which I am very grateful. Surely you won't deny my request after the pleasant times we shared at Lord Melevoir's castle.

"And we will not stay here," he hastened to add. "We will go to my home, Caer Coch. I assure you, the accommodation is much finer."

"I appreciate the sentiment behind your actions, my lord," she said, trying to remain patient. "Nevertheless, I must insist that you take me back to my family *today*."

"I regret I cannot do that, my lady," he said, still with his usual smile.

Before she could say more, he rose swiftly and faced her. "A month is not so long, my lady, and little enough after what you led me to believe at Lord Melevoir's, as you yourself have said. At the end of the month, if you wish to go to Craig Fawr, I will have you escorted there. You have my word."

Rhiannon's gaze faltered. He sounded so sincere. Perhaps her father had been wrong about Lord Cynvelin. And she *was* to blame for his misconception.

Surely she could persuade Cynvelin to take her home before the month was out.

She got to her feet. "Very well, my lord. I see no harm in staying a little while, especially if my father had given his permission. Has my father gone on to Craig Fawr?"

"I hope so."

She gave him a quizzical look. He smiled. "I believe that was his plan, my lady. I am afraid I was so pleased that he had given his permission, I was not as attentive as I should have been."

"Oh." She wished Cynvelin was more knowledgeable, but it was probable that her father would either journey toward Caer Coch, or continue to Craig Fawr. She would rather be sure, though.

"If you would be so good as to have a servant show me to my quarters, I would like to retire, my lord," she said.

"Very well, my lady. There is a chamber prepared for you in the keep, and you will find some gowns and other garments there. Again, you have my apologies for the less-than-appropriate accommodation, but it is only for tonight. However, I hope you will join us in the hall for the evening meal."

"No, thank you, my lord," she said. "I would prefer to eat alone. I am very tired and would not be good company."

He frowned slightly, then quickly gave her another wistful smile. "If that is what you would prefer, although I shall be desolate without your charming company."

He again took hold of her hand and pressed a kiss upon the back of it, and this time she did not pull it away.

"Please look upon Annedd Bach as your own for tonight, my sweet lady," he said. He spotted one of the maidservants near the entrance. "Ula!" he called out. "Please show Lady Rhiannon to her quarters."

The girl nodded, and Rhiannon followed her out of the hall.

Cynvelin watched Rhiannon follow the wench out the door and turn toward the keep.

Then he rubbed his fist into his palm in frustration.

This was not going as he had planned. She was supposed to be happy to see him, grateful for his desire that had made him abduct her, anxious to share his bed. Instead, she dared to say that *he* had made a mistake.

The little fool! She had certainly acted as if she had fallen in love with him at Lord Melevoir's, smiling and laughing and dancing, looking at him with adoration. How could he be to blame, especially when he had been at such pains to make it so? Other women would have willingly run to his bed with much less effort on his part.

He wanted Rhiannon DeLanyea to be passionately in love with him. She would be his wife, and she would bear his children. She would be so in love with him, she would turn against her father and believe whatever he, Cynvelin ap Hywell, chose to make her believe.

Which would torture Emryss DeLanyea for the rest of his life, a fitting vengeance for being turned out of Craig Fawr like a common thief.

Not only that, Cynvelin reflected with a scowl, but as the baron's son-in-law he could use DeLanyea's power as leverage for his own schemes, even without the man's knowledge or agreement.

Not to mention the prospect of Rhiannon herself for his wife, a beautiful, accomplished lady who would make a fine chatelaine, as well as most beddable spouse, at least while she still had novelty to add to her charms.

Aroused, he contemplated what he would do this night, for frustrated urges made a man liable to foolish mistakes.

That serving wench again? He thought not. She had lain on the bed like a dead fish.

If memory served, there was a village an hour's ride away with an inn, and the serving wenches there were pleased to earn some extra money. He would go there tonight.

Cynvelin smiled slowly. A whore tonight, out of

necessity, but soon enough, one way or another, Rhiannon DeLanyea would be in his bed.

Glaring at the old female servant, Bryce stamped his foot in frustration and pointed again at the pile of bedding in the storeroom. "I want you to take those to the bedchamber in the keep," he told her.

The servant gazed at him with all the apparent intelligence of a somnambulant cow as he thrust his finger toward the keep, which was across the cobbled courtyard from this virtually empty building.

Ermin had told him that there was no bedding for the lady. Disgruntled, Bryce had found one of the female servants and come to the storeroom himself to find that there was linen right in plain sight. Now if he could only make the hag understand what she was to do with it.

It seemed he had been trying to make her understand for an eternity.

Or perhaps it seemed so long because of his unconquerable curiosity to know what was passing between Lady Rhiannon and her betrothed.

Not that it was any of his business. He had done what Cynvelin had asked, and obeyed as he had been ordered.

As if he were the lowliest servant in the castle.

He may be a hireling, but he was most certainly more than a servant, and he deeply resented the manner in which Cynvelin had addressed him.

In front of Lady Rhiannon, too.

"I want those taken to the lady's chamber," he repeated slowly and loudly, pointing at the blankets on the dusty wooden shelf. He knew the problem was not the servant's ability to hear but to understand a foreign tongue. Still, he felt better for raising his voice.

"*Pa beth?*" the crone queried.

"I want these taken to the keep bedchamber," he said.

The hag gave him a blank look and shrugged her scrawny shoulders.

"Oh, never mind!" Bryce snarled.

He gestured for the woman to go and, after another shrug of her stick-thin shoulders, she did, tottering off toward the kitchen where she would likely eat whatever she could lay her claws on.

Bryce picked up the first blanket. It was riddled with small holes.

"Oh, sweet Savior!" Bryce muttered as he grabbed one of the others. It was in the same condition. And the next.

He discovered that the blankets also smelled. Who could say when these had last seen the light of day, or fresh air?

"Excellent," he murmured sarcastically, tossing the blankets back onto the shelf in a heap. "Lord Cynvelin might have let me prepare before this little game commenced. Now I'll have to try to make somebody understand that the blankets need to be mended and aired."

He could ask Lord Cynvelin for guidance in this matter, but that would mean interrupting his conversation with his almost-betrothed. Worse, it might look as if Bryce were incapable of handling even a small domestic problem, and that might lead Lord Cynvelin to question his competence to oversee an estate.

In the meantime, however, Lady Rhiannon had to have some kind of covering. In the night. In her bed.

He closed his eyes. He simply had to ignore his burning desire. She belonged to Lord Cynvelin, and she was going to marry him. Soon enough she would be gone, while he would remain, doing his best to revive this estate and train the garrison so that he would once again be a titled man. *That* was what he needed to remember.

At the very least he should be able to control his growing jealousy, especially in view of her apparently immodest behavior.

Apparently? She had to be a shameless hussy, or else why would she tempt him when she was as good as betrothed to another? Why else would she let Lord Cynvelin kiss her like that? Why else would Lord Cynvelin imply that tonight they would be sharing the same bed?

What good was all this thinking doing him?

He would take his own bedding to the keep bedchamber. It was not luxurious, but better than nothing, and no matter how uncomfortable he might be without it, that was the simplest solution.

A sudden vision of Lady Rhiannon under his blanket, her waist-length hair loose about her, her eyes and lips smiling, nearly took his breath away.

"God's wounds," Bryce growled as he left the storehouse to go to the barracks for his bedding, "I will be glad to see them gone!"

* * *

Rhiannon stood in the small round room in the upper level of the keep of Annedd Bach and looked around the chamber. It was sparsely furnished with a narrow rope bed and a feather mattress naked of coverings, as well as a table sporting a basin and ewer. There was a stool in one corner and a medium-sized leather-clad chest in the other.

At least everything seemed relatively clean.

She glanced at the thin, pinched-faced serving wench who had shown her here.

"Is that ewer filled?" she asked, thinking she would feel more herself when she was clean of mud and better able to think what to do next.

"No, my lady." The servant hurried forward and snatched up the ewer, obviously intending to fill it at once.

"Wait a moment," Rhiannon said. "What is your name?"

"Ula, my lady."

"Have you been a servant here long?"

Ula nodded. "I've lived at Annedd Bach all my life."

"Is Lord Cynvelin a good master?"

The girl's face betrayed no answer. "I'll fetch you the water now, my lady," she muttered, turning to leave.

Rhiannon hurried after her and grabbed Ula's arm to make her halt. The girl looked down at Rhiannon's hand and she let go at once.

"Ula, please listen," she urged. "This has all been a terrible misunderstanding. Lord Cynvelin thinks I care for him a great deal more than I do. There will be no repercussions if I return to my father, and perhaps even a reward if someone were to carry a message asking him to come for me,'' she finished hopefully.

Ula's only answer was a frown.

Then they both heard footsteps on the stairs leading to the upper chamber. A frightened look crossed Ula's face before she darted out the door, while Rhiannon moved back quickly.

Scowling, Bryce Frechette appeared on the threshold, carrying a bundle of cloth.

For a moment, Rhiannon felt a strange combination of dread and excitement. She could not have said if she was afraid he would try to kiss her again, or afraid that he wouldn't.

He strode into the room, halted and bowed toward Rhiannon, who acknowledged his presence with an inclination of her head. He glanced at the naked feather bed, and her heart seemed to stop, only to begin to beat wildly.

What kind of power did this man have to make her even consider sharing a bed with him after what he had done?

He held out the bundle in his hand. "I brought you some bedding, my lady."

She blushed, feeling as if he could read her shameless thoughts.

"Thank you," she replied haughtily, determined to maintain what dignity she still possessed. "I am surprised that you would do a servant's task."

"I regret there is no place finer for you," he said,

ignoring her comment, the words apparently yanked out of him against his will.

"I regret I must be here at all," she snapped as she stepped forward to take the bedding from his hands. "I was wondering if I would have to sleep on the floor. Now you may go."

His brow furrowed in puzzlement, but only for an instant. "I'm sure Lord Cynvelin wouldn't have allowed that to happen," he replied with an equally defiant expression. "He likes his comforts, too, I'm sure."

Her eyes narrowed suspiciously. "What are you implying?"

"Me?" he asked with mock innocence, for she saw the implication in his eyes. "Nothing at all."

"I am no wanton wench!" she declared.

"No, of course not. The stores here are meagre at present," he continued before she could respond. "However, we have what Lord Cynvelin has brought. Fortunately, the cook here makes better bread than one might expect, and I'm sure good wine has been brought. Will you join us for the evening meal, or would you prefer that I send a servant here with some light refreshment?"

She was impressed by his realization that she might not care for company, something that seemed beyond Lord Cynvelin's powers of discernment. However, she wasn't about to forget his previous insulting implication.

"As I said to Lord Cynvelin, I am tired and would rather not join the company this evening. I would be grateful for whatever food you can provide."

"Very well, my lady." His face expressionless, Bryce Frechette bowed and swiveled on his heel as if to leave.

"Frechette!" She stepped forward and almost held out her hands beseechingly, but the realization that she might appear to be begging made her clasp her hands together tightly instead.

"Frechette," she said firmly, "I want to go back to my father."

"I told you, I am ignorant of your ways, my lady."

She took another step closer. "You don't understand. I have asked Lord Cynvelin to take me back and he has refused. He insists I stay with him a month."

Bryce cocked his head as he regarded her. To be sure, she sounded desperate to be away from here, but he had seen her with Lord Cynvelin at the feast, and kissing him, too. Besides, he had no idea what else might be involved in these strange Welsh marriage rituals and perhaps these protestations were part of the game. "If Lord Cynvelin wishes you to stay, then I think you should stay," he replied noncommittally.

Her large green eyes flashed and her face flushed, bringing a pink glow to her cheeks. "I tell you, I want to go home!" she cried like a spoiled child.

"And I tell you, my lady, if Lord Cynvelin thinks you should stay, I will not go against his orders."

"What kind of man are you, Bryce Frechette?" she demanded. "Are you just a sword to be hired out? A warrior to be bought, like an ox or a horse?"

His jaw clenched at her words. Custom or no custom, game or no game, he would not be insulted. "I am in the service of Lord Cynvelin ap Hywell, my lady, and it is my duty to do as he commands."

Her lip curled disdainfully as she turned away. "Ah, your duty and your honor are available for purchase, then. Perhaps I should have said my father will pay you well if you convince Lord Cynvelin to let me go back to him."

Bryce abruptly reached out and grabbed her shoulders, forcing her to look at him. "I don't know what kind of pleasant diversion you and your lover are enjoying here, but that is between the pair of you. Not me."

"Lover? He is not my lover!"

"Call him what you will, as long as you understand, my lady, that I hold whatever honor I have left very dear, even if I lack a title. And you should know that such things can change. They *will* change. I will make it so, and Lord Cynvelin is offering me a way to begin again. Therefore, I am beholden to him, and it is my duty to obey his orders."

She did not look away. She did not flinch beneath his angry gaze. Instead, her gaze held his firmly. "I hold my honor dear, too," she declared. "I am not Cynvelin's lover. I will *never* be his lover."

"What are you saying?" he asked, truly puzzled, scarcely daring to believe what her words seemed to be indicating, yet hoping he was right.

"I am saying that there has been a mistake. Lord Cynvelin acted with undue haste."

"If you do not wish to stay—"

"I don't."

"You should ask Lord Cynvelin to escort you."

"I have and he will not."

A part of Bryce could easily understand why a man in love with Lady Rhiannon DeLanyea would not want to do anything that took her away from him.

"Would you help me?" she asked softly, a pleading look in her eyes.

A trusting look. A look that made him feel an honorable man again. "Are you certain you do not want to stay?" he whispered, taking a step closer.

"You have to take me back right away."

Her order, for so it sounded, cooled his ardor and destroyed his hopeful fancy. "Or what?"

She flushed and blinked as if uncomprehending.

"Or what, my lady?" he persisted. "You won't kiss me again? You won't let me touch you? You won't entice me?"

"I...I didn't mean to entice you," she stammered, not meeting his harsh gaze.

"Let me guess. You must return to your father before the wedding or some such nonsense, and you must convince someone to take you, in whatever way you can, is that it?"

"No! I do need your help," she said, regarding him with her big green eyes.

"Oh, please, my lady! You have played Delilah for me twice, for reasons I cannot comprehend, and I have been twice fooled. Will this not content you? Or must you involve me in more games? Will you now tell me this willingness to abase yourself by kissing me is a part of the custom, too?"

"No, you don't understand—"

"As you say, I don't understand," he growled harshly. "Nor do I care to."

He marched to the door and put his hand on the latch.

"I didn't know you were going to kiss me!" she cried.

He faced her again, crossing his arms over his broad chest. "Oh—and you did not kiss me back that first time? Sweet Savior, lady, you are a marvel of innocence! I suppose now you would tell me you knew nothing of this ridiculous abduction nonsense?"

"Of course I know the custom but—"

"But now you must return to your family," he repeated mockingly. "I see. Of course. And if that requires a kiss or two or more, you will do it. You Welsh are the most immoral people I've ever met!"

"Immoral?" she retorted. "I am not the immoral one!"

"No need to sound so mightily offended, Lady Rhiannon," he replied sardonically. "This chamber was for both you and Lord Cynvelin. He said so himself."

"Then he said too much!"

"More hypocrisy will now be added to the mixture? You will share your bed with a man before marriage, but heaven forbid it should be spoken of!"

She glared at him, her hands on her hips. "I have never shared my bed with any man!"

"I don't care if you've shared your bed with the entire garrison," he replied just as hotly. "Just as I don't care for your stupid customs." He made a scornful bow. "I wish you joy in your marriage, my lady. Good day."

"Yes, go," she ordered, pointing as arrogantly as any noblewoman he had ever met. She ran a contemptuous gaze over him. "When you next see your master, tell him he had better take me back to my father."

"Tell him yourself!"

"I will!"

"Of course you will," he muttered sarcastically before making a swift obeisance. He spun on his heel and went out, slamming the door behind him.

Chapter Seven

As enraged and upset as she had ever been in her life, Rhiannon picked up the bundle of bedding and threw it with all her might. It hit the back of the door with a dull thud, then landed on the ground, the bundle falling apart into linen and a blanket.

Tears of anger and frustration stung her eyes, but she wiped them away angrily. How dare he speak to her that way! She was no Delilah, any more than he was Samson with that hair of his!

Nevertheless, she would be thrilled to see a temple tumble down around Bryce Frechette's stubborn, stupid ears! And if a falling column would rid her of Lord Cynvelin ap Hywell as well, she would be a happy woman!

Panting, she tried to calm herself. Such extremes of emotion weren't going to help her; that was Dylan's way, and many a time she had criticized him for it.

Slowly she drew a deep breath, then she began to pick up the fallen linen, tossing it onto the bed.

Despite her resolve to calm herself, she couldn't

stop being upset with Bryce Frechette. How dare he imply that she would share her bed with Cynvelin ap Hywell, that she probably already had! How dare he call the Welsh immoral, the Norman lout!

How dare he claim she had kissed him because of some coy desire to play games?

She looked down at the blanket she clutched. She ran her hand over the rough wool, remembering the feel of Frechette's leather tunic beneath her hands.

Why. *had* she kissed him?

Because he kissed her, of course, and she had returned his kiss because...because...

She threw the blanket onto the bed, too. She didn't know why. She had no answer, except that as she learned more about him, her attraction for him became more natural, and harder to condemn.

What did it matter why she had kissed him? Right now her main task was to convince Cynvelin ap Hywell that he could never win her love, regardless of her behavior at Lord Melevoir's or the customs of their people.

She marched to the door, then halted. She was distraught, she was tired, she was muddy—hardly the best of states to be in when she had to be both firm and diplomatic. If she spoke to Lord Cynvelin now, she might wind up in tears, and that would be too humiliating.

Besides, it was growing too late to travel anywhere, for it was already getting dark.

Therefore, she decided, she would keep to this room tonight, and in the morning, when she was rested and cleaner, she would find Lord Cynvelin and tell him that she was sorry, but she simply could not stay.

While the servants hurried to finish putting up the tables for the evening meal, Cynvelin, seated in a chair like a king upon his throne, gave Ermin a pointed look and held out his hand expectantly. The Welshman placed the heavy iron key to the keep in his master's hand.

Before he could move back, Cynvelin struck Ermin across the cheek with it. "Next time, don't be so slow!" the nobleman said harshly, and loud enough for all to hear. "When I want something, I want it at once, do you understand, you oaf?"

Holding his cut cheek, Ermin nodded.

"Good. Tell one of those fools who passes for a groom that I want my horse saddled after the evening meal. Find Madoc and Twedwr and have them get ready to go with me then, too. Now get out of my sight, you stupid peasant!"

Ermin bowed and hurried to the door. As he went out, Bryce Frechette entered.

Cynvelin immediately stopped scowling at his departing countryman and smiled. "Ah, Bryce! Here you are," he called out merrily.

The Norman did not look happy, Cynvelin noted. No doubt Rhiannon had been as haughty and proud as all the rest of her family, hardly conduct to win a Norman's regard. He had counted on that when he had asked Frechette to take her. "Is something amiss?"

"Besides the lack of linen and food, my lord?" Bryce replied sarcastically.

"I told you, you are free to correct any faults with Annedd Bach however you see fit."

Bryce's only response was a brief bow.

"Where have you been?"

"Doing as you ordered, my lord. I went to try to find some linen for the keep bedchamber."

"Ah!" Cynvelin leaned back in his oak chair. "With no success, I assume from your frustrated face?"

"No. What linen I could find was not suitable for the lady."

"Or me," Lord Cynvelin added.

Bryce nodded abruptly. "Or you, my lord."

"Well, no matter. I have more among my baggage. A bundle of straw in the stable was good enough for last night, but it will not do for in the keep with my lady."

"There is bedding, my lord," Frechette replied flatly.

"Indeed? I confess I am truly impressed that you managed to communicate your wishes to the slothful servants in this godforsaken place."

Bryce colored. "That I had less success at, my lord, but there is bedding, nonetheless."

"Good."

Bryce gave Cynvelin a sidelong glance, his lips pursed as if in thought before he spoke. "Lady Rhiannon says she doesn't want to stay here. She wants to go back to her father."

Cynvelin fought to keep an annoyed expression

from his face. "When did she say this? When you brought her here?"

"Yes, my lord. And when I took her the bedding."

Cynvelin leaned forward and gazed at him intently. "*You* took her the bedding?"

"Yes, my lord," Bryce replied stoically. "I regret I couldn't make the servant understand me, so I took my bedding myself."

"And *your* bedding, was it?"

"I could find nothing else suitable."

"No doubt the lady was pleased by your sacrifice."

Bryce's expression changed, and in a way that Cynvelin was glad to see.

"I didn't tell her it was mine."

"You look as if she was not happy to see you."

"I believe she will be happy never to see me again," Bryce replied.

Cynvelin noted the irritation in his tone. "And you? I gather my love was somewhat rude, a characteristic I can lay at her arrogant father's feet, but one I'm sure will be amended with time."

"I will gladly do what I must in her service, since she is to be your wife, my lord."

Cynvelin smiled and relaxed. "No doubt she will be happy not to see Annedd Bach again, at any rate. This place is barely more than a hovel."

"Yes, my lord," Bryce agreed stonily.

"A pity you sacrificed your bedding, although I appreciate it. It need only be for this night, since we will go to Caer Coch in the morning."

"Yes, my lord."

* * *

Sometime later, when Bryce had finished patrolling the wall walk and making certain all the guards were awake and not dozing, he stood in the courtyard and looked up at the keep.

He had not encountered Cynvelin on his rounds and had no doubt of his overlord's whereabouts.

He reminded himself that his goal was to win back what he had lost, not gain a black-haired temptress.

Even if she had the eyes of an angel.

Nor would he sleep in the hall tonight. He could easily guess the comments and jokes that the men would bandy about as they settled down to sleep.

He might not understand the language, but the tone would be familiar, and more than he could stand.

The next morning, Rhiannon rose from the feather bed, determined to find Lord Cynvelin and convince him that she had no wish to remain in his company. Despite his apparent regard, she would make him understand that he could not court her in this fashion.

And she had to get away from the confusing Bryce Frechette, whose merest touch seemed to send the blood throbbing through her body, addling her wits and making her act like a moonstruck simpleton.

His kisses had made her forget who she was and where she was, her only awareness being of him and her desire for him, yet he would not help her.

Clad in her shift and shivering in the morning's chill, she looked at her gown, laid out to dry on the back of the chair. On the table stood the remains of

her light meal that the sullen Ula had brought, together with an empty goblet of wine.

Unfortunately, her dress was obviously still very
wet and stained with mud. She would hardly look
like the lady she was in such clothing and, by heavens, she needed to remember she was a lady.

Her gaze then went to the chest, and curious, she
threw open the lid.

It was filled with women's garments, and fine
ones, at that. She pulled out the top one.

It was a lovely gown of rich crimson brocade,
heavily embroidered in gold and silver about the
curved neck and the cuffs of the long sleeves.

She would have been delighted with it, under other
circumstances. She looked deeper into the chest, and
discovered a linen shift and some slippers of soft
leather. There was also a brush for her hair, and some
scarves.

She could not fault Lord Cynvelin for his taste or,
she realized when she put the garments on, his ability
to guess her measure. The gown was a little tight but
otherwise fit surprisingly well. She would leave her
head uncovered.

Now feeling as if she were attired for battle in
more appropriate armor, Rhiannon opened the door
and hurried to the hall.

When she entered the large room, the first thing
she noticed was Bryce Frechette sitting at the high
table, wearing nothing but his leather jerkin and
breeches despite the cool air. Beside him was Lord
Cynvelin, who was in black, as usual.

Suddenly her mind leapt to a comparison between

the two men, one so bitter and remorseful, the other so apparently carefree and careless.

And the way they kissed, Bryce Frechette with gentle longing, Cynvelin ap Hywell possessive and selfish.

She shook her head and told herself to think only of getting away from both of them.

She came farther into the room and realized that the soldiers gathered there for the morning meal seemed to be divided into two camps. One group was well dressed and arrogant, sitting at the tables nearest Lord Cynvelin. The others, in an assortment of ill-kept clothing and morose, sat below the salt or at tables at the back of the hall.

She didn't see Ula or any of the other servants.

Cynvelin shoved back his chair and got to his feet when he saw her. "Ah, Lady Rhiannon!" he cried happily. "How delightful that you are joining us!"

"I must speak with you, my lord," she said as she fought not to look at Frechette. "Alone."

"We have only just begun to eat, my lady," Cynvelin replied. "Perhaps afterward we can be alone."

"I would rather talk now."

Bryce rose at once. It was obvious he had no wish to linger any more than she wished him to be present. "If you will excuse me, my lord, I have many duties—"

"Which can wait," Cynvelin interrupted. "I must insist that you join us for the meal, just as I must insist, my love, that our discussion wait until later."

Rhiannon's teeth clenched at his endearment.

"If the lady wishes to speak with you alone—" Bryce began.

"My lord, I think you must agree—" she said simultaneously.

"Now stop complaining, the pair of you. Lady Rhiannon, surely you are not going to suggest that I send my loyal Frechette from the hall," Cynvelin protested. "He did a good day's work for me yesterday, for which I shall be forever grateful. As for you, Frechette, I will not have you sup upon a crust of bread in the stable or some such thing because you are so determined to win a knighthood that you work yourself to death."

Rhiannon glanced at the Norman sharply. Perhaps he was not just a rather unwilling participant doing as he was told. Perhaps he was eager to follow Cynvelin's orders, if a knighthood was to be his prize.

She would ignore his physical presence, difficult though that may be, and she would put all memory of his passionate kiss from her mind.

"Please sit, both of you." Cynvelin's words were more of a command than a request. "Lady Rhiannon, I would have you on my right, and Bryce beside you. You shall be the rose between thorns."

Trying not to scowl, Rhiannon reluctantly obeyed while Cynvelin smiled complacently at his joke. Out of the corner of her eye, she saw Frechette slump into the chair beside her. He looked no more pleased than she was.

She felt trapped, as if the men were the walls of a cell and she their prisoner. She almost wished she had stayed in the keep.

"Isn't this fine?" the nobleman remarked. "My bride-to-be beside me, and my new knight beside her."

Both Rhiannon and Bryce turned to regard Cynvelin with stunned expressions. He smiled warmly. "Well, if all goes as I hope," he added. His hand covered Rhiannon's. "Especially the first."

She slipped her hand into her lap. "So, you are knighting Frechette," she said quietly in Welsh.

"If he deserves it," Cynvelin replied, giving her a searching look that she didn't like. "I like to have loyal, trustworthy people around me."

"By that you mean people who will do as they are told, whatever it may be?" she asked, watching the cowed servants, noting the difference between them and the arrogant men of Cynvelin's personal guard. "If so, then knight Frechette, by all means."

The maidservants, including Ula, brought bread, meat and wine to the table. The girl never looked up, not at her, or Frechette or Lord Cynvelin. Indeed, she trembled as she set down the platter of bread, as if she were afraid.

"You sound as if you dislike the man," Cynvelin noted.

Rhiannon flushed hotly, telling herself she did dislike him. If she was tempted by him, it was only lust and nothing more, and she would soon have control over whatever wayward sensations it sent to plague her. "I did not come to speak of Frechette."

Cynvelin turned to her with another smile. "I am happy to hear that. What did you wish to speak of?"

"Returning to my father."

She saw his eyes narrow slightly, but went on nonetheless. "Truly, my lord," she said firmly, "if you have any regard for me, or my reputation, you will agree."

Cynvelin sighed softly. "My lady, you are indeed breaking my heart! Is my presence so odious to you that you cannot bear it even a little while?"

Rhiannon regarded him steadily, glad that she could speak without Bryce Frechette understanding her. "Did you tell Frechette that we were lovers?"

Lord Cynvelin looked shocked. "My lady!"

"Did you?"

Obviously guessing the source of that information, Cynvelin glanced at Bryce, who continued to eat without so much as a glance in their direction. The Norman's revelation might cost him his knighthood, but Rhiannon didn't care. He couldn't purchase that with *her* honor.

Cynvelin gave her a winsome smile. "My dearest lady, I might have said something about *wanting* to be your lover when I was in my cups and not thinking clearly. Perhaps I did. You must understand I was only voicing my greatest wish. Indeed," he went on, his voice dropping to a husky whisper, "I could ask for nothing more than to be your lover, except to be your husband."

Rhiannon flushed beneath the Welshman's steadfast, persuasive gaze.

Suddenly feeling that he had stomached all he could, in more ways than one, Bryce set down the loaf in his hands and got to his feet.

Lady Rhiannon claimed she didn't want to be here, but she was certainly acting as if she were pleased by Lord Cynvelin's attention.

Indeed, she was behaving as coquettishly as she had at Lord Melevoir's, blushing and averting her eyes as coyly as any modest maiden.

And to think he, Bryce Frechette, apparently the biggest dunderhead in all of Britain, had nearly been swayed into believing that her request to return to her father was in earnest!

Obviously Lady Rhiannon was one of those women who sought to inflame a lover's passion by acting contrary. Yesterday she had struggled and protested and complained only to make her love that much more the prize. No doubt the pleading vulnerability he had seen in her lovely eyes before he had kissed her was only a woman's wile, intended to make him do whatever she wanted.

Indeed, she had probably kissed him because it amused her. No doubt she had been laughing at him and complimenting herself on her ability to win men's love.

Well, she couldn't win *his!*

He could never love such a trickster. She was using him for some game of her own, and he had been too blinded by desire to see it.

He knew better now, and he would keep away from the lying, duplicitous, tempting woman.

He made a brief obeisance to his overlord. "If you will excuse me, I had better see to my duties."

"The burden of command calls you forth, does it?" Lord Cynvelin asked lightly. "Well, I suppose

I have kept you from it long enough. You do seem preoccupied.''

Bryce had no intention of looking at Lady Rhiannon. He had no wish to be captured again in the spell of her luminous eyes.

But he did. Their gazes met and held, until hers faltered.

As it should, now that he knew what she was about.

Bryce turned on his heel and left them, cursing himself for a blind, impetuous fool, and he felt as if the wine in his belly had turned to poison.

As he marched toward the gatehouse, determined to see that the watch was in place, he thought of his sister, who had married a man who, by rights, she should have hated. Etienne DeGuerre had been given their family estate and forced Gabriella to choose between leaving, or remaining as a servant.

When Bryce had finally returned, Gabriella had confessed that she had fallen in love with Baron DeGuerre and was happy to be his wife. At that time and ever since, Bryce had believed it was Gabriella's soft heart and vulnerable circumstances that had contributed to her seemingly impossible conduct.

Now he was not so sure. After all, he was not known to be softhearted or vulnerable.

He could not be. He would not think about Rhiannon DeLanyea. He would focus all his energy on Annedd Bach and win himself a title.

"I'm afraid Frechette's manners have suffered for the time he has spent out of noble company," Lord

Cynvelin noted mournfully as Bryce strode from the hall. "Forgive his rudeness, my lady."

Rhiannon acknowledged the Welshman's remarks with a nod, then reached for her wine and tried not to think of the censure she had seen in the Norman's eyes.

He had no right to look at her so! She was the aggrieved party here, not him, whatever he might think.

Besides, he had kissed the woman he believed his overlord wanted, and yet he claimed to be an honorable man.

But, chided the small voice of conscience, she had kissed him, too, and she was an honorable woman.

Wasn't she?

"That gown suits you, my lady," Lord Cynvelin said. "Although its loveliness is nothing compared to that of its wearer."

She gave him a feeble smile.

"I like to see you look happy," he said. "I would like to hear you laugh again, as you did at Lord Melevoir's."

"Perhaps if I could find something amusing, I would," she noted dryly.

Cynvelin's dark brows lowered, but he continued to smile. "I suppose I should be glad you don't consider me a figure of fun."

"Oh, no, my lord, I do not."

"Good. I would do almost anything to make you happy," he said softly. "Nothing would give me greater joy than to try to make you happy all the days of your life."

When she didn't respond, he sighed deeply, then reached for an apple. He drew a dagger from his belt and proceeded to peel the fruit in a long, single coil, the fruit gliding lightly between his slender fingers.

He handed the peeled apple to her. She hesitated, then took the offered fruit.

Suddenly a loud crack of thunder boomed directly overhead. Rhiannon jumped, dropping the apple, and everyone else looked startled, too. Then they could hear the rain, a seemingly torrential downpour, strike the stone walls as if it were a cascade of pebbles.

Bryce Frechette ran into the hall, shaking his head like a dog who had run through a stream. "It's hail, my lord," he announced. "You cannot ride out in this."

Cynvelin muttered an astonishingly obscene curse. When he saw Rhiannon's shocked face, he made a placating smile. "Forgive me, my lady. I did want to take you to Caer Coch today. It would be so much more comfortable for you."

"I want to leave, too, but not—"

"I assure you, I am equally disappointed."

As the rain continued to pound on the roof, Rhiannon realized there would be no purpose pressing him to take her to her father immediately. No one could go anywhere in this weather. The roads were too primitive in this part of the country to venture forth in such a storm.

Nevertheless, in one way she was glad of it, for her father would not be going anywhere, either.

Surely he had gone back to the monastery, or the closest inn, and even if he had thought to return to

Craig Fawr or continue to Caer Coch, he would not be able to until the weather cleared.

She watched as Bryce Frechette spoke to a thin, dark-haired man, who seemed to relay his orders to the men who had been below the salt. "If you will pardon us, my lord," the Norman said, addressing Lord Cynvelin, "I will go with the garrison to the barracks."

The motley assortment of men who comprised the garrison rose from their places. The other men, hardened, rather vicious-looking soldiers who had sat in the more favored place, therefore had to be Cynvelin's personal guard.

She would have realized that, of course, if she had not been so intent on her purpose.

Maintaining a dignified expression, she told herself that she was a Welsh baron's daughter, and so must be quite safe with a Welsh nobleman, no matter what manner of men comprised his guard.

"By all means," Lord Cynvelin agreed.

The garrison filed out, Bryce Frechette leading the way. Out of the hall. Leaving her with Cynvelin and his men.

"We shall have to entertain ourselves, somehow," Lord Cynvelin said softly.

Rhiannon flushed at his low tones, then bent to retrieve the apple. She looked around and saw a dog eating it.

She was rather relieved.

"It is a pity there is no minstrel," Lord Cynvelin reflected after another thunderclap shook the hall.

The drumming of the hail was replaced by the steady sound of heavy rain. "Then we could dance."

Rhiannon could scarcely imagine dancing with him now. She certainly didn't want to encourage any physical proximity. "I would be too tired."

"I could sing, if you would like."

He didn't wait for any encouragement or suggestions for a particular tune.

He simply started to sing.

He had a marvelous voice, very rich and full of feeling, and his choice was a mournful lay of lost love. All the men ceased eating and talking to listen, and even the servants stopped moving.

The music made her want to cry, for it was filled with loneliness and longing. She thought Bryce Frechette would appreciate it and that it was a pity he was not there to listen.

Her gaze returned to Lord Cynvelin, who was watching her with obvious desire in his eyes. Surely no one could sing those words of hope with such passion unless they knew the emotion, she reflected.

Perhaps Lord Cynvelin did love her. Perhaps he wanted her as much as the man in the song yearned for his lover. Maybe she was wrong to think so ill of him.

She had been wrong about Frechette. He cared very much about his family, and she believed him when he said he had stayed away and sent no word of his whereabouts because he was trying to help them in secret.

How difficult those days must have been for him! Being here, away from her family, she could appreciate his loneliness all the more, and even, when she thought of her regrettable behavior, the pride that had kept him away.

Was he still ashamed and full of wounded pride? Was that why he was so desperate to regain a title?

And he must want to earn it himself. His brother-in-law was a powerful baron. Surely, if Bryce's sister requested it, the Baron DeGuerre would find a way to bestow a knighthood on Bryce.

She could admire his determination to seek a title on his own merits.

If she stayed here awhile, maybe she could learn if Bryce Frechette was truly worthy of such a reward, and she could convince Lord Cynvelin to knight him before she left. Then all this trouble would not have been completely for nought.

The song ended, the last, long, sad note echoing in the hall. Her mind full of thoughts of Bryce and his troubles, she smiled absently while the men of Cynvelin's guard shouted loud approval and stamped their feet.

Only Ula did not clap, Rhiannon noted, her smile disappearing as her puzzlement increased. The maidservant had listened politely; now she simply began serving more ale, her expression blank.

"Well, my lady?" Lord Cynvelin said softly. "Would I have been able to sing my way home as a minstrel, as your father did, do you think?"

"Yes, yes, I believe you could," she stammered, still distracted by Ula's manner.

"You seem very quiet, my lady. I hope my singing has not put you to sleep," he said softly.

"Not at all. You have a very fine voice."

"I'm sure yours is as wonderful as the birds themselves, my lady. Perhaps you will grace me with a song yourself."

"Perhaps."

The soldier who had insulted her that day called out, "We're going to our barracks, too, my lord."

Lord Cynvelin nodded his approval. "Don't lose all your money, Madoc," he remarked genially as his men began to file out, covering their heads with their arms before disappearing into the curtain of rain.

Cynvelin turned to her. "They are going to gamble. I will be lucky if someone does not get hurt before the day is out."

"You allow gambling?"

"Unlike some men, I see no harm in it," he replied.

"My father thinks it makes for bad feelings, as you yourself have just implied."

"The men need something to do, and since there are few women here for them to sport with, I think gambling is harmless enough, even if there are a few arguments."

Rhiannon turned away to hide her shock at his blunt remark about the lack of women. While that may be true, he should not have spoken so to a lady.

Indeed, she was fast coming to the conclusion that Lord Cynvelin ap Hywell, for all his smiles, charm and flattery, was much less of a gentleman than...say, Bryce Frechette. At least with the Norman, she always had a sense of underlying respect, even when he was being completely impertinent.

That made little sense; nevertheless, the respect was there, deep in his eyes.

What lurked in Lord Cynvelin's eyes? Desire, perhaps, but respect? She didn't think so.

"If you will excuse me, my lord, I would like to go back to the keep."

"Why? There is nothing there for you to do. I will have one of the servants fetch my chessboard, shall I, and we will have a game. You do play, do you not?"

"Yes, but I am not very good. I have little patience for games of strategy."

"Well," he said kindly, "if you tire of that, we shall find some other way to amuse ourselves."

She glanced at him sharply, but his expression was all innocence as he summoned Ula and told her what he wanted.

The girl went out at once.

Leaving Rhiannon alone with Lord Cynvelin.

She rose and went to look out the door. The rain was like a waterfall, and looked to last for quite some time. Turning aside from the door, she began to pace beside the hearth as she waited for Ula to return.

She would welcome the chess game, if only because her mind would be occupied with pieces on a board, not men in a hall.

Agitation was a good sign, Cynvelin thought complacently as he watched Rhiannon pace. He was sure she was upset because she didn't know quite what to think anymore, whether to believe his declarations of love and desire, or to believe her father's condemnation.

He had seen a panther once when he had traveled to France, kept in a cage only large enough for it to take a few steps and then turn around. Rhiannon DeLanyea reminded him very much of that animal, with her dark hair and fierce shining eyes as she paced in front of him.

His smile broadened and his eyes gleamed hungrily. Kindness, flattery, the proclamation of an eternal passion—he knew many tricks and stratagems. It would take time, but eventually Baron DeLanyea's daughter would be his.

It suddenly struck him that her love might be a rare and blessed gift.

Then he remembered who she was, and what her father had done to him. He, Cynvelin ap Hywell, had been shamed by that half-Norman bastard, sent away like a child, made to feel unworthy, all because he had sported with some peasant girl whose protests he had ignored.

They were alone here. Would Rhiannon protest if he kissed her now? Would she cry out if he did more? What would she do if he pushed her back against the wall and thrust his knee between her legs while he pulled her skirt upward? Would she fight and scratch, as that girl had, or would she welcome his fierce embrace?

Cynvelin took a deep, calming breath. Not here. Not yet. He was making progress, as her altered behavior amply proved. Too much haste would surely once again turn her into that complaining, determined harpy.

Nevertheless, it took a mighty effort not to leap from his chair, capture her in his arms and crush her lips with his own, to take possession of her mouth and then her shapely body. He yearned to show her how powerful he was, in every way.

Not now, he told himself. Not yet.

He felt the key in the purse on his belt, satisfied that he had no need of it yet. Indeed, he might never need it.

She was his captured creature in a cage of his making and his ultimate vengeance would come when she grew to love her keeper.

Chapter Eight

The monastery of St. David was a large one, and prosperous. Located on the main road leading north into Wales and containing a *hospitalis,* it was used by many on their travels, especially those who were ill or injured.

A week after Rhiannon's abduction, Baron De-Lanyea paced before the hearth in the large chamber where the brothers took their meals, occasionally stopping to listen to the rain falling against the outer wall.

The heavy rain that had started the day after Rhiannon had been taken from them still continued to fall, making the roads a muddy, slippery, dangerous morass. Every time it seemed to let up, it proved to be only a brief respite. Torrential rain began before they could even get their horses saddled.

But the baron was also pleased by the weather, for it kept Cynvelin at Annedd Bach and away from his stronghold of Caer Coch.

The baron glanced at his son sitting in the shadows on a bench at the side of the hearth. The chill of the monastic chamber was dispelled somewhat by the low fire, which cast feeble rays of light.

Griffydd leaned against the wall, as still as if he were part of it.

"I wonder how long this rain will last?" the baron mused. "I would hope until Dylan and the others can get here."

Griffydd's voice came from the shadows. "Do you think they will be traveling in such weather?"

The baron glanced at Griffydd. "Think you a storm would stop Dylan? He would say, 'What is rain to a Welshman?' and ride on."

"If he is with Morgan and Fitzroy, they might have steadier heads and make him wait for clearer weather." As he spoke, nobody observing Griffydd DeLanyea would have an inkling that he had any feelings at all, let alone the extent of the anger and frustration contained within him. Or his smoldering hatred of Cynvelin ap Hywell.

"Not Morgan. Hotheaded as Dylan, that one. As for Fitzroy, when he hears the reason Dylan has come, it would take more than foul weather to keep him at home." The baron began to pace again. "Still, let us hope they arrive soon. Who can say when Cynvelin might take it into his head to go on to Caer Coch? That's one of the most defendable castles in Wales."

"But you think we still must wait?"

"Aye."

There was a moment of silence before Griffydd spoke again. "Easier it will be to rescue Rhiannon while they are on the road."

"Yes, but we must be sure to win any skirmish with them, and we need more men for that."

Griffydd's face betrayed no emotion. "Frechette will be a hard man to beat in battle."

"Aye, there's that, too."

"What if we could take him alone, or Cynvelin?"

The baron's eyes narrowed. "What are you saying? They have never stirred out of Annedd Bach, have they?"

"Cynvelin spent the first night they were there in a tavern a few miles from Annedd Bach. With a whore."

The baron halted and swiveled slowly on his heel to regard his son. The two men might have been mirror images of each other, save for the difference in age and the baron's scar. "What?"

"I had one of our men follow him," Griffydd answered. "He waited outside until Cynvelin and his men left before dawn."

"Why did you not tell me sooner?" the baron demanded.

"By the time the man returned, Cynvelin would have been back at Annedd Bach. I have told the men watching to let us know if he ever sets foot outside the gates again, but he has not.

"He spent the night with a whore," Griffydd growled, some of that hatred finally finding voice, "this man who thinks to woo my sister."

"Thank God!"

"Thank God?" Griffydd repeated incredulously. "Thank God this is the man who wants Rhiannon?"

"Wanting is not wedding, my son," the baron replied. "If he spent the night with a whore, he was not with Rhiannon. I would wish he spent every night that way until we have Rhiannon back again."

"Cynvelin is a scoundrel, but surely he wouldn't dishonor her," Griffydd said.

A look of sorrowful dismay crossed the baron's face. "Do you remember Peulan the Nose?"

"Of course," his son replied. "The shepherd with the big nose."

"Do you remember his daughter, Cathwg?"

"The pretty one, wasn't she? About the same age as Rhiannon, I think."

The baron nodded slowly, then began to pace once more. "Glad I am that Dylan is not hearing this, or he would attack Annedd Bach single-handed."

Surprised by his father's remark, Griffydd asked, "What is it? What about Cathwg?"

The baron halted and regarded his son steadily. "Cynvelin ap Hywell raped her. That is why they left our land and why I sent him from Craig Fawr in disgrace."

Griffydd's expression didn't seem to alter, but there was a change in the depths of his eyes. "She was only a child."

"Yes, Cathwg was only ten years old when it happened."

"Why did you never accuse him of the crime?"

"When Peulan told me, I immediately summoned Cynvelin to hear what answer he would make to the charge." The baron looked at the toe of his boot, then raised his eyes to his son. "He laughed. He said we should try to accuse him before his peers. He is a rich and powerful man, Peulan and his daughter only peasants.''

The baron averted his gaze. ''I told him he was to consider himself confined to the castle. By that time, I had seen enough of him to believe he was capable of such a crime, but I also knew he was right. A Norman court would likely let him go free.

''I decided to visit Cathwg myself in the morning, to be absolutely certain she knew who had attacked her, to satisfy myself because of what I was going to do.''

Griffydd eyed his father warily. ''What was that?''

''What Welsh justice demanded. I would give Cynvelin to Peulan and his sons, and take the consequences myself, if any Norman lord questioned my judgment.''

Griffydd nodded with approval.

''But when I went to see Cathwg, the whole family was gone. Nobody ever learned where they went, so we had no witness. It would have been too risky to charge him without the girl to speak against him.

''So I did all I thought I could. After I warned Cynvelin that I would speak against him if he was ever similarly accused in the future, I sent him home to his father.''

Griffydd got to his feet. ''For once, I would act as Dylan. How can we wait, knowing what kind of man he is?''

The baron shook his head. ''No. To attack with such a small force would be foolish.'' He sighed again. ''Did you see him when he spoke of her? He honestly believes Rhiannon cares for him.''

"But you don't?"

Emryss DeLanyea shook his head and the ghost of a smile crossed his face for a fleeting moment. "No. And she never will. Still, I think he will keep his word a while yet until he realizes that his cause is a hopeless one."

Griffydd leaned into the light, regarding his father steadily. "I cannot wait much longer, Father."

"Not easy, I know, my son." Sympathy struggled with anger on the baron's face. "We have to be remembering Cynvelin's threat if we move against him. If we lay seige to Annedd Bach, Rhiannon will be in even greater jeopardy."

"Cynvelin's threat also means, I suppose, that we cannot go to the king?" Griffydd asked.

"That scoundrel will likely find out if we do, or I would have done it already," the baron affirmed.

"What if Cynvelin hears we've sent for help?" Griffydd asked.

"Even if Cynvelin does catch a whiff of something, Hu had left Craig Fawr to make his fortune before Cynvelin came. Cynvelin might not know the name."

"He'll have heard of him, surely—a Welshman knighted and married to a Norman's daughter."

"Maybe, but I'll risk it." The baron shook his head regretfully. "I should have brought more men with me."

"Who could have known this would happen?" Griffydd replied. His frown deepened. "Father, do you think it's possible...do you suppose Cynvelin might be able to win Rhiannon's affections, as he claims? He is a handsome fellow.''

''She will see him for what he is. He will stand no chance with her.''

''But…''

''But what?''

''Well, Father, Cynvelin was telling the truth. You *did* kidnap my mother.''

''And let her go the next day, unharmed. Different that was, my son. Be giving your sister credit for a good head on her shoulders. She'll not be swayed by any man's handsome face or flattering words, and certainly never enough to marry one like that.''

''Do you think he'll really let her go if she refuses him?''

The baron didn't meet his son's unwavering gaze. ''No, I do not.'' He sighed. ''Still, the man is conceited enough to believe he could persuade her to take him, and we will have to count on that and hope that for once, he keeps his word. He would be a fool to harm her, since I have friends, too.'' His voice lowered. ''Unfortunately, he is not a wise man. But I vow before God and the Holy Virgin, we *will* get her back.''

Griffydd's gray eyes darkened with anger, and his deceptively slender fingers, which had far more strength than many opponents realized, balled into fists. ''Aye, Father. We will. And if that devil hurts her in any way, I will kill him,'' the young man vowed.

The baron faced his son, his familiar face twisting

into something cold and forbidding. "If he hurts her in any way, that will be for me, my son."

"Then I will have Frechette."

Emryss DeLanyea nodded his agreement. "If any harm comes to Rhiannon at their hands, you may have him, and may God have mercy on both their souls."

"Damn the rain," Lord Cynvelin muttered as he stood looking out the door of the hall. "We can't leave today, either, unless we want to take a boat."

Madoc and Twedwr and the men of his guard exchanged sullen looks. They started to mumble amongst themselves, then Madoc took out a dagger and threw it at one of the beams in the roof, apparently as an expression of dismay.

"This place needs enough repair without you adding to the damage," Bryce noted from the other end of the hall where he stood with the men of the garrison. Like Cynvelin's guards, they had been forced to stay inside for most of the past seven days.

Bryce very much wished it could be otherwise, for it had become abundantly clear that the men of the garrison and the men of the Cynvelin's guard despised one another, although all were Welshman.

It was easy enough to see why. Cynvelin's men were arrogant, impertinent rascals who seemed to think everything that didn't personally belong to Cynvelin was theirs by right. The food, the bedding—even the women. More than once Bryce had had to break up a dispute, and the women had taken to keeping in the kitchen, for which he could not fault them.

When Lord Cynvelin did witness some of the arguments, he seemed to find it all vastly amusing, and never sought to intervene. Bryce assumed the Welshman considered that *his* task, so he did his best to keep the two factions apart.

Fortunately, Cynvelin and his men would be leaving eventually, and hopefully before Cynvelin's baggage carts were completely devoid of food.

Although Bryce didn't look forward to that nearly as much as he had when he first brought Lady Rhiannon here.

He had been trying his best to ignore her, given what had passed between them, yet no matter how often he reminded himself that she was already betrothed, he couldn't help noticing that she seemed far less pleased with Lord Cynvelin now than she had been at Lord Melevoir's—and shouldn't the opposite be true? She should be delighted to be with the man she loved.

If she loved him.

Lady Rhiannon was the most vibrant, interesting woman he had ever met. In addition, she was everything a gracious chatelaine should be. She was easily the most patient person in the hall, never complaining about the weather or the accommodation. She ate whatever was served with good grace and spoke kindly to the servants. When he watched her play chess with Lord Cynvelin, always losing with good humor, it was all he could do not to hover about her like a bee, drawn to the sweetness of her smiles.

He struggled to decipher her behavior and reactions. Was she truly that kindhearted and patient, or was that merely another part of her deception? Did she care for Lord Cynvelin, or were those hints of strain and displeasure merely fatigue and a desire to get away from Annedd Bach to the more luxurious accommodation of Caer Coch?

She had to be a shameless temptress. After all, she had enticed him into the shadows at Lord Melevoir's. And for all her indignant denials, Lord Cynvelin apparently spent the night in the keep with her. Apparently, because Bryce always retired to the stables to sleep before they left the hall. Although it was weak and foolish, he could not bear to see them depart together. He also wished he could stop imagining the intimate embraces they no doubt shared.

All this should have been enough to make her unappealing to him, but it wasn't. If she came to him and said she wanted him, he wouldn't have hesitated for a moment to accept her love.

Her love. He must be mad.

It would be foolish to even dream that she might care for him in any way, supposing she were an honest, worthy lady. He had nothing to offer such a noblewoman. No home, save this that he held under rather tenuous circumstances. No wealth. No power. Not even a title.

How could he compete with a man like Cynvelin ap Hywell?

Madoc muttered something in Welsh, which made his friends smile and the garrison frown.

Bryce tried to ignore him. Instead, he signaled to

the slim, dark-haired Ermin, who was still his translator. "Tell my men we shall be practicing our swordplay later, if the weather allows," he said.

Ermin nodded hesitantly, then spoke in Welsh to the men, who exchanged cautious, as well as somewhat annoyed, glances.

Lord Cynvelin sauntered toward them. "A recalcitrant lot, are they not, Frechette?" he observed. "Have you been able to do anything with them at all?"

"They are wary of me, my lord," Bryce replied. "Given that I am a Norman, I am not surprised. Unfortunately, we can only practice close fighting in the barracks. However, they are much improved in that regard, even in so short a time."

"I really should not have kept away from here for so long," the nobleman said with a sigh. "They've gone too wild, I think. It will take a strong hand to bring them back in line."

"Perhaps," Bryce replied noncommittally.

"Well, you might have to have your practice inside again today," he said, looking out the window, "unless they want to get soaked through for their trouble. Nobody should go out in this wet."

As if she purposefully sought to contradict him, Lady Rhiannon hurried into the hall, throwing back the hood of her cloak. "Gracious heavens!" she exclaimed. "I thought I would drown."

"I am so delighted you have come!" Lord Cynvelin cried.

He hurried toward her and helped her remove the cloak, which Bryce assumed was another gift from her lover, as was the gown of green, with a gold and green brocade overtunic. A girdle of worked leather was around her slender hips, which accentuated the sensual grace of her walk. Her head was covered by a scarf, and a wimple surrounded her face. Bryce had thought the frame of her hair showed her beauty to perfection; however, the plain whiteness and severity of the wimple seemed to make her luminous eyes even larger and her skin more rosy.

"I thought you might stay in the keep, like Noah in his ark," Cynvelin said.

"I was going to," she confessed, "but it is too quiet there for me. I am used to company."

No doubt, Bryce thought sardonically.

"I am happy to hear it," Cynvelin said. He gave Madoc a hard look. "The lady requires a seat."

Lady Rhiannon gracefully sat in the chair the lumbering Madoc vacated. "I believe the rain is letting up," she observed.

"Is it, Frechette?" Lord Cynvelin called out.

He went toward the door, trying not to get very close to Lady Rhiannon, who even smelled beautiful, of fresh flowers or the first breeze of spring. "Yes, my lord, it is."

"Excellent! Maybe we can be on our way today!"

Bryce tried to keep his expression absolutely non-committal, but he couldn't help noticing that Lady Rhiannon didn't seem particularly pleased at the thought of leaving.

"At least it is easing for the time being, my lord," he continued. "There are çlouds on the horizon, though, that look as though they might herald another storm."

Cynvelin swore softly. "I am sick to death of this place," he muttered to no one in particular. "Well, perhaps we should wait awhile yet to be certain."

"Nevertheless, I think I will take the men to train in the meadow beyond the castle," Bryce announced. He looked at Ermin, who gave the order in Welsh to the men of the garrison. "Good day, my lord, my lady."

With that, he signaled to his men and they all went out the door.

Rhiannon watched Bryce Frechette leave, noting the way the men didn't hesitate to follow his order. For a Norman, he had done well to gain their respect in so short a time. Indeed, he had done well for any commander, for she had heard snatches of the men's conversations and knew they thought him a seasoned warrior worthy of their esteem.

She was less certain of what the garrison thought of Lord Cynvelin, yet she suspected it would not be so flattering.

Bryce Frechette was not like Cynvelin, who could be arrogant and callous. To be sure, the Welshman behaved in a gentlemanly manner to her, but she had overheard him speak to the servants and even the men of his own guard with dismissive scorn, especially when he was not aware that she was nearby.

Nor was Bryce like Griffydd, who commanded great respect, but whose demeanor didn't inspire a sense of camaraderie. The Norman wasn't like Dylan, who was such a friend to his men that he complained they didn't respect him, not seeing that a commander and a friend were not the same. Her father understood that, and while friendly, no man ever forgot he was their overlord.

She had to admit Bryce Frechette was as fine a leader as her father, if more intimidating to her. She found his physical presence discomfiting, especially his dark, fierce eyes and intense gaze that seemed to reach to a part of her soul she hadn't even known she possessed. When she was trying to play chess with Lord Cynvelin, it was all she could do not to ask for Bryce's opinion on her next move and try to keep her attention focused on her pieces. He was so distracting, in fact, that she had yet to win a game.

It took only the mention of his name to make her recall the kiss they had shared. When he had touched her, she had felt suddenly more alive, as if some of the vitality he emanated had somehow jumped into her flesh.

When he was not present, all she felt was stifling ennui and annoyance, even though Lord Cynvelin had been the epitome of the hospitable host, making light, amusing conversation as they talked together in the hall.

If they had been at Lord Melevoir's or her home, she might even have enjoyed his company. As it was, she felt oppressed, both by his continual meaningless banter, and his apparent inability to believe she would know her own mind.

As for Bryce, he had not actually spoken to her since that second day, and she had tried to tell herself that she had quite enough to think about without troubling herself with him.

Such as trying to convince Lord Cynvelin that as admirable as he might be, she didn't want to be his wife. After hearing him sing that morning, and other times since, she was more inclined to pity him than to be angry with him. Unrequited love was not at all pleasant, although she really knew nothing about that.

The men of the castle seemed equally out of sorts. No doubt they regretted being confined to Annedd Bach nearly as much as she did. They probably wanted to get to Caer Coch; she just wanted to go home. Unfortunately, with the continuing poor weather, there was little point insisting that Lord Cynvelin take her there immediately.

Ula and another maidservant came to sweep out the hearth. They paid no heed to the nobles, but went about their tasks in the most desultory fashion.

The only person who seemed to move with any vigor in all of Annedd Bach was Bryce Frechette, and she wondered how far it was to the meadow.

"I hope this cursed rain will cease enough to make the roads less of a muddy mess so that we can go to Caer Coch," Lord Cynvelin declared, approaching her.

"Is not the state of the roads your responsibility since you are overlord here?" Rhiannon asked, giving him a sidelong, speculative glance.

"I am not to blame for the rain," the Welshman answered petulantly.

"No, of course not," Rhiannon replied soothingly, treating him as she would a peevish child.

Cynvelin smiled and all trace of irritability apparently vanished. "I have many estates, and this one is so small, it is easy to forget about. Of course, it shall now be dearer to me, because of your presence."

She rose and walked away from him toward the empty hearth. "It would seem to require a more dedicated overseer," she remarked.

"That is why I have put Frechette in command, although—" Lord Cynvelin seemed to hesitate worriedly "—I may have made a mistake with him."

He came so close to her she had to resist the urge to nudge him away with her elbow.

"My lady, I fear I have been deceived."

"How so?" Rhiannon demanded, eyeing him warily as she stepped away from him.

Mercifully, he didn't follow. "Have you noticed anything odd about Ula?"

"She is very quiet and rather...unfriendly," she said hesitantly. She didn't want to get the girl in trouble.

"Do you have any idea why?"

"Not really."

"Bryce Frechette," Cynvelin said with a significant look.

"Bryce Frechette? What has he to do with Ula?"

Cynvelin cleared his throat delicately. "He, um...and Ula...well, she was not terribly willing, you see."

Rhiannon immediately understood what he was

implying—that Bryce Frechette had taken advantage of the girl, that he had raped her.

She didn't believe it. Not for an instant.

Why not? Why should she be so unwilling to believe that a man like Bryce Frechette was capable of hurting a woman?

Because after what she had seen of him, she simply knew he would not.

"What evidence do you have to support this charge? Did Ula accuse him?"

"Ula never says much at all, as I'm sure you've noticed." He gave Rhiannon a puzzled look, and when he spoke, there was an unfamiliar edge to his tone. "Are you saying you doubt what I am telling you?"

"No, my lord, not precisely. But I find it hard to believe that he would do such a thing."

"You seem anxious to rush to his defense."

"I would have evidence before I condemn him, that's all," she replied truthfully.

"Then you are different from your father," Cynvelin said with as much of a frown as she had ever seen him make.

"What do you mean?" she asked, startled by his reference to her father.

The Welshman shook his head. "Nothing. Pay no heed to my ramblings. I have slept poorly these last few nights, and my head aches."

"Perhaps you should rest, then," she suggested.

"Perhaps." He gave her a meaningful look. "If I could have some company."

She stiffened, but before she could speak, he hurried on. "God save me, my head hurts! Yet if I lie down, it hurts even more. Perhaps if you would keep me company, talk or sing to me, it will ease the ache."

Rhiannon relaxed a little. He did look ill. "It could be the change in the weather, if there is another storm coming."

"I hope it comes no closer," Cynvelin said. "However, I fear there is another cause." His face was a picture of melancholy. "Indeed, it is all your fault, my lady."

"My fault?"

"Yes. I could not sleep last night for thinking of you. Have I told you that you are the most beautiful creature in the world?"

Rhiannon smiled wearily. She, too, had not slept well, so she was in no mood for flattery. "Thank you."

"Would you sing to me, my lady?" he asked, giving her a pleading look. "A song is not much when I am nearly dying of love for you, and I'm sure your beautiful voice would ease my head."

Turning away, she made a skeptical face that he couldn't see. His continual avowals of his devotion were growing more tiresome with every passing moment. "Or I might make it ache more."

He smiled. "Nothing you could do would hurt me, unless you broke my heart."

"What sort of song would you like?" she asked, conceding to his request, because if she sang, he wouldn't talk.

"Anything you choose, as long as you sit beside me and hold my hand."

"I would rather not," she said, very unwilling to touch him, or to have him touch her. "I do not think it proper."

He shrugged his shoulders with a mournful sigh. "Very well," he said, "it is enough that you are near me. But you will sing for me, won't you?"

He made it sound as if she would be the hardest-hearted woman in Christendom if she begrudged him a song. She followed him to the chairs. When she sat, he slumped into the other and closed his eyes.

Then she started to sing a quiet, gentle song that some mothers sang as a lullaby.

As Rhiannon crooned her lay softly, Cynvelin watched her through half-closed lids. The room was warm, her voice was soft, and in a few moments she was pleased to see that he was asleep.

Rhiannon looked around the hall. The women had finished and left; no one was there.

She sighed and regarded the sleeping man, trying to consider her feelings rationally.

Suppose, she asked herself, suppose Lord Cynvelin was liked by her father. Would she want him then?

She thought not. He was charming, occasionally amusing and he could sing...yet he did not excite her. He bored her with his shallow banter and empty flattery. It was as if he were all surface and no depth. A puddle of emotion, compared to the ocean of feelings that lurked in Bryce Frechette.

She had had tantalizing glimpses of those depths

when she was alone with Bryce or watching him in the hall when he did not know it. Now she wondered what it meant that he had revealed to her something of the troubled feelings within him when they had been alone.

He didn't do so to impress her, of that she was certain. It was more as if he couldn't help himself.

But then he had accused her of acting dishonorably, when he was the one who had kissed her first! For the past week he had ignored her as if she had some kind of disease. Not that she wanted his attention.

She could not want it. He was a dishonorable scoundrel who had deserted his family and helped to take her from her father and brothers. Surely she couldn't feel any affection for such a man. Any love...

Her own head was starting to ache. The thought that she might have to remain inside today, too, if another storm came, prompted her to rise, moving as quietly as she could so she wouldn't disturb Cynvelin.

Hurrying to the door, she looked out. The clouds were gathering in dark gray menace over the hills, but it was not raining yet.

A brisk breeze blew the damp scent of the surrounding hills through the confines of the courtyard. Rhiannon sighed, breathing in the clear coolness of it. Her head felt better almost at once.

She would go outside while she could, and she would enjoy being alone.

She heard a hearty burst of male laughter outside

the gates, as if several men were gathered there and sharing a joke. They sounded happy and carefree, so she gave up the idea of passing her time in solitary— and no doubt pointless—meditation to join them. After all, she could use some amusement.

As she went toward the gate, she glanced up at the darkening sky. Another storm *was* moving in. A low rumble of thunder sounded in the distance, and the breeze quickened.

Whoever was laughing, they had better get inside soon.

She reached the gatehouse. Just beyond, soldiers of the garrison lay upon the grass, regardless of the fact that it must be wet. Their chests heaved and several gasped for breath, red in the face. A few men stood, bending over, their hands on their knees, rocking with laughter. Another had his back to her, and two swords with blades snapped off at the hilt dangled uselessly from his hands. His shoulders shook because, she realized, he was laughing, too.

She had seen that back before, but then he had not been half-naked, leaning his weight on one muscular leg.

She almost turned back to return to the hall, but the thought of any more time in that place with only a slumbering Cynvelin or his unruly men for company was enough to make her decide to find out what could amuse both the Welsh soldiers and their Norman master.

Madoc, the brawny Welshman whose insult she had not forgotten, stood at the gate, leaning on his spear. Ignoring him, she went to go past him when he suddenly laid the spear across her stomach.

"Sorry, my lady," he said in Welsh, "but there is to be no going out the gate for you."

Rhiannon DeLanyea was not the daughter of a powerful baron for nothing, as the look she gave him attested. She raised her chin in an imperious manner and haughtily said, "By whose order?"

"Frechette's," the man replied.

Rhiannon raised one dark eyebrow. "Really? He must be mistaken." She crossed her arms over her chest and tapped her foot impatiently. "Frechette!" she called out, his name a summons.

The Norman swiveled slowly on his heel and looked at her.

Chapter Nine

Rhiannon didn't quite know where to look. Certainly not at Bryce Frechette's dark, questioning eyes, or frowning, sensual lips, or sweat-slicked chest, or anything lower. Except his muddy boots.

"Yes, my lady?" he inquired, his tone nearly as impertinent as the guard's had been.

"Is it your order that I cannot leave Annedd Bach?"

Frechette muttered something that sounded suspiciously like a curse, tossed the sword hilts onto the ground beside his leather tunic, then strolled toward her. She raised her eyes and tried to regard him steadily, even if he was half-naked.

"It was Lord Cynvelin's order, my lady. I gather he fears for your safety outside the walls, or so he told the garrison. Isn't that right, Madoc?"

The Welshman didn't respond.

"He doesn't understand you," Rhiannon reminded him, pushing aside the Welshman's spear and walking toward Bryce.

"Oh, I remember, my lady," he replied. He

dropped his voice to a loud whisper. "But I have discovered that he only pretends not to understand me."

Madoc scowled, and Rhiannon nearly smiled at the man's discomfort. It was small enough recompense for his insult.

"I will answer for my lady's safety," he told the Welshman.

Madoc's only response was a non-committal grunt.

Leaving the shelter of the gatehouse, Rhiannon and Bryce began to walk toward the other men, who were watching with obvious curiosity. Bryce nodded at them. "They, however and unfortunately, do not know a word of French."

"Nevertheless, you seem to be able to amuse them," she noted.

"When two men are staging a mock fight to demonstrate defensive stances and both blades snap clean off at the same time, soldiers tend to find that amusing."

His tone was grim but she thought she heard laughter lurking in his voice.

She would never have imagined that such a warrior would find a potentially embarrassing situation funny. She had not suspected Bryce Frechette had the capacity to take himself less than completely seriously.

Then she remembered that she should be more careful of her reactions around this most disconcerting man. "I see no reason I shouldn't leave the castle if *they* are outside."

Seeing the mirth disappear from his eyes, replaced by that cold detachment she was more familiar with, filled Rhiannon with a regret she attempted to dismiss.

"As long as you stay where I can see you, my lady," he said flatly, "I suppose his lordship would not take it amiss." He frowned. "But where is he, my lady? He should be the one whose permission you seek."

"I don't need his permission."

"His company, then."

"I do not…" She hesitated. This man didn't have to know anything about her feelings. "I am not a prisoner here," she observed.

"Oh, no, my lady. Most certainly not. You are a very favored guest."

She didn't like his mockingly deferential tone. "Then I should be treated with some respect." She ran her gaze over his sweat-slicked chest.

She was pleased to see his face color, but he made no move to fetch his tunic. "I have been training the men. It is warm work and some things are better done unencumbered by clothing, as you know."

She flushed hotly. "No, I do not!" she said emphatically before walking past him along the muddy path toward the men. The ones who had been lying down scrambled to their feet, and all bowed when she approached.

Bryce caught up to her. "It's going to rain soon, my lady. Shouldn't you return to the hall? Perhaps you should go back to Lord Cynvelin."

"He is asleep."

"Ah!" he said with another meaningful look.

She glared at him. Depths of emotion, indeed! She must have been mad to find him fascinating. "What are you suggesting?"

He widened his eyes with mock innocence. "I, my lady? Nothing. Nothing at all."

"You are the most impertinent, discourteous Norman I have ever met!"

To her chagrin, he smiled and bowed.

She flounced toward a stump and perched upon the edge. "I believe I shall stay to see this miracle, how you train men who do not understand you."

He didn't even have the courtesy to answer. He simply shrugged his shoulders and turned back to the men.

One of them, the thin, dark-haired steward named Ermin, came to stand next to him. He seemed nervous, although whether it was because of his proximity to the Norman, or the coming storm, she couldn't tell, for he glanced at both the man beside him and gathering clouds with equal anxiety. It took another moment for Rhiannon to realize the dark-haired man was acting as translator.

Or at least he tried. He paused often when Bryce was talking, clearly searching for the proper word.

The men listened, albeit with desultory interest. Bryce's voice got progressively more impatient, even though his expression remained outwardly calm.

After a little while, Rhiannon rose from her perch and approached Bryce. "They are not stupid," she announced, interrupting as he repeated his caution about keeping their grips loose enough to avoid jarring their wrists.

Both men turned to face her, Ermin obviously surprised, Bryce annoyed. "They aren't attending to a word I say," the Norman grumbled.

"If they are like the men on my father's estate, and I see no reason to suppose they are not, they are not being attentive because they do not usually fight with swords. They think such an oration does not apply to them," she explained.

"Oration?"

"Lesson. Harangue, call it what you will. How many men here even possess a sword?"

"Five brought them," Bryce muttered. "I assumed the others forgot."

She made a disgusted face. "Forgot? Like they were simple? Did you not wonder when you saw the state of the weapons that they did bring? The rusted and broken blades should have told you something."

Bryce's eyes narrowed. Although her words would be an explanation for the deplorable lack of swords and the decrepit state of the five he had seen, he wished she would stop talking, stop looking at him with those vivacious green eyes, and stop standing within a hundred yards of him. He was finding it extremely difficult to concentrate as it was. Her simplest remark, even spoken with sarcastic frustration, seemed to strike at the chords of his heart rather than anger him, and with one look from her beautiful, sympathetic eyes she was able to pierce the armor he had built around himself. When they had been alone, he had said things to her he would never have revealed to another soul.

She was dangerous, with those eyes and that tempting smile.

He had to avoid her, this woman who belonged to another, lest he say or do something that would cause him to forfeit his chance for advancement. And he would hope the weather would stay clear, so they could leave him in peace.

If he could ever truly be at peace again, knowing that Lady Rhiannon could never be his.

It was only with the firmest resolve that he was able to attend to the business at hand, and that made him sound far angrier than he was. "They let them rust on purpose?" he demanded.

Ermin gasped with dismay and shook his head. "No, no, sir, we don't! Not on purpose!"

"I should have been more explicit. They don't neglect their weapons on purpose, any more than they didn't forget to bring a sword. Welshmen prefer bows."

"Bows?"

She nodded. "They will use swords in close quarters and spears, too, if they must. Have you ever seen a Welsh bow?"

"I once saw an archer shoot an arrow through a plank four inches thick. They said he was a Welshman."

"And the bow itself? What was it made of?"

"Elm, they told me," he recalled. "It was the ugliest weapon I ever saw. Too rigid and so long, it seemed unwieldy."

"Yet it sent an arrow through a four-inch plank," she noted, the glimmer of a smile on her lips and in her eyes as she looked at him.

Ermin muttered something to the men, and they all seemed to wake up.

"Is this true?" he asked Ermin. "Do they prefer bows?"

"Aye, sir," Ermin replied.

"Very well, then. Tomorrow, they will bring their bows and arrows, and I shall see if they are as good a weapon as the lady thinks."

Ermin nodded, but again he glanced upward, as if what Bryce were saying was far less important than the sky.

"What is it?" Bryce demanded. "What's wrong? Is it the storm?"

"No, sir," Ermin replied. "It's…it's…"

"Tell me!"

Ermin gave Lady Rhiannon a beseeching look, then a barrage of rapid Welsh poured from his lips.

Bryce turned to her questioningly. She smiled kindly at Ermin, then looked at Bryce, her lingering smile seemingly for him alone. "It's his wife. A woman brought word she's in labor and he wants to leave here to be with her." The lady's steadfast gaze grew sympathetic. "He says she lost their last child and almost died herself. He humbly asks to go home. He will return as soon as the babe is born."

If Lady Rhiannon had given Bryce such a look and asked him to jump from the battlements, he would have agreed. "I remember well how I felt when I heard my father was dead, and how I wished

I had been with him," he murmured. "Of course he may go."

She smiled, her eyes shining with approval.

He abruptly cleared his throat, then turned to the nervous Ermin. "We have to stop now anyway," he said, his voice husky with suppressed emotion, "or be wet through, and their weapons are rusted enough as it is. Go, Ermin—and take a horse from the stable and come back when all is well." He grinned ruefully as Ermin smiled broadly and with great relief. "I would not take a horse belonging to one of Cynvelin's men, if I were you."

Ermin nodded eagerly. "Thank you, sir! I will not!" He started to run toward the gatehouse, looking back over his shoulder to shout, "Thank you! Thank you!"

Suddenly a clap of thunder made them all jump, then turn to the west. "We had better get inside," Bryce said brusquely and to no one in particular.

As his men whispered among themselves, he bent to pick up his tunic. When he straightened, Lady Rhiannon was already nearly at the gatehouse.

Just as well, he told himself. Let her go without him. Let him learn to live without her.

Let her return to Lord Cynvelin, the most fortunate of men.

Rhiannon came to an abrupt halt when Lord Cynvelin, shrouded in a long, black cloak that made him look like a carrion crow, stepped out of the shadows to stand beside Madoc. "My lord," she cried. "You are awake."

"Indeed I am," he replied with a bow. "Imagine my surprise when I awakened and found my lovely lady had flown. I was very concerned, my dear."

Out of the corner of her eye, she noticed Madoc grinning at her as if party to some great joke. Had he gone to summon Lord Cynvelin, to tell him where she had gone like some kind of spy?

Why should she not be free to go where she would? She was a guest here.

"I had grown tired of being inside so much," she said with a glance at the stone-faced Madoc. "That fellow told me I couldn't go outside Annedd Bach."

Cynvelin waved his hand dismissively. "For your safety, my lady. I promised your good father that you would not come to any harm while in my care. The woods here may harbor outlaws." He smiled with apparent commiseration and held out his arm. "It will be better when we get to Caer Coch. The gardens are lovely, although naturally I shall approve any changes you think necessary. In the meantime, we should get inside before the storm hits. Unfortunately, I fear we shall have to stay here awhile yet."

"Yes," she answered, fighting both the urge to turn to see if Bryce Frechette was behind her, and to refuse Cynvelin's proffered arm.

Indeed, she was sorely tempted to turn and run out of Annedd Bach and try to find her father, storm or no storm. Then she would be away from both these men, especially the very puzzling, very contradictory Bryce Frechette, who seemed so cold and aloof sometimes, so warm and approachable and attractive at others.

"Frechette," Cynvelin said.

Rhiannon turned slightly to see the Norman acknowledging Lord Cynvelin with a nod of his head as he came through the gate. "My lord. My lady."

She was relieved to see that he had put on his tunic. And that he was not looking at her directly.

Not that he shouldn't. There was no reason he could not. They had done nothing wrong. He hadn't touched her. He hadn't kissed her. Not this time.

He would never kiss her again, and all too soon she would be gone. She should be happy about that, and eager to return to her father.

She would certainly be eager to be free of Lord Cynvelin's company, at any rate.

"Was that Ermin I saw running to the stable as if the building was on fire?"

"Yes, my lord," Bryce replied evenly. "He needs to get home. His wife is having a baby."

A loud rumble nearly drowned out the Welsh lord's response. "Why did he go to the stable, then?"

"I told him he could take a horse," Bryce said.

"I don't recall you asking my permission for such an order."

"Forgive me, my lord," Bryce said, his tone only slightly contrite. "I did not think it required your permission, if I am in charge of the garrison."

Rhiannon's gaze darted from man to man as they spoke. She realized Bryce was far from pleased but determined to remain calm. Although Lord Cynvelin smiled, she noted the narrowing of his eyes.

Despite his loss of rank, by allowing Ermin to go,

Bryce had displayed an understanding of noblesse oblige that Cynvelin himself would do well to emulate, and with a true spirit of kind concern that was rare, indeed.

She was more certain than ever that whoever had mistreated Ula, it was not Bryce Frechette.

Another loud crack of thunder surprised them all. The horse Ermin was leading out of the stable whinnied and pranced nervously. The thin man tried to control it as rain began to fall again.

Without waiting for his overlord's dismissal, Bryce walked away from Rhiannon and Cynvelin. As he strode toward Ermin, she heard him ask if the Welshman was still determined to leave in the storm. Ermin nodded, and Bryce held the horse for him to mount.

"I suspect that will be one horse we shall never see again," Lord Cynvelin said sarcastically.

Rhiannon moved back against the wall to let Ermin ride past. He nodded at them as he urged the horse out into the driving rain, while Bryce continued toward the barracks. "You think Ermin will steal it?"

"Or it will get stolen while he waits for his wife to have her brat."

Rhiannon turned to stare at the Welshman.

Cynvelin laughed. "You know how these peasants are, my lady. They have babies as if they were rabbits."

"I think that is a heartless thing to say, my lord," Rhiannon charged, remembering Ermin's face when he told her of the baby who had died. "Peasant or not, he wants to be with his wife, and I think it very kind of Frechette to allow him the use of a horse.''

"I'm sorry to upset you, my lady," Cynvelin replied, frowning slightly. "Please forgive my hasty remark. Sometimes I speak without thinking.''

Since Rhiannon herself was guilty of this sin, she could scarcely hold that against him, although she did fault his lack of feeling.

"If you will share my cloak, my lady, we should get inside the hall before the courtyard is awash.'' With a pleasant smile, he held open his cloak, obviously expecting her to come beneath it, close beside him in what would be almost an embrace.

The idea of being in such close proximity with Lord Cynvelin ap Hywell did not please her at all.

"What is rain to a Welshman, my lord?" she chided mirthfully as she lifted up her skirt and dashed nimbly away from him, across the courtyard and into the keep.

With a set face, Cynvelin watched her go, then turned to Madoc. "What did you see?" he growled.

Madoc shrugged his beefy shoulders. "They talked, then she watched, then they talked.''

Suddenly Cynvelin shoved Madoc against the wall, his forearm against the soldier's throat. "How did they talk, you fool!''

Madoc, his face growing red, spluttered, "They talked, that's all. I...I didn't see nothing suspicious, my lord!''

"On your life?''

"I swear! If I thought there was anything amiss, I would have come for you.''

Cynvelin relaxed and stepped back, while Madoc gasped for breath. "Good. I want you to make sure she doesn't go outside the walls again."

Madoc nodded.

"She stays here, and if she goes near Frechette again, tell me."

Madoc looked at his master questioningly. "You don't think—"

"No," he said to himself as much as to his companion. "She would never choose him over me. But Frechette could be trouble."

"Then kill him," Madoc suggested matter-of-factly.

Cynvelin gave the man a skeptical glance. "Known for your cleverness are you, Madoc? You must remember, then, that Frechette's sister is married to the Baron DeGuerre. With him as my underling and the daughter of Emryss DeLanyea for my wife, I will be allied to the two most famous warriors in England."

Madoc's eyes widened with respect.

"Of course, should Frechette prove to be less than amenable to my commands...well, his reputation is against him, poor fellow, so if I must find fault with him and send him away, no one will question it."

Feeling better than he had since he had first spied Rhiannon standing next to Bryce Frechette, Cynvelin smiled and wrapped his cloak around him like a shroud before sauntering out into the rain.

Rhiannon hurried into the bedchamber and closed the door behind her, panting from the exertion of running up the steps.

And the need to get away from Lord Cynvelin.

"My lady?"

Rhiannon whirled around. She hadn't noticed Ula, who had obviously been tidying the room, for the few articles Rhiannon had left scattered about were nowhere to be seen, and the bed had been made.

"Your dress is wet, my lady," the maidservant observed.

"I was watching the men train and it started to rain," Rhiannon answered.

"Best you should be getting out of those wet things, then."

As if to confirm Ula's suggestion, Rhiannon sneezed. "I think that blue gown would be the warmest," she said, realizing she was shivering.

As the maidservant untied the laces at the back of Rhiannon's gown, Rhiannon spoke in a casual tone. "Tell me, what do you think of Lord Cynvelin?"

Ula went to the chest and lifted out the woolen gown of deep indigo blue that looked warm and comfortable.

"I don't think about him," Ula answered. "It's not my place to think about him."

Her voice wavered slightly, and Rhiannon realized that her hands had started to tremble.

Rhiannon started to wiggle out of her damp gown and asked her next question as if it was not important. "Is he considered a good overlord?"

Ula didn't answer as she took the wet dress and laid it on the bed.

Clad only in her shift, Rhiannon regarded the younger woman. She caught a glimpse of an expression that looked like anger, dismay and defiance combined in Ula's eyes. "Are you afraid of him?"

"Who, my lady?"

"Lord Cynvelin. Has he ever hurt you?"

Ula hesitated. "No, my lady."

Rhiannon realized she was not going to get an honest answer, but she thought the girl's trembling hands told her some of what she wanted to know.

Ula was afraid of Cynvelin.

The maidservant held up the blue dress. Rhiannon slipped her hands into the arms and Ula lifted it over her head.

"What of Frechette?" she asked, her voice muffled as the garment went over her. "Is he a good master?"

Ula didn't respond as she began pulling it down.

Then the gown seemed to go slack, as if Ula had let go, leaving Rhiannon to tug the bodice into place. "Ula?"

She glanced over her shoulder—to see a smiling Lord Cynvelin, his black cloak over his arm, standing on the threshold of the bedchamber.

"My lord!" Rhiannon gasped as he tossed his cloak onto the bed.

Realizing they were alone, she hurried to the far side of the room, holding her loose bodice over her breasts.

"Where is Ula?"

"I sent her away," he replied lightly.

"Please leave!" she ordered. "I am not properly dressed."

"Allow me to help you," he said, sauntering closer.

"You, my lord? No, thank you. I can tie the laces myself."

His voice dropped to a provocative whisper. "You have no maid nearby."

"I can do it myself, thank you," she said sternly.

His gaze seemed to intensify, and not in a good way. "Allow me, my lady," he said, and the words were an order as he advanced on her.

"No, truly, I—"

"There is no need to be so coy." He shoved her shoulder, so that she had to turn, then she felt him pick up the laces and begin to pull them tight.

Too stunned to move, surprised by the change in his manner, she said no more.

"All finished," he said. When she turned to face him, he was near the door, holding his arms wide. "You see. I only wanted to help."

"So now you have helped and now you may leave."

He frowned sorrowfully. "My lady, why are you so harsh with me today? Is it something I said? Have I offended you in some way?"

"You come into the room when I am not decently attired and are surprised to find I feel offended?"

"I thought you wanted me to follow you."

She gave him a critical look. "You seem to have a great facility for misunderstanding me, my lord."

"Perhaps that is because you are unlike any woman I have ever met," he said. "You are the most beautiful, the most graceful, the most desirable."

Once again she felt trapped. "My lord, we...we should not be alone together here," she stammered.

"No, my lovely Rhiannon? Not alone? Then when may I tell you how much I adore you? How much I love you? How much I need you?"

She backed away, not sure what to do, only sure that she should not be alone with him. "You could court me properly, not keep me here like a prisoner."

He stared at her with wide-eyed innocence. "What makes you say such a thing, my lady?"

"You won't let me go outside the gates, and I think you have set your men to spy upon me."

Cynvelin's expression grew sorrowful. "You hurt me, my lady! You are not a prisoner here, except for your own good! I have not set my men to spy upon you. I came looking for you."

His explanation was reasonable, and yet she wanted him gone. Indeed, she wanted to be away from him completely. "My lord," she began, "I think I should go back to my father immediately."

"Travel in such weather? You cannot be serious."

"I assure you, Lord Cynvelin, I am very serious."

"You want to leave me that much? And Frechette, too?"

"What is Frechette to me?" she asked, coloring.

Cynvelin strolled over to the small table and started to examine her toilet articles. "That is what I have been wondering. I thought you disliked the man. I thought you considered him dishonorable. What has happened to change your mind?"

"Nothing," she replied, knowing that she lied. Many small things had happened to make her realize she had originally judged Bryce Frechette in haste, without really knowing him or why he had done what he had. Her opinion had changed greatly, all for the better. "I was telling him about Welsh bows."

"Is that so?" He glanced up at her sharply. Critically.

"Yes, my lord, it is," she retorted. "Would you dictate to whom I may speak or what I may say?"

He picked up her hairbrush and began to smack it against his palm with light, rhythmic taps. "I would rather you did not speak to him. He is not a fit companion for you."

"Yet you saw fit to hire him and set him in command here," she observed.

The brush stopped moving. "To command a garrison in this godforsaken part of Wales is what he is fit for. And nothing more."

"If you say so, my lord."

Cynvelin set down the brush gently and gave her a winsome look. "Please, my lady, do not be angry with me."

He smiled guiltily, like a little boy caught stealing apples from the orchard. "I am jealous."

"Jealous?"

"Of any man who looks at you, let alone talks with you," he explained. "I was even jealous of Ula when I came into the room. That is why I sent her away. I begrudge anyone who has your attention, when it is not me."

That he was in earnest she did not doubt. But his jealousy only made her feel as if he thought he already possessed her.

He came toward her, holding out his hands beseechingly. "Rhiannon, you know I love you. I would do anything to have you. Will you not make me the happiest man in the kingdom by agreeing to be my wife?''

Out in the courtyard, she heard a man's voice raised in command. Bryce Frechette's voice.

She suddenly felt as if she were standing on the edge of an abyss, and that Bryce Frechette was calling her to safety.

''My lord,'' she said softly, yet with determination. ''I cannot. Please do not ask it of me! Let me go back to my father.''

''Why must you make this so difficult, dearest Rhiannon?'' he asked, the pleading tone of his words at distinct odds with the frustration she saw in his eyes.

''It does not have to be difficult,'' she answered. ''Indeed, what I ask is simple indeed. Return me to my father.''

His gaze faltered and he slowly nodded his head. ''I see that it is useless for me to plead with you more,'' he said softly.

He raised his eyes, and she thought she saw so genuine a disappointment she almost feared she had misunderstood him, as he had misunderstood her.

''I will do what I must,'' he muttered.

With that, he slowly turned on his heel, picked up his cloak and left the room, closing the door quietly behind him.

Sighing, Rhiannon sat on the bed.

And told herself that she should be glad she was going away from Annedd Bach, and everybody in it.

Chapter Ten

Bryce and the men of the garrison rose when Cynvelin sauntered into the barracks.

As they made their obeisance, the nobleman took off his cloak and shook it, wetting the nearest sleeping pallets without concern.

His gaze swept over a chessboard, the pieces scattered in the players' haste to stand, a harp held in one man's grimy fingers and Bryce's distance from the others, for he had been alone in the corner, the cloth and sword in his hand betraying what he had been doing.

"Well, Frechette," he said, ignoring the men and addressing only their commander, "surely these men are not resting?"

Bryce put down the cloth and sheathed his sword. "Our practice was cut short by the rain."

A strange look crossed Cynvelin's face. "What is rain to a Welshman?" he asked. He tossed his cloak onto the sleeping pallet. Bryce noted the disgruntled expression on the face of the man who slept there, but said nothing.

"Of course, since you saw fit to send your interpreter away," he continued, "and Lady Rhiannon is not here to help you, I perceive the difficulty in trying to get your men to do anything other than entertain themselves."

"A garrison requires a certain camaraderie to be effective, my lord," Bryce replied.

"So I have been told."

"With that in mind, I saw no harm in allowing them some diversions."

"And also with that in mind, don't you think these men should be in the hall spending time with the men of my guard?"

"Given the animosity between your guard and the garrison, I've ordered the garrison to keep to the barracks as much as possible."

"Animosity?" Cynvelin said, apparently surprised. "That seems a harsh term. I would call it a friendly rivalry."

Bryce thought friendly didn't enter into it. "Whatever you wish to call it, my lord," he said frankly, "such weather tends to make men short-tempered, and I thought it best to keep them apart."

"I see." Cynvelin smiled. "There is another way to inspire that sense of unity you deem so important. I would set you and your men a task."

"Yes, my lord?"

"I want you to take the best men of the garrison and ride out to the far border of the estate. I have heard reports of an outlaw camp there, and the sooner such a thing is eradicated, the better."

"In this weather, my lord, and so late in the day?"

Cynvelin's eyes narrowed and Bryce realized the man was angry. No doubt the weather and the delay in the journey to Caer Coch was making the Welshman short-tempered.

No wonder Lady Rhiannon had not looked happy when he had last seen them together at the gate.

A lover's spat might explain a certain shortness of temper, too, and the lady's apparent annoyance with the Welshman.

"Are you questioning my orders, Frechette?" Cynvelin asked.

Bryce wanted to, very much. Although sending out a small armed party on a foray was very different from a full guard escorting a lady, it was raining hard. The road would be slippery and he didn't want to risk getting lost again. Most of all, he didn't want to leave Lady Rhiannon, not even for a little while, not even if she belonged to another.

"Well, Frechette, do you intend to obey me, or not?"

Bryce knew he could hardly refuse Lord Cynvelin's direct order unless he wanted to give up all hope of a knighthood from the Welshman, which, he reminded himself, was what he needed to keep foremost in his mind. All else was nothing more than a futile dream. "Yes, my lord. But what of guarding Annedd Bach? That is the job of the garrison, and there will not be enough men for the watches."

"My men will be here to protect Annedd Bach and take a turn on watch."

"Then we shall leave at once, my lord," Bryce replied.

Cynvelin eyed the men and gave a few brisk orders in their language. Bryce saw their surprise and displeasure, which matched his own, as well as their sullen expressions and disgruntled glances at Cynvelin ap Hywell.

"If the hour is late, that is all the more reason to start at once," Cynvelin observed, reaching for his cloak. "Madoc knows the way. He can show you, and he can interpret for you."

"If you are sure he understands me, my lord," Bryce said, not quite keeping the sarcasm from his voice.

Cynvelin grinned. "That is his little joke. I assure you, he will understand enough. I expect you will be gone all night, so take what provisions you need with you. I shall give your regrets to Lady Rhiannon when you are absent from the evening meal."

Bryce inclined his head in acquiescence as Lord Cynvelin turned on his heel and left the barracks.

The moment he was gone, the men erupted in a jumble of what Bryce knew had to be curses and complaints, although they kept their voices low.

He didn't blame them. He didn't want to do this any more than they did.

It was not only the rain and the lateness of the hour. He didn't like the thought of Lady Rhiannon alone with Lord Cynvelin, with only his guard nearby.

He told himself to quit being a jealous fool and get about his business, no matter how unpleasant.

Rhiannon rose when she heard a commotion in the courtyard. She hurried to the window and hiked herself up on the wide sill, looking out through the teeming rain.

Men were gathered there with their horses, preparing to ride out. Perhaps Cynvelin had changed his mind and was willing to take her to her father now, despite the rain.

Bryce Frechette strode out of the stables, leading his stallion. He must be part of her escort.

She took a deep breath. Maybe Cynvelin would not come with them. Once she was gone from Annedd Bach, she would likely never see Bryce Frechette again. Maybe she would get a chance to say something—anything—to Bryce Frechette before they parted ways.

She watched him mount his horse and realized that no one had come to fetch her. Then the portcullis began to open.

These men were leaving without her. They were not her escort, but must be about some other business for Cynvelin.

Disappointment washed over her. Where was Bryce going, and why? Would he return before she left here to go to her father?

Would she get a chance to say goodbye?

Then she told herself maybe it was better this way.

She turned away from the window. And maybe it would not hurt so much if she didn't see him go.

"Oh, Rhiaaan-non!"

Rhiannon nearly fell off the stool when she heard Cynvelin call. The hour was late; indeed, she had heard the men going to the barracks some time ago, and the only light illuminating her bedchamber was from the moon, which peeked out occasionally from behind the thick, scudding clouds.

If she thought she would be able to sleep, she would have gone to bed long ago, too, instead of sitting by the table deluding herself that she should brush her hair again.

Her grip on the brush tightened as she frowned at the door, wondering why Cynvelin would bother her. She had told Ula to convey her regrets that she would not join him in the hall, pleading a slight indisposition. Could her countryman not even appreciate that?

"Oh, my lovely Rhiannon!" Cynvelin's voice sang out again, and she speculated that perhaps he had imbibed too much wine.

"Are you awake, my beautiful Rhiannon?" Cynvelin asked from the other side of the door. "Wake up, my dear one! Wake up. The man who adores you is here."

She scowled when she saw the latch move and realized he was opening the door. First he dared to intrude when she was not dressed; now he would accost her in the night? Quickly she shoved the chest against the door. She had no wish to talk to him anymore, and certainly not now.

The door opened, then hit the chest with a thud. "What have you done, my beautiful bride?" His tone altered slightly. "Are you trying to keep me out?"

"My lord, this is most improper!" she declared. "I have nothing to say to you at this time of night!"

"Nothing to say, Rhiannon?" he remarked, more anger in his voice as he shoved at the door again. "You usually have so much to say. To me. To Frechette. To Ula. Even to Madoc."

The chest moved again and she realized he was pushing against the door. She was very glad she had not started to disrobe.

"My lord!" she said irritably, "will you not go away? I do not want to see you now!"

"Why should you be alone when I am nearby? You seemed to enjoy my company at Lord Melevoir's, and here, too."

"It was not the middle of the night then!"

"It is not the middle of the night now," he replied. "It is only the beginning of the night. There are many hours of darkness yet that we could share."

He must have given a strong shove, for suddenly the door opened, pushing the chest into the room.

"My lord!" she cried, the words a shocked condemnation as he strolled into the room as if he had every right to be there.

"My lord, leave me!" she ordered.

"You are a DeLanyea to your very bones, aren't you, my dear?" he speculated, none the whit disturbed by her tone, apparently. "So sure of yourself, so proud, so imperious."

"Cynvelin, this is most improper, as you well know."

He began to circle her slowly, and for the first time in his presence, she started to be afraid. "Please, my lord, go away."

"No."

"I thought you said you would take me to my father."

Smiling, he stopped in front of her and shook his head. "This time, I fear you misunderstood me, my lady. I said I would do what I must, and so I shall."

A shiver of dread ran down Rhiannon's spine. What had happened to the pleading supplicant? "What...what do you mean, do what you must? You have to let me go."

"No, my dear. At Annedd Bach, I don't have to do anything."

"If there is any honor in you," she said, "why not let me go from here? I could never marry you."

"Never?" he asked, a chill in his voice that she had never heard before. "Why not?"

She straightened her shoulders, willing herself not to be afraid. "Because I cannot marry a man I do not respect."

His expression grew more stern. "You do not respect me?" he asked, not loudly, but the way he spoke added to her dread.

She had wanted him to understand that she could not marry him, but she had not expected this cold, heartless response. Nevertheless, she would not turn away from her course now. "I cannot respect a man who lies."

"Not even for love?"

"I would say especially not then. A husband and wife should trust each other."

"You sound very sure and certain, my dear."

"I am," she answered simply and honestly.

He smiled and laughed softly, but it was a hollow,

mirthless laugh. "I am not the only one who lies, my lady who claims she cares nothing for Frechette."

She flushed and said nothing, watching him warily, for this was a man she had never seen before. He continued to circle her, smiling his usual smile, and that was perhaps the most chilling thing of all. "It doesn't matter what you think of him. He knows he dare not question my orders, not if he is to get the knighthood he so desperately craves."

She stood motionless as he walked around her. "Will you give him that, or is that another lie?" she asked.

"What is it to you?"

He halted behind her, leaning forward so that his hot breath was on her ear. "Shall I tell you how and why I learned to lie with such convincing skill, my virtuous lady?" he asked. He came around in front of her. "I learned it at my mother's knee. It was the best way to avoid my father's wrath, so that he would not beat me."

He seemed to expect an answer, so she said, "I am sorry to hear it."

Cynvelin's smile widened, but it did not reach his eyes. Indeed, his eyes gleamed with something far different from happiness. "Is that a hint of pity on my lady's face? Well, I do not need pity now. I discovered early what to say so that my father would not strike. My mother, unfortunately, did not lie as well as I, and so he hit her more."

He gave her another eerily unhappy smile. "But no matter. He is dead now, you see. Fell from the wall walk of Caer Coch, his body broken on the rocks below. All the bruises and broken bones repaid in one instant, as it were. A fitting way for a man like that to die, would you not agree?''

That he was speaking the truth she did not doubt. Nor did she doubt that, for once, she was seeing beneath his shallow mask to a hint of something deeper.

Something evil and rank and poisonous, a hatred that had warped him.

Unlike Bryce, Cynvelin had no regrets. No remorse. No shame.

He advanced upon her, gazing at her intently. ''Your pity or your love,'' he said, lifting her hand and brushing a kiss across her palm. ''I will take either one, my lady.''

''Cynvelin, please, don't,'' she whispered.

''Don't what?'' he murmured, turning her hand over to press another unwelcome kiss upon the back of it. ''Stop telling you how much I desire you? How I cannot sleep for thinking of you sharing my bed? How I will pleasure you?''

''I am a noblewoman,'' she blurted, her stomach churning with fear.

He raised his eyes, a sly smile on his face. She could scarcely believe she had once thought him handsome, or honorable.

''I know that, my lady.''

''You should let me go to my father.''

''Surely by now he has gone home to Craig Fawr.''

''No!'' she cried, pulling away from him, desperately hoping she was right. ''He wouldn't go anywhere while I am here.''

"Surely there is no need for such theatrics, my dear."

"Theatrics? I am not playacting! I want to go to my father!"

"You are never leaving me," Cynvelin said coldly. "I will not permit it."

"You will not...? I am not asking you, my lord," she said sternly, hugging herself tightly. "I am ordering you to take me to my father!"

She watched in horror at the angry wrath that came to Cynvelin's face as he looked at her and shook his head. "No. You are going to be my wife."

The cold deliberation of Cynvelin's words added to Rhiannon's growing fear.

She took a step as if she would run, but just as suddenly, she knew she could not flee. She couldn't outrun him, or his guards. She couldn't get to a horse before he could stop her.

Cynvelin knelt in front of her and took her hands in his, pressing them between his warm palms, once again the charming courtier. "Surely you do not think it will be a bad thing to be my wife, my lady."

She looked at him beseechingly. "Why...why do you want me?" she whispered, her throat dry.

"You do not believe I love you?"

She couldn't answer.

The pressure of his hands increased until he was hurting her. "You do not believe I love you?" he repeated, and again she saw hostility in his eyes.

"I...I believe you," she lied.

Another smile twisted his handsome face. "You see how easy it is to learn to lie, my lovely bride?"

He turned her palm upward and nuzzled it. "But I don't care if you love me or not. I want you for my wife, and so it shall be."

"My father—"

He abruptly let go of her hands and stood. "Still refusing all that I offer?" he challenged, glaring at her. "It doesn't matter, Rhiannon. I want you and I have you. You will never leave me, and your father will suffer for the rest of his life knowing that you belong to me in the eyes of God and man. That I can take you when I will, and that the children of your body—*his* grandchildren—will also be mine."

Her eyes widened as the full horror of his words and demeanor struck her like a backhand blow. "You hate him that much? Why?"

"He shamed me."

"All he did was send you from Craig Fawr!"

"And you think people did not hear? That other nobles didn't wonder why? Since the great baron of Craig Fawr didn't want me, they assumed there must have been a good reason." He cocked his head and gave her a sardonic smile. "You had heard of Frechette's scandalous behavior. It's a wonder you never heard the whispers about *me*."

She wondered at that, too, and then, because she knew her father, she straightened her shoulders and said, "I don't think there were any whispers. You were treated as a welcome guest at Lord Melevoir's. You were not shunned like Bryce Frechette."

Her voice grew stronger. "I know that without proof, my father would make no accusations. He would start no rumors. Indeed, I can believe he would put a stop to such talk if it ever reached his ears. If you think people are whispering about you behind your back, that is your own guilty conscience.''

To her dismay, she realized Cynvelin was unmoved. ''He wronged me, and I will have my revenge.''

She clasped her hands together. ''No matter what you think my father is guilty of, Cynvelin, *I* have done nothing.''

Cynvelin grabbed her hands again, his grip so strong that tears stung her eyes. ''Nothing except be the child of Emryss DeLanyea, as well as a beautiful, desirable woman. I could love you, Rhiannon.''

He wrapped his arms around her and she felt as if she were entwined in a snake's coils. ''Let me love you,'' he whispered, and she felt him kiss her neck.

She thought there was only one kind of love Cynvelin was capable of, and she would rather die than experience it.

He was stronger than she, but her father had taught her to defend herself. Motionless, she relaxed in his arms, waiting for the opportunity to lift her knee and kick.

It didn't come, because he moved away. ''Very well, my dear. I am in no humor for battle, nor am I some kind of monstrous creature. I can be very kind when I am pleased.''

He went toward the door, then paused on the threshold to look back at her, that horrible smile still on his face. ''Of course, I can be very cruel when I am not. I shall let you muse upon that for a while, shall I? Otherwise, I might hurt you.

"I think you need a little discipline, too, therefore I believe you should stay here alone, my dear, all alone, with no food and no water. After a day or two of that, we shall see if you find my company so unbearable."

He went out the door, banging it shut behind him.

Rhiannon stared at the back of the door with eyes that had been opened.

Cynvelin didn't even care for her at all, except as a prize in his private battle. Her rank would not protect her. Her family would not help her.

She had to get away. Now. At once.

She ran to the door, to discover that it was locked.

She tried the latch again and again, but there was no mistake. She was Cynvelin's prisoner, as surely as if she were locked in the deepest cell of the most terrible dungeon.

Was there no one here from whom she could seek aid?

Bryce Frechette came immediately to mind. Yet he had kidnapped her and—

And he had spoken of her abduction as a custom, which it was, provided the bride was willing.

Even she had not suspected Cynvelin of any baser motive than the one he had espoused in the beginning—that he was desperate to court her and could think of no other way to be near her, given her father's dislike.

It could be that Bryce believed that, too. Knowing little of the Welsh—if anything at all—he would probably accept whatever a man so outwardly honest and charming as Cynvelin ap Hywell told him about Welsh customs…and whatever else he chose.

If Cynvelin had told Bryce that she returned his love, perhaps even going so far as to claim that they were betrothed, what would Bryce, or any truly honorable man, make of her willingness to kiss him?

That she was shameless and immoral, tempting him when she belonged to another.

Gasping, she covered her mouth with her hand, everything suddenly clear. She was just as suddenly certain that he would help her, once he knew the truth.

But Bryce wasn't here. Cynvelin had sent him away.

Her fear returned a hundredfold. Why had Cynvelin done that? When would Bryce come back? What if he never came back?

She shook her head. No, his absence must only be temporary, or he would not have any of the men of the garrison with him.

But who could say when he would return? Maybe it would be after Cynvelin had lost what patience he possessed.

At the thought of Cynvelin attacking her, she felt sick and helpless. She was only a lone woman, completely at his mercy.

Her father had been alone, all those years ago in the Holy Land when King Richard and the others had left him for dead on the field at Acre. He had been alone for ten long years as he made his way home with no money, no horse, no armor.

She was Emryss DeLanyea's daughter, as Cynvelin had said, and she would not disgrace his name by giving up.

Nor would she ever marry Cynvelin ap Hywell and join his name to that of her family. Not even if he raped her.

Determined to protect herself as best she could, she shoved all the furnishings in the bedchamber against the door to create a makeshift barricade.

She would get out of this place somehow, some way. She ran to the narrow window. Placing her hands on the sill, she raised herself up. The window narrowed, but if she turned sideways and was very careful, she could get through it. She climbed up and perched on the sill, looking out.

Then down.

A long way down.

But the walls of the keep were very rough, the stones rugged with age. A skilled and nimble climber like Dylan wouldn't hesitate to descend, especially if there was a pretty girl waiting for him.

Not her. She dared not risk it without a rope.

She jumped down from the sill and looked around the room, her eyes lighting on the bed, whose linen was supported by ropes.

She hurried to it and threw back the coverings.

The knot fastening the end looked as if it had been there for the past one hundred years. Crouching down and biting her lip, she tried to untie it.

She kept trying, even when the rough hemp cut her fingers. Tears of frustration stung her eyes as she worked the knot, trying to get it loose.

It was no use. The knot was too tight and she had nothing with which to cut it.

She sat back on her haunches and wiped her eyes. She would get out of this place, somehow.

She looked at the chest of clothing.

She could make her own rope, she thought with a glimmer of rekindled hope. She could tear a garment into strips and braid them together. She promptly pulled one of the linen shifts out of the chest, thinking that would be the easiest fabric to tear.

It was not.

With the zeal of near desperation, she took the fabric in her teeth and worried it like a dog with a bone until she made a hole. Then she ripped.

Cynvelin put his hand on the cold wall, trying to calm his rage.

Anger burned in him, furious, roiling wrath that threatened to overtake his reason.

But he wouldn't let that happen. Not again. Not with Rhiannon. He needed her for his glorious plan.

Straightening, he saw Ula standing at the bottom of the stairs, a covered bowl held carefully against her chest, and a wineskin in her other hand.

"What are you doing?" he demanded, jogging down the rest of the stairs.

"I am bringing Lady Rhiannon some stew and wine since she did not come to the hall tonight."

"Come here."

When Ula didn't obey at once, he snatched the wine from her and yanked out the stopper. He took a long pull on the wineskin, then wiped his lips with the back of his hand. "Take that back to the kitchen," he ordered, nodding at the bowl.

"But she'll be hungry," Ula protested.

"I want her hungry!" he snarled as he knocked the bowl away from Ula.

The cover flew off and the contents spilled on the wall and floor. Tossing aside the wineskin, he glared at the shocked Ula.

Then suddenly he reached out and grabbed her hair, tugging her toward him. "What were you talking about, eh?" he demanded. "Me?"

"No!" the frightened girl answered.

"Liar!" he growled, forcing her head back. "Did you tell her how I took you?"

"No!" Ula started to weep, and that pleased him.

Nor did he require Ula for any plan. "You're a liar. You told her what I made you do."

"No!" She sniveled as he pulled harder.

Then, slowly, he smiled.

Chapter Eleven

The next day, soaked to the skin and thoroughly miserable, Bryce sat wearily upon his horse as it plodded through the thick mud on what was supposed to be a road. Behind him, Madoc and the others were likewise sodden from the continuing rain.

The mud made sucking noises every time his horse took a step. The only other sounds were the rain and the occasional discontented mutter from one of the Welshmen.

Not that he blamed them for complaining. He was beginning to believe this had been a fool's errand from start to finish.

There had been no outlaw camp, nor any signs of one. Bryce and his men had reached the edge of the forest late last night and made what camp they could on the wet ground. They had started to search this morning as soon as it was light, or as much light as could penetrate the mist. So far they had not found so much as a questionable stick.

If he were a suspicious man, Bryce mused, he

would think Lord Cynvelin simply wanted to get him out of Annedd Bach.

If that were so, what cause would he have to want him gone?

Bryce thought of the previous day and wondered if the Welshman suspected Bryce of having inappropriate feelings for his betrothed. Bryce had tried to hide his growing regard, but likely with inadequate results. He had never been able to hide his emotions completely.

But then why would Cynvelin not say something to him? Why keep him in his company if he surmised such a thing?

Because Bryce was a valuable warrior?

He was not feeling very valuable at the moment.

Suddenly the hairs on the back of his neck stood up.

They were being watched. He couldn't see anything through the rain and the trees, but he was sure of it nonetheless. Perhaps he had discounted the notion of outlaws too easily, his mind clouded by thoughts and feelings he should not be harboring.

With a deliberately casual gesture, he signaled for Madoc to ride forward beside him.

The Welshman rubbed his dripping nose on the sleeve of his tunic and gave Bryce a quizzical look.

"We have companions in the woods," Bryce said quietly.

Madoc started and half turned before Bryce spoke. "No, don't look. I don't want the outlaws to know we're on to them."

Madoc nodded and opened his mouth to speak, but

Bryce didn't give him a chance. "Pass word among the men, but don't do anything suspicious."

"Aye," Madoc muttered.

His gaze darting from bush to tree to road, Bryce slowly rode on ahead as Madoc fell back among the others. He noted that the forest opened out a little on his right, and there was a small rise in the distance.

On that rise sat a lone horseman, unmoving in the rain, as if he were a ghost, or a statue, watching them.

There was something familiar about the man, the way he sat on his horse, or something else that Bryce couldn't quite name.

By the time Madoc and the others had caught up to him, the stranger had turned his horse and was disappearing beyond the ridge.

Madoc gasped what sounded like an oath, then murmured, "DeLanyea!"

"The baron?" Bryce asked, surprised. He hadn't been able to see the man's face clearly in the rain, yet there was that about the stranger that made Bryce think it was not Lady Rhiannon's father. "What would he be doing here?"

Madoc only shook his head for an answer and nudged his horse forward. Bryce did the same, until he was abreast of the Welshman. "Why would the baron or his men be watching us?"

Madoc shrugged his shoulders. "A mistake I made. As you say, why would he be here?"

Exactly, Bryce thought. It was more likely outlaws or rebels. The garrison seemed to respect him and follow his leadership, but he knew rebels could be clever. Perhaps this was a trap.

Suddenly the sound of a galloping horse came to his ears. Bryce pulled his horse to a stop, jumped from his saddle and drew his sword. Madoc did likewise, and the rest of the garrison took the bows from their shoulders.

At least he might discover if Lady Rhiannon was right about Welshmen and their bows, Bryce thought sardonically as he braced himself for an attack.

A horse came careening around the corner of the road, then came to such an abrupt halt, it almost fell.

There sat Ermin, dripping wet and grinning from ear to ear. "Sir!" he called out happily.

Bryce relaxed, but not completely. Not after the sight of the man on the ridge.

Ermin continued to speak excitedly as the men of the garrison swarmed past Bryce and surrounded their companion, leaving Madoc scowling behind them.

"You can tell Lord Cynvelin there was no need to be concerned about the horse," Bryce said to Madoc as he sheathed his sword.

"Be telling him yourself," Madoc muttered.

Bryce glanced at Madoc and noted the man's tense posture. Indeed, he kept looking back over his shoulder as if he expected an attack from the rear.

"It's a boy, sir!" Ermin cried as he dismounted and led the horse toward Bryce. "A fine, healthy boy! And my wife is well, too."

"I am glad to hear it. I'm also glad you didn't break your neck riding that way, or injure the horse."

Ermin's face fell.

"You didn't bring any rebels with you?"

Ermin was obviously shocked. "Rebels? No, sir!"

"Good," Bryce said, believing the man. "Let's get back to Annedd Bach so we can all get dry."

"Yes, sir!" Ermin relayed Bryce's order to the others, who did as they were bid.

"Madoc, you go to the rear."

"Me? Why?" the soldier demanded hotly.

Bryce regarded him steadily, recognizing fear beneath the apparent anger. "Are you afraid?" he asked quietly. "Is there something I should know?"

"No!"

"Then go."

Madoc scowled and reluctantly obeyed. As he went to the back of the line, Bryce gestured for Ermin to join him. "Do you know why somebody would be spying on us?"

"Sir?"

"Someone was watching us, back there a ways. I think it was one of the baron's men."

"I saw him, too," Ermin revealed, giving Bryce another surprise. "It was Griffydd DeLanyea."

"Why the devil would he be watching us? Why haven't they gone ahead to Caer Coch, or home to prepare for the wedding?"

Ermin gave Bryce a puzzled look. "Because you took his sister."

Bryce felt as if a stone had dropped into his stomach. "That's the tradition. Isn't it?"

"Aye, it is," Ermin admitted.

"Lord Cynvelin said this was all expected. That they were as good as betrothed."

"Did he?" Ermin said hopefully. "Maybe we was all wrong, then."

"What are you talking about?"

"Those men of his, Madoc and the others, the way they talk, Cynvelin hates the Baron DeLanyea, and the baron hates him. They don't seem to think it's much of a love match, if there is to be a marriage."

Dismay and a wild surge of hope battled for supremacy within Bryce. "Many a father and son-in-law have no love for each other," Bryce observed. "Lady Rhiannon seems to find him attractive."

Ermin's face became unusually enigmatic. "Does she?"

Bryce thought of the last time he had seen Lady Rhiannon with Lord Cynvelin, and then how they had appeared at Lord Melevoir's.

Something had changed, that was certain.

What if Cynvelin had lied? What if there was more to this business than mere custom?

Perhaps Lady Rhiannon's behavior at Lord Melevoir's was simply the friendly activity of a spirited young woman. That would explain her conduct toward *him* as something other than a woman's wiles. Even as he thrilled to think that might be so, another realization assailed him.

That would also mean her protests and requests to be returned to her father were not merely feigned for the sake of a custom. She had been in earnest, and he had not helped her.

The things he had said to her! The way he had dismissed her pleas!

No, that could not be. Cynvelin would not do

something so base as to kidnap a woman and force her into marriage. Nor would he have to, given his title, wealth and personal attributes.

Even as Bryce spurred his horse to a gallop through the thickening fog, leaving the others behind him without so much as a second glance, he told himself that couldn't be true.

Because if Rhiannon DeLanyea's abduction had not been a Welsh custom, what had he done?

Rhiannon heard the portcullis slowly rattle upward and, leaving on the bed her braided makeshift rope that she had finished a little while ago, she went to see who had arrived.

As she did, she wet her dry lips with her tongue. She had never been so thirsty in her life, or hungry, either. Although she had been convinced nothing could ever compel her to welcome Cynvelin's company, she was beginning to understand that solitude and lack of food could be powerful inducements.

She couldn't take the chance that her resolve might weaken with her body. Tonight she would escape.

The fog was worsening, yet she knew at once who rode into the courtyard and her hopes soared.

Bryce Frechette had come back!

Maybe she would have no need of the rope. He was an honorable man; once he realized something was amiss, he would help her.

If he realized something was amiss. She, of all people, knew that Cynvelin, with his smooth tongue and charming manner, might convince him otherwise.

Desperately she lifted her hand and waved, trying to catch his attention.

She went to call out but stopped herself. It might not be wise to draw the attention of the guards, whose loyalty was surely to Cynvelin first.

She waved again, frantically, but Bryce didn't look her way. Instead, he marched straight toward the hall.

Disappointed, she leaned against the side of the window. If only he had looked up—what? Would he have known something was wrong?

Even if he did, would he give up his chance for knighthood for the sake of a woman he hardly knew, no matter what emotions seemed to exist between them? She thought he might, but she could not be completely sure.

The only thing she could be absolutely certain of was the need to get away from Annedd Bach and Cynvelin ap Hywell.

Once inside the hall, Bryce stood dripping on the threshold as he surveyed the room. Cynvelin was seated at a table near the hearth, awaiting the noon meal. Those men not on watch lounged about on benches as a few of the servants put up the trestle tables. A welcome fire burned in the hearth.

Nothing seemed unusual, except that Lady Rhiannon was nowhere to be seen. Her absence seemed suddenly sinister, and Bryce's hands balled into fists as he strode toward the Welshman, very aware that he was alone among Cynvelin's guard.

As alone as Rhiannon must have felt when he had not listened to her.

"Ah, Bryce!" Cynvelin called out cheerfully. "You have returned earlier than I expected. Come and eat. Did you find the outlaws, or was that only a rumor?"

Bryce began to doubt his own assumptions. He had always been impetuous and that had led to disastrous consequences. What if he was wrong about Cynvelin? Could any man truly be so blasé if he were guilty of such a heinous crime?

"A rumor, I presume, my lord, and hardly worth the effort," Bryce replied, trying to sound as if nothing at all were wrong.

"Sit," Cynvelin ordered, gesturing at the chair to his right.

Bryce glanced questioningly at the empty seat beside his overlord as he obeyed.

"Lady Rhiannon will not be joining us," the Welshman replied calmly to Bryce's unasked question. "She is unwell."

"I trust it is nothing serious, my lord."

"No, nothing at all. Just her women's time. She should be fine to travel tomorrow."

"Tomorrow?"

"Yes, tomorrow. I did have another purpose for sending you out in such weather," Cynvelin replied with a smile. "How are the roads?"

"Bad."

"I feared it would be so. Nevertheless, I have decided not to stay here any longer. We cannot remain cooped up in Annedd Bach forever."

"Does Lady Rhiannon agree with that decision?" Bryce asked.

Cynvelin gave him a surprised look. "Of course."

Then he looked at the door, and Bryce eagerly followed his gaze, hoping to see Lady Rhiannon.

It was Ermin.

Cynvelin chuckled and Bryce told himself that no one could be so merry if he was indeed holding someone against their will.

"I see you are a better judge of human nature than I am," Cynvelin remarked.

"He brought the horse back, too," Bryce noted.

After Ermin came the equally soaked members of the garrison who had been on the patrol. The servants, including the old crone who had been relegated to the kitchen ever since Bryce's frustrating attempt to get her to comprehend him, began to serve bread, roasted chicken, stew and ale. The men of Cynvelin's guard, in typical fashion, began to commandeer the first offerings.

"I believe the men of the garrison who went with me should be served first, my lord," Bryce said as his men cast hostile glances at Cynvelin's guard, who were warm and dry.

"Really?" Cynvelin replied calmly. "Then order it, since you are the commander here."

Bryce did so, ignoring the angry expressions on Twedwr and the rest.

"I'm very pleased with the rapport you've established with the garrison," Cynvelin said next, reaching for the roasted chicken placed before him. He ripped off the leg. "They seem to get along well with you, even if you are a Norman."

"Perhaps," Bryce answered noncommittally, "but

there may be those who do not welcome me, or any Norman.''

Cynvelin turned toward him with an interested expression. "Such as?''

"My men and I were watched on our return journey today.''

The chicken leg halted its progress to the Welshman's mouth. "Is that so?'' Cynvelin asked before taking a bite. "By whom?''

"I do not know, my lord.''

"More than one peasant, was it? Or do you suspect rebels? This would not be the first time they have troubled this part of the country.''

"Ermin thought it was Griffydd DeLanyea, and I believe he could be right.'' Bryce watched Cynvelin's face carefully and saw him color slightly.

"Ridiculous!'' Cynvelin cried. "Why would they set a watch?''

Bryce shrugged and cut a slice from the loaf in front of him. "That's what I would like to know, my lord. Would they—and why?''

"They wouldn't, and you should not be listening to a milksop like that anyway, a man who has to run to his wife just because she's having a baby. You surprise me, Frechette, you really do. I thought you had more sense.''

Bryce fought to subdue his displeasure with his overlord's remarks and fixed a shrewd gaze on Lord Cynvelin, whom he was now certain was being less than forthcoming. "I was expecting you to say this was part of the custom, too.''

Cynvelin threw back his head and laughed. "No,''

he said when he stopped, giving Bryce a wry grin. "It's another custom that the peasants particularly enjoy. Badger the Normans."

Bryce was not amused. "What is the next part of the custom, my lord? Attack the Normans? Kill the Normans?"

Cynvelin stopped grinning. "Depends on the Normans, that does. I think you will be safe enough, Bryce Frechette," he said, seemingly not the whit concerned that Bryce and his men had been spied upon by Griffydd DeLanyea, or anyone else.

If there was no love between Baron DeLanyea and Cynvelin, that might explain Cynvelin's deceit.

Or it might not.

Bryce abruptly pushed back his chair. "If you will excuse me, my lord, I should see that all is in readiness for your departure in the morning, if you are determined to leave."

"How very efficient of you," Cynvelin noted. "I am. Very determined."

Bryce gave a brisk nod and strode from the hall.

Rhiannon once again tested the strength of her rope. The braided cloth seemed strong enough. She would assume it was and would not have any fear that it would break.

She simply couldn't wait any longer. She had thought that perhaps Bryce might come, but he had not.

Rising from the stool, she flexed her fingers, which were stiff from braiding the linen strips. She ignored the empty feeling in her stomach and her exhaustion.

She couldn't take the chance that the fog might dissipate, either. Fog would make it more difficult to find the road, but it would also make it harder for someone to see her.

Rhiannon knew what she had to do. She had to climb out of the keep, then cautiously find a secluded place on the wall walk from whence she could climb to the ground outside the walls. It would be dangerous, but she had no choice.

Then she would make her way, skirting the road until she found someone of whom she could ask directions to the monastery of St. David. She hoped to find her father there, but if he was not, surely the holy brothers would give her sanctuary, and then she could think of a way to send word of her escape home.

She went to the window.

She had taken the empty basin from the table and set it on the sill, so that part of it was out the window. Now the basin was half-full of rainwater, and she gratefully took a drink, sipping it slowly to make the most of it.

Outside, she couldn't see the hall, or even light from the windows. It was as if the keep had been spirited away to some distant, isolated island.

She again glanced at the distance from the window to the ground and swallowed hard. It was not going to be easy.

Indeed, she thought as she regarded the window, she wouldn't be able to wear her gown. Not only was she not certain that she could fit through the narrow window with such a large skirt, the rain would make it dangerously heavy. She would have to wear only her shift but, aware of the chilly damp, she would wait until she was ready to go before she took off her warm gown.

She didn't even know what hour it was, and could only hope that all the men except the few necessary guards would stay inside.

She picked up her makeshift rope and looked around for the best place to attach it inside the room. The biggest piece of furniture was the bed; unfortunately, that formed the major part of her barricade against the door. If she moved it away and Cynvelin returned...

She would hope to be gone.

Pressing her lips together, she began to move aside the stool, table and chest. She grabbed the bed and began to drag it toward the window.

"My lady?"

She stopped, holding her breath.

"My lady? I must speak with you. Please! I fear I have done you a terrible disservice."

It wasn't Cynvelin. Her heart raced as she recognized Bryce's voice. "Please let me in."

"It's locked."

She heard what sounded like scratching at the lock. In another moment, the door began to open.

Bryce stood on the threshold, looking at her, a thin dagger in his hands. He sheathed his weapon, then came into the room and closed the door behind him.

She moved back cautiously, watching him. She had been so wrong about one man; perhaps she should not trust Bryce as completely as her heart urged her to do.

"Are you betrothed to Lord Cynvelin?" he demanded.

"No!"

"Do you want to be betrothed to him?"

"No!"

He muttered an oath. "Then you did not expect to meet him on the road? You were not prepared to go with him?"

"Certainly not," she replied, more hopeful than ever.

"That lying blackguard!" He held out his hands in a gesture of supplication, as Cynvelin had done, and yet so very different. "Forgive me, my lady, for having wronged you," he said. "If I had known the truth, I would never have had anything to do with your abduction."

"Why did you?" she asked, still not absolutely sure she could trust him.

"Cynvelin told me the kidnapping was only a custom, and all arranged between you. That you were already as good as betrothed. What do I know of Welsh customs? I believed him."

He sounded so desperate, so honest, and yet...

"You took me from my father," she said cautiously.

"To my shame, lady," he replied fervently. "If I had known this was done against your will, I would have refused to help, knighthood or no. Whatever else you think of me, you must believe that."

"As you believed Cynvelin?"

"Yes...no! Anyone watching the two of you at Lord Melevoir's feast might think you were more than mere acquaintances."

She flushed at that, knowing that he spoke the truth. "I would never have been in this trouble if I had behaved with more prudence there," she acknowledged bitterly. "Still, the fact that my father and brothers were so angry should have told you this was no game."

"I didn't understand what was being said, and Cynvelin told me your father didn't like him."

"He hates him, and so do I."

"And so do I, for what he has done. Has he...has he hurt you?"

She shook her head. "Not yet."

"I will lay down my life to get you away from here, my lady, if you will allow me that honor," Bryce declared.

Simple words, sincerely spoken. Rhiannon gazed into his eyes, very aware that they were alone together. That she had been wrong about him. That he was an honorable man.

That he cared about her and she could trust him with her life.

"I hoped you would help me, once you learned the truth," she confessed.

His eyes widened. "You did?"

"Yes," she admitted. "The trouble was, I didn't see how I could convince you after I took so long to discover the truth about Cynvelin myself. I thought I would have to get away without anyone's aid."

"How?"

She pointed to the braided fabric on the bed. "I was going to go out the window and climb down."

"You could have fallen to your death!"

"Better that than…"

He nodded brusquely. "I should have realized—"

"You have."

He held out his hand. "Come, my lady."

She hesitated a moment. "What will you do afterward?"

"It doesn't matter. But I will not serve Cynvelin ap Hywell a moment after I have delivered you safe to your father."

An unwelcome thought intruded into her mind. "He will not be happy to see you, Bryce. He will give you no reward. He might even kill you for what you have done. Perhaps you would do better to help me get out of Annedd Bach, then flee for your life."

Bryce slowly shook his head. "I will not be happy until I know you are back with your family."

"Happy it will make you, to see me safe?" she asked softly.

"Content, then." He regarded her steadily. "If your father does take me prisoner, would you not plead my case for me, my lady?"

His low, solemn question touched her deeply. "Yes," she whispered.

"I ask no more than that for my reward. Come, my lady," he whispered. "We have lost too much time as it is."

She nodded, then put her hand in his and let him lead her forth.

To encounter Cynvelin and Madoc, as well as other men of Cynvelin's guard, waiting on the stairs.

Chapter Twelve

A few of the men held torches, and the light flickered on Cynvelin's face, accentuating every angle, plane and shadow.

"Isn't this an unexpected pleasure," Cynvelin remarked coldly. "Well, perhaps not completely unexpected."

Bryce realized they were outnumbered at least ten to one.

He didn't care. He had participated in Lady Rhiannon's abduction, even if he had not understood the true nature of what he was doing, and he would die to right his wrong, if need be.

"I am taking this lady away from here, as she desires," he replied sternly.

"Is that all she desires of you, Frechette?" the Welshman snarled. He slowly drew out his sword. "Or is this one of many rendezvous you have shared? I believe I was wrong to put you in a position of trust, after all."

"Who are you to speak of trust?" Bryce demanded scornfully, his hand on the hilt of his sword.

"You are a liar, a dishonorable villain. And you have made me a party to your despicable plans."

"Harsh words from a dispossessed earl who has become nothing more than a hired sword."

Bryce pulled out his blade. "Let us pass!"

Rhiannon held him back. She would not have his death on her hands. "If there is any honor in you at all," she urged Cynvelin, "you will let us leave this place unhindered."

"So that you may run to your father?" He shook his head. "Oh, no, my lady. That I cannot permit."

Bryce took a step forward. Rhiannon hurried to stand in front of him at the edge of the top step. "Why must you persist?" she pleaded. "I will never marry you."

Cynvelin smiled that same diabolical smile, and it nauseated her. "Yes, you will, Rhiannon. I wanted you to marry me of your own volition to make my triumph all the sweeter, but if that cannot be, no matter. Bryce, if what I am going to do distresses you so, you may go."

"I will not leave without the lady. She doesn't want you."

"What she wants is unimportant. *I* want *her.*"

"So you would take her honor, too, as you have stolen mine?" Bryce charged.

"What honor of yours have I stolen? You agreed to come here. You agreed to take her."

"I didn't know what you were doing."

"I would go while I could, Bryce, if I were in your boots. Of course, it will not be easy for you. Even if there are those who might believe your claim that you acted in ignorance, no nobleman would have such a suspicious fellow in his hall, or his garrison. You will have nothing. You will *be* nothing. You might have to take up begging in the streets, or go back to Europe. That would be better than being dead, I suppose.''

Bryce could well believe that it would unfold as Cynvelin said, as he could well believe that Cynvelin would do whatever evil thing he vowed.

"Oh, poor child," Cynvelin mocked. "Poor, foolish boy." His expression hardened. "A fool you have always been, Frechette. An arrogant, well-trained warrior of a fool, but a gullible fool all the same." He moved back among his men. "Bring them to the hall."

Bryce shoved past Rhiannon. "You wretch!"

Cynvelin ducked behind Twedwr, so Bryce's blow struck Twedwr in the arm instead. The soldier howled in pain as he dropped his sword and clutched a huge gash.

Rhiannon grabbed Twedwr's fallen sword, ready to fight.

The others fell back before Bryce and Rhiannon, until Madoc blocked the way, his large, solid body filling the stairway. Bryce raised his sword to strike and brought it down, but Madoc parried the blow, turning the blade aside and pinning it against the wall. Encouraged by Madoc's action, the guard swarmed forward.

Rhiannon tried to stab at Madoc. He saw her, guessed what she was about to do and twisted away. Although her attack freed Bryce's blade, the mo-

mentum of her action made her stumble forward.
Cynvelin lunged and stopped her from falling. Then
he grabbed her wrist with a grip so tight she had to
drop the weapon.

"Frechette!" he shouted.

Bryce froze, motionless as a deer hearing the first
pounding of the beaters, while Rhiannon tried to free
herself from the Welshman's grasp.

Cynvelin laughed cruelly, all vestige of civility
gone, "Come with me, my lady, and don't try to be
difficult, or by God, you will rue it."

"Don't let them hurt him!" she cried, planting her
feet as firmly as she could and desperately looking
back over her shoulder.

Cynvelin dragged her down the steps. The rest of
his men surrounded Bryce.

"Hear that, men?" Cynvelin shouted sarcastically.
"Be gentle with him, for the lady's sake. And mine,
for I have another task for him before he dies."

"You can't kill him!" Rhiannon declared, struggling to get away.

"Oh, can I not?" Cynvelin muttered as he tugged
her down the stairs.

He pulled Rhiannon out of the keep and across the
courtyard, through the dank mist and regardless of
the puddles on the ground, then shoved her through
the entrance to the hall.

The servants and men of the garrison who were
there stared, wide-eyed and openmouthed.

"Get out!" Cynvelin snarled. "Everybody out!"

They obeyed slowly and with obvious reluctance
as Rhiannon stood next to the hearth, panting heavily

and thinking of Bryce, who had been going to help her and who was now in the hands of Cynvelin's men.

"Get out!" Cynvelin shouted again, waving his sword threateningly.

The servants quickened their pace.

Rhiannon turned, ready to run toward the kitchen corridor.

"Oh no, you don't!" Cynvelin cried, taking her again by the arm. "You cannot get away from me, Rhiannon. Not now and not ever!"

He pulled her close and she struggled to escape his embrace. "Fight me all you want, here or in our bed. I don't care. I like a woman who fights me. I like a girl who fights me, like that shepherd's daughter. What was her name? Ah yes, Cathwg."

Shocked at the mention of that name, Rhiannon stopped moving.

Cynvelin's smile was mocking and cruel. "You look confused, my dear. Did your bastard father not tell about the shepherd girl who dared to accuse me of rape?"

Rhiannon mutely shook her head. She remembered Cathwg, and that when she had returned from visiting friends one summer, Cathwg and her family had disappeared, but she knew nothing of any accusation. Her father had tried to find them, with no success.

"If he had told you, you might know that I am not to be trifled with. Still, even he does not know what I did to her and her family."

"You killed them," Rhiannon whispered, certain of it.

"Not me," he chided, chucking her hard under her chin. "Madoc and some others. I couldn't take the chance that your father, who always hated me for no good reason, would presume to take me to trial if they lived. Me—Cynvelin ap Hywell! Accused on the word of a peasant."

He cocked his head, and she heard the sounds of many feet on the stones of the courtyard. "The others are coming, my love. Poor Bryce. He wanted so much to be a knight. Not enough, I fear," he said disdainfully. "He would risk it all for a woman."

"He is a more chivalrous knight than you could ever be!" She shoved hard at Cynvelin's chest and, surprisingly, he let her loose.

She gasped as Madoc and Twedwr dragged Bryce into the hall, his face cut and bleeding, his lip split and one eyelid already bruised and swelling.

They let go and he fell to his knees. As he struggled to his feet, Rhiannon ran to him, wrapping her arms around him and helping him to stand erect.

"Hold her," Cynvelin ordered, looking at Madoc.

"There is no need," Rhiannon replied with as much dignity as she could muster. "I will not leave if he stays. You have to let us both go."

"You don't understand, do you?" Cynvelin demanded incredulously. "I'm never letting you go. You are going to be my wife."

"Set her free!" Bryce ordered Cynvelin, glaring at the Welshman with the eye that wasn't swollen shut.

"Who do you think you are to order me?" Cynvelin asked scornfully. "The Earl of Westborough?

I think not. Indeed, I think perhaps I should kill you for interfering."

"Cynvelin," Rhiannon said, the necessity of saving Bryce making her bold, "*you* are a fool if you think you can keep me forever, or that killing Bryce Frechette would be wise. My father will come for me, and you seem to be forgetting that Bryce is the brother-in-law of Baron DeGuerre."

"Bryce Frechette is the man who kidnapped Rhiannon DeLanyea, and your father is not coming for you. If he tries to take you back, he knows I will kill you."

"What?" she breathed. "Then that is why—"

"He has not come? Of course." He advanced on her, smiling once more. "Fortunately for you, I would rather marry you than kill you. Then I can take my pleasure of you again and again, until you learn to like it." He ran his hand over her breasts. "You will learn to like it, Rhiannon."

She glared at him with eyes full of hate and anger, all her fear gone. "Then you had best learn to sleep lightly, my lord, lest your wife slay you in the night."

He stepped away from her as if she already had a dagger in her hands.

She saw the fear and uncertainty in his eyes, and his attempt to hide it.

"Besides, Rhiannon," he said, his tone lacking some of his arrogant confidence, "think of your dear family. Even your dolt of a father would rather see you married than dead, or he would already have tried to rescue you, don't you think?"

"God's blood, I will kill you!" Bryce snarled, lunging for Cynvelin, only to be thrown to the ground by his captors and held there, their knees pressing on his back.

Cynvelin laughed. "You could try, but Madoc or one of the others would slay you in an instant. And Rhiannon would still be mine."

"You dishonorable coward!" Rhiannon said through clenched teeth.

Cynvelin raised his hand and with a force that made tears start in her eyes, slapped her full across the face.

Glaring at Cynvelin like a caged wolf, Bryce struggled even more to get free. "You despicable snake," he hissed, adding a scornful epithet. "I curse the day I ran afoul of you!"

"Fine language in front of a lady is that," Cynvelin remarked sardonically. "As for your strong words, my bride," he said, facing her, his eyes full of anger, "they are ones that I would not repeat, if I were you.

"And if you think to accuse me of wrongdoing, think again. I have friends enough that they will gladly take my word against yours. And know, my dear Rhiannon, if you dare to speak against me, I will tell the king that your father is plotting rebellion in that Welsh stronghold of his."

"That's a lie!"

"So you say. So the Baron DeLanyea will say. Yet it would plant the seeds of doubt in the king's mind. Every Norman knows the Welsh plot rebellion with every breath. Likely your father and brothers would find it difficult to win support at court after that, even if men do not quite believe them capable of treason.''

"Do *you* plot rebellion?" Rhiannon demanded. "Is that why you want my father's influence?"

Cynvelin barked another laugh. "No! What do I care if Wales is free or not? I want his influence at court because I deserve it. I've deserved it for years, but everybody knew the great, the marvelous Baron DeLanyea had sent me from his household. No reason given, so they were free to speculate. And they did, whispering behind my back, smirking. Even my father—" He paused, then straightened his shoulders. "But the baron is about to repay me for all of that. With you, my dear."

"No!" Bryce shouted, bucking and twisting like a stallion being broken to the saddle.

"Take him to the dungeon," Cynvelin ordered. He smiled coldly at Bryce. "You did not know it existed, did you, in the lower level of the keep? Yet you think yourself worthy of a knighthood, you who doesn't even bother to learn all the secrets in a castle. Well, no matter now. Nor will you be alone. Ula will keep you company." He gasped, his eyes dancing merrily as he covered his mouth. "Oh, but it's too bad she won't be able to warm you. She's dead."

Rhiannon moaned with dismay, and Bryce stared in shock.

"She fought me rather too hard, Rhiannon. Let that be a lesson to you. Now take that fool out of my sight."

"Bryce!" Rhiannon reached out for him.

Madoc and Twedwr shoved her away and she fell to the ground while they started to drag Bryce out.

"Forgive me, my lady!" he called out, staring back at her with anguished eyes.

"Forgive *me!*" she cried.

"How very touching," Cynvelin said as he took hold of Rhiannon's hand and pulled her to her feet. "But it is most inappropriate for the betrothed of Cynvelin ap Hywell to be on her knees to anyone except me."

She twisted out of his grasp and glared at him defiantly. "I will never be your wife! I would rather die!"

"How many times must I tell you? I do not want you dead," Cynvelin replied, fighting to maintain what was left of his self-control. "Do you want to save his life, at least for a little while?"

He saw understanding dawn in her luminous eyes. "Do you?"

She slowly nodded her head. "Yes."

"What are you willing to do?"

She continued to regard him with a determined, unwavering gaze, full of hate and defiant pride even yet. "Whatever I must."

"Then come." He held out his hand.

She hesitated for a moment, then placed hers within his grasp.

A feeling of triumph joined that of his anger. He had won. She would be his, and the baron would suffer, now and forever.

He marveled that she did not weep as he led her across the courtyard toward the keep and up the stairs to the bedchamber, not even when he pulled her into the room. Instead, she faced him with dignity and composure, like a nobleman facing the headman's ax.

"God's blood," he muttered, wanting her even more though he knew that she was in earnest when she said she would prefer death to marriage to him.

He wanted her alive so that the baron's torment would be continuous, like a sore that could never heal.

He wanted her in his bed, this woman of passion and fervor. It would have been better if she had believed herself in love with him, but he would take her anyway.

But not now, although never had he craved her so much. Not when he was still struggling to contain his rage. Otherwise, when she fought him, as she undoubtedly would because a woman of such spirit would never submit without a battle, no matter how much hung in the balance, he would surely kill her.

He had done that before. Cathwg had fought him; Ula had fought him. There had been others, too, whose names he had forgotten. He recognized the surging anger that would make him do it again.

He could not kill Rhiannon, no matter how tempting it was to take her by her fine white throat and slowly watch her fight for breath, staring at him with those green eyes, knowing that he had absolute mastery over her at last. That was not part of his glorious vengeance.

So he managed to subdue both the anticipation and the anger. "How did he open the lock?"

She stared at him, her brows knitting in puzzlement as she crossed her arms over her chest.

"How did Frechette open that lock?"

"I don't know."

Cynvelin strode to the door and examined it. "It's not broken. Good." He caught sight of something on the floor, a long line of fabric. "What the devil is this?"

She didn't reply as he walked over and picked up her makeshift rope as gingerly as if it were alive. "Clever, my lady, clever," he muttered, glancing up at her. "We cannot have you climbing down walls. What if you were to fall? My heart would break."

"You have no heart."

"Perhaps not. Perhaps my father beat it out of me." He gathered up the rope and she watched him warily as he put it on top of the chest, his back to her. "I shall have to take these with me," he remarked as she sidled toward the door.

"Stop!" he commanded, whirling around suddenly. "I am not a simpleton, my lady. I want you to consider that. I would have you consider many things, including how you could best help your doting friend."

With that, he lifted the chest and staggered out the door. He set down the chest, then pulled the door shut. The key turned in the heavy iron lock.

He had left her. He had not...

Why? Was he going to kill Bryce now? If she had gone to him more willingly, if she had begged and pleaded and given herself to him without a whimper of protest, could she have delayed Bryce's death at his hands?

Bryce was going to die for trying to help her. If she had not encouraged Cynvelin, however unwittingly, this trouble might have been averted and Bryce would be safe.

Wrapping her arms about her body, she sank to the floor, rocking back and forth.

"Oh, God forgive me!" she cried in anguish, choking sobs racking her body. "God save him!"

What could she do? How could she help Bryce?

She could stop crying. She would not allow herself to give in to despair. She had not known the extent of evil lurking in Cynvelin ap Hywell. Neither had Bryce.

This was not her fault, any more than the abduction was his.

Somehow they would triumph over Cynvelin and his wicked schemes.

She got to her feet and her gaze came to rest on the stool. Quickly she grabbed hold of the leg and smashed the stool onto the stone floor. It broke apart and the leg splintered, the end a point.

Rhiannon began to rub the sharp end over the rough floor, twisting and turning as she shaped it into a fine and lethal point.

She would make a weapon and she would climb down the wall, even though Cynvelin had taken her rope. If Dylan could do it, so could she. Then she would find Bryce and help him get free, even if she had to kill.

Her rational mind told her that her plan was doomed to fail.

But she paid it no heed, because she was listening to her heart.

Bryce crashed into the wall as the men threw him into the dank, dark cell in the lower reaches of the keep. His forehead struck the slimy wall before he slumped to the floor.

Madoc growled something in Welsh that set the others laughing cruelly before they went out, the door banging shut behind them. The key turned in the lock as he shook his head to try to clear it.

Despair enveloped him like the dark. Cynvelin was right. He *was* a fool, a blind, stupid fool who should have seen the signs that all was not as Cynvelin claimed: Rhiannon's persistent struggles and insistence upon being taken back to her father, her revulsion at the idea that Cynvelin was her lover, the way she looked at *him,* and especially the passion in her kiss.

If only he had not been so selfish and so anxious to make up for his past mistakes by earning a knighthood that he had not taken the time to learn more of the man to whom he would be beholden! If only he had listened to her as his heart bade him, and not told himself to pay no heed to her impassioned words. If only he had not been so swift to believe the lies of a seemingly benevolent man.

Instead, all his previous failings paled before what he had done to Rhiannon.

Cynvelin was right about the dungeon, too. He

should have had Ermin go through the castle with him. Then he might have known about the small wooden door beneath the stairs that led to this lower level.

Again despair threatened to engulf him, but he fought it off. As long as Rhiannon was in danger, he would not give up. He would try to find a way to help her.

Madoc and his men had taken his weapons, including his dagger. He had learned many things in his travels, and how to pick a lock was one of them. That wouldn't have made a difference here, though, because there was no opening in the door.

Perhaps there was something in the cell he could use as a weapon when they came for him. Even a bucket would be something.

It was too dark to see, so he began to slowly make his way around the cell holding onto the wall.

His foot touched a large object. It didn't move, nor was it hard.

He guessed what it was and knelt down, gently feeling the shape.

Yes, it was Ula's body. Another woman he should have protected, and had not. Like his sister. Like Rhiannon.

Then Bryce thought of Rhiannon, alone and in that man's hands, and a fresh wave of anger, hatred and determination filled him.

Somehow he would get free, and he would rescue Rhiannon.

And then he would kill Cynvelin ap Hywell.

Chapter Thirteen

There was nothing in the cell except Ula's body. Bryce kept a lonely vigil beside it, trying to think of some way to escape. If only Madoc and one of the others came to take him out, he thought he stood a chance to overcome them—but then how to help Rhiannon? Where was she? Cynvelin might even have started for Caer Coch and taken her with him.

With these and the thoughts of his own culpability to torment him, it seemed a long time before he heard voices and footsteps. The cell door opened and Bryce squinted at the sudden influx of light, even though the torchlight wasn't bright.

Madoc held the torch. Several other men of Cynvelin's guard waited behind him, including the two brawniest. The Welshman grunted and gestured with his head to indicate that Bryce was to come with them.

He had no choice, especially when the two big men grabbed his arms. As they led him out into the courtyard in the feeble light of the morning, he thought of trying to overpower them, wondering if the men of the garrison could perhaps be called to his aid, but he just as quickly dismissed the notion. For one thing, he couldn't be completely certain of their loyalty, or that they would help. Worse, not a one of his men was on guard at the gate, or standing sentry on the wall walk. It was not inconceivable that if Cynvelin had reason to doubt their loyalty to him, he would have sent them away.

Then he realized that the presence of so many of Cynvelin's men might be a good sign, indicating that Cynvelin and Rhiannon were still in Annedd Bach.

The guards took him into the hall. The men of the garrison, silent and watchful, were there, off to the side, arranged in rows. Cynvelin sat by the hearth, the rest of his men gathered around him.

Rhiannon wasn't there, and a chill of dread ran through Bryce's body.

Cynvelin, as well dressed as always and with a calm expression, watched dispassionately while Bryce was hauled before him.

But not so calm, Bryce thought, for Cynvelin played nervously with the leather gloves he held, twisting and turning them in his hands.

"Where is she?" Bryce demanded. "What have you done with her?"

"I see a night of solitary contemplation has not mellowed you," the Welsh nobleman said with something between a grin and smirk. "She is quite well, all things considered."

"What 'things'?"

Suddenly Cynvelin stood and hit Bryce across the

face with his gloves, on the same side as his swollen eye.

It hurt like the devil, but Bryce didn't move. He wouldn't move or do anything until he knew about Rhiannon. Angry mutters arose from the garrison, and their reaction encouraged him. If they were against Cynvelin, there was more cause for hope.

"I have heard it said that simpletons and madmen don't feel pain the way gentlefolk do, and I see that is quite correct," Cynvelin said, returning to his seat.

"Where is Lady Rhiannon?"

Cynvelin smiled very, very slowly. "In the bedchamber. Just think, Frechette, last night while you were with Ula—or at least her body—right above you, I was…" He let his words trail off suggestively.

Rage filled him, but Bryce knew he could not let his emotions overtake him. That had been the way of his past, and that was disaster. He had to think, to be ready to take advantage of any opportunity. "I hope for your sake you have not hurt her."

"Hurt? Oh no, not yet. And that is what you must tell her father."

"What?"

"Don't look so shocked, my friend," Cynvelin replied, the gloves still twisting and turning in his hands. "It is a simple task, really. You are to go to the monastery of St. David and fetch a priest, for I will not wait anymore. I will marry Rhiannon today. Of course, I would not be surprised if you should find the baron there. No doubt it was one of his men spying on you, as Ermin guessed."

The steward shifted uncomfortably when he heard

his name, although Bryce doubted he understood all that Cynvelin was saying.

"I doubt it was the one-eyed bastard himself. That grim-faced son of his, more likely. Whoever it was, it doesn't matter. They are probably there, and just as probably watching everyone who goes in or out of Annedd Bach. So he may wish to speak with you. If that is so, naturally you should tell them what I have said." He smiled again. "Further, tell them I regret I cannot invite them to celebrate with me, but I have no food for a feast. If they try to prevent you, say to the baron it has already been *caru yn y gwely.*"

"What does that mean?"

"He will know, and that is enough."

Bryce thought he knew, too. *Oh, Rhiannon!* he wanted to wail, imagining her terror and the outraged honor of a proud woman.

But at least she lived, and that was what mattered most. He would think only of that.

"What if they kill me?" Bryce asked grimly.

"They had better not, or more than I will suffer, as they know. As you know."

Bryce did know, and at the thought of Rhiannon's life in this man's hands, he wanted to do more than wail. He wanted to choke the life out of Cynvelin ap Hywell.

Yet if ever in his life he needed to subdue his emotions, this was the time. Acting on his impulses would only get them both killed.

Cynvelin's expression hardened. "Tell them whatever you like, as long as you return with a priest to bless the marriage between Lady Rhiannon and myself before the sun sets.''

''I am surprised you would wish a priest,'' Bryce said disdainfully.

Cynvelin laughed, a joyless sound that seemed less than human. ''You *are* a fool, Frechette! I don't care if the union is blessed or not. I want the DeLanyeas to know what you have to tell them.''

He walked up and gently tapped Bryce's face with his glove as he continued to speak, enraging Bryce even more, making it more difficult for him to control his anger with every passing moment. ''They've been watching us ever since we took her, oaf, but don't dare to raise a finger. The great baron is afraid—of me!''

''Only the worst villain strikes at a man through his children.''

Cynvelin's glove struck Bryce hard in the face again, and his eyes seemed to grow even more demonic. ''You are a bold fellow. I can admire that. Indeed, if you do as I order you, I may even reconsider and give you the knighthood you crave.''

''You must be mad,'' Bryce said incredulously. ''Do you think I still want a knighthood if your marriage to Lady Rhiannon is to be the price?''

''Not mad, Frechette. Determined. Determined to have the lady for my wife, and determined that her father know it. Surely a man like you can appreciate determination, and surely a man as determined as you would accept the reward of a knighthood. You may as well, for I will have the lady anyway, Frechette. Take what gain you can.''

"You use me as your agent for an evil scheme, you lock me in a dungeon, you propose that I use a lady to purchase a title and you think I will agree?" he demanded. "You *are* mad!"

"If you do not want the knighthood, so be it. Now you had better get on your way."

Bryce regarded him steadily. "Why, after all that has passed between us, would you send me on such an errand?"

"Who better?" Cynvelin said, making that damnable, cruel and mocking smile. "You will come back, for the lady's sake if nothing else, to see her again and know that she is unharmed.

"Besides, you are the finest fighter I know. If anyone tries to stop you, such as the baron or his sons, I'm sure you will manage to return."

"If I do not return, it may not be my fault. Would you harm her anyway?"

Cynvelin raised one dark eyebrow scornfully. "Just make sure you do. If you betray me, or if you do not return before sunset, I am liable to lose my patience, and that would be the worse for my beautiful Rhiannon. Do you understand me, Bryce?"

"Yes," he answered grimly. "Am I to go alone?"

"Madoc and some men will go with you."

Bryce heard the sudden intake of Madoc's breath and glanced at the man's frightened face.

Cynvelin also saw the Welshman's reaction and spoke harshly to his underling in their language. Madoc stammered an answer, not looking at his lord.

Suddenly Ermin stepped forward. "We will go," he said in French. "We are for Frechette." He ran a contemptuous gaze over Madoc and the men of the guard. "We are not afraid."

Despite his anger and his fear for Rhiannon's safety, Bryce was grateful and proud of their loyalty.

"You bloody well should be afraid of that one-eyed bastard," Cynvelin muttered as he returned to his seat. "But very well. Go with him."

"Am I to get a sword?" Bryce asked.

"As I've said, I'm not mad. No."

Bryce's hands balled into fists, but again he subdued his rage. His own feelings were not important anymore. All that mattered was saving Rhiannon.

"Just remember what I said, Frechette. Tell the baron I am marrying his daughter today, and bring the priest. If you fail me, she will be the one who suffers. Do you understand?"

"Yes, I do."

Cynvelin scowled. "Remember, if you do this well, you may yet receive a knighthood."

Bryce gave him a scornful smile. "I wouldn't take that from you now for all the gold in Christendom," he said.

He looked at Ermin. "Come, my friend." Together they turned and walked out of the hall, followed by the whole garrison of Annedd Bach.

Rhiannon heard the men in the courtyard. Clutching her sharpened stake, she went to the window, wondering about the noise, and looked out to see a sight that both shocked and thrilled her.

Bryce was mounted at the head of the garrison, obviously preparing to ride out.

"He lives!" she whispered, offering up a silent, fervent prayer of thankfulness.

But where was he going?

Did it matter? He was alive and getting away.

He would come back for her. In her heart, she knew it, with a complete assurance that added to her relief.

As the gate swung open, Bryce suddenly turned in his saddle and looked up at her window. She didn't know whether Cynvelin was somewhere watching, nor did she care.

"God go with you!" she called out, and waved her hand.

His face was grim as he nodded, and then he lifted his hand, the gesture a bond between them.

The garrison likewise turned to look at her, pity on their faces.

Then Bryce turned away, punched his horse into a gallop and led them out the gate, while Rhiannon pressed her tear-dampened cheek against the cold, unyielding stones.

"Where is the monastery?" Bryce shouted at Ermin as they galloped along the road leading away from Annedd Bach.

"Along this road, then left at the first fork," the Welshman panted in response.

Bryce nodded and urged his horse onward the way Ermin had indicated. He had to get to the monastery, and he had to get there soon. If the mounts of Ermin and the others could not keep up with his stallion, so be it. He would not wait for them.

Nevertheless, he prized their loyalty and would have to find some way to show his gratitude when this was over.

After he had saved Rhiannon.

For Bryce now had a plan, one that depended upon the baron's cooperation, if he could make the man listen to him and if Rhiannon's father would trust him.

Bryce rounded a corner in the road and saw the fork. At nearly the same time, he saw a group of men riding down the other road that met the one he was on. Three men rode abreast at the head of the well-armed troop.

Bryce recognized the man in the middle. He had been one of the men in the baron's party. As for the others, he had no idea who they were, nor did he care. All he cared about was saving Rhiannon.

"Frechette!" the man in the center shouted, drawing his sword and digging in his heels so that his horse leapt forward. The other men also pulled out their weapons.

"Listen to me!" Bryce cried. He reined his horse to a halt. "Listen!"

The man didn't. Instead he continued to charge, although Bryce had no sword or other weapon to defend himself.

Bryce slipped off his horse, putting the animal between him and his attacker.

"Come away, you coward!" the man roared. "Where is she, you lout? If anybody's touched a hair on her head, by God, I'll kill them!"

"Dylan!" one of the other leaders called out

sternly. He was tall, dark haired, well muscled, of middle years, with hawklike features. "Put up your sword. Can you not see he has no weapon?"

"He is the one who was with Cynvelin, Fitzroy. He's the one who took Rhiannon," Dylan snarled, not taking his eyes off Bryce.

"If killing him you are, he won't be able to tell us anything," the third man said in a reasonable tone, his voice having a Welsh lilt to it. He was younger than the hawklike fellow, but older than Dylan. Like the other man, he looked to be a seasoned warrior.

Bryce refused to be intimidated. "Where is the Baron DeLanyea?" he demanded. "Is he at the monastery of St. David?"

"Why should I tell you?" Dylan demanded.

The third man rode closer. "Can you not see he has something to tell?" he asked. "I am Sir Hu Morgan, a friend of the baron's. Why do you seek the baron?"

"I have news regarding his daughter's welfare."

Morgan glanced at the man Dylan had called Fitzroy, then Dylan. "Is she well?"

"She lives," Bryce replied. "But we have no time to lose. For God's sake, and hers, take me to the baron!"

Suddenly Ermin and the others came around the corner. "It's a trap!" Dylan cried.

"No, no!" Bryce responded fervently as his men stopped and stared. "Please, listen to me!"

"Why should we?"

"Because Rhiannon is in serious danger."

"We know that!"

"Listen to me," Bryce urged. "I must see the baron. You have to help me get her out of Annedd Bach today. We haven't a moment to lose!"

Dylan finally lowered his sword. "Why would you want to help Rhiannon? Are you not in Cynvelin's pay?"

"I agreed to be in his company, to my shame, but no longer. It is to my disgrace that I took part in the abduction of Lady Rhiannon, and I am willing to do whatever I can to help restore her to you. I have a plan to do that, if you will take me to the baron and let me put it to him."

"I don't believe it," Dylan said firmly. "This is a lie, or a trick, or a trap or all three! I will not trust you, for I know all about you, Frechette.

"You are a lazy, arrogant rogue who argued with his father and finally left home in a fit of temper, not even coming back when your father lay dying." He glared at the others. "I cannot believe you would all be so willing to believe whatever he chooses to tell you!"

"What would you have us do?" Morgan queried. "Kill him first and questions later?"

Bryce marched around his horse toward the young warrior and stared into the Welshman's eyes. "I don't give a tinker's damn if you believe me or not. I come to plead my case to the baron, not to you, and I demand that you take me to him. My men can wait here, if that will content you."

Dylan glared at him and looked about to make a heated retort as Fitzroy rode forward. "Dylan," he said in a tone that would make any man hesitate, "we will take him to your foster father."

"But—"

Morgan shook his head. "We should be letting Emryss hear what he has to say, and if this Norman is willing to leave his men here, with ours to watch them, I see no reason to fear tricks or schemes."

"Please!" Bryce pleaded, willing to forget his pride in his need to speak to the baron. "Bind me if you must, but we cannot waste any more time!"

"Oh, I'll bind you all right, you cur," Dylan muttered.

He grabbed hold of the leather lacing at the neck of Bryce's leather tunic and jerked it out of its holes.

Bryce meekly turned around and thrust back his hands. "Ermin," he said, his tone proud because he was getting what he wanted, "stay here with these others. I'll be back as soon as I can."

"Aye, sir, whatever you ask of us, that we will do."

Never in all his life had Bryce seen such an imposing figure as that of Baron DeLanyea seated in the great room of the monastery, enthroned on a large oak chair. With his shoulder-length, iron gray hair, piercing gaze and well-built, muscular frame, he was like an ancient warrior king waiting to pass judgment. There was only the slightest hint in the dark circle beneath the man's remaining eye and the tension in his shoulders that he was as worried as any father might be if his daughter had been kidnapped.

He simply hid his fear better than any man Bryce had ever met.

Bryce felt like a condemned criminal, his hands bound behind his back. Nevertheless, he tried to put any thoughts except those concerning Rhiannon's rescue from his mind. He had to think clearly and speak concisely if he was to compel the baron to listen and believe.

"Baron DeLanyea—" he began.

"Where is Rhiannon?"

"In Annedd Bach. I saw her with my own eyes before we rode out."

"Is she well?"

Bryce could not meet the baron's steadfast gaze. "She lives, my lord."

"Why do you come here?" the older man demanded after a moment's hesitation, again with only the merest suggestion that Bryce's words had touched him. "How can you dare to show your face to me?"

Bryce straightened his shoulders and lifted his chin, determined to make this man trust him. "I want you to help me save your daughter."

"You want me to help you save my daughter?" the baron repeated skeptically. "Are you telling me you would be her savior?"

"Yes, if you will let me."

The baron rubbed the scar beneath his eye patch, his expression belligerent. "You it was took her. Why should you help her now?"

"Because I didn't know then what I did."

Dylan emitted a scoffing laugh, until the swift

glance of the baron fell upon him. Then he merely scowled.

"Am I to understand that when you carried her off, you were in some kind of trance?" the baron asked coldly.

Bryce shook his head. "No. But Cynvelin told me it was only a custom, and that she was expecting it."

The other men exchanged cynical glances and Bryce felt the sweat trickling down his back. "You have to believe me!"

"What kind of dolts do you take us for?" Dylan demanded hotly, springing forward and raising his hand to strike.

The baron, with a swiftness Bryce could scarcely believe for one of his years, deftly intercepted the younger man and blocked the blow. "Stop!" he commanded.

Dylan grudgingly obeyed.

"My lord," Bryce pleaded, trying to ignore the interruption and to keep his focus only on the baron.

He went to go closer to the man, until the others put their hands on the hilt of their swords. He halted, looking at the man beseechingly, willing the baron to believe that he spoke the truth. "He said that kidnapping your betrothed was a Welsh custom."

"What kind of nonsense is this you're talking, man?" Morgan said suspiciously. "You do not look to be a simpleton."

"Did my daughter appear pleased to be with that piece of dung?" the baron demanded. "Was her behavior not a sign? Was not mine?"

Bryce gazed steadily at the baron, his hands twisting in their bindings. He would have gone on his knees to beg, if he thought that would help. "It's the truth, whether you believe me or not. But that doesn't matter. We have to get her out of there, at once!"

"I know that better than you, man," the baron growled.

"We must get her away from him *today*."

"Why today? He said he would give her a month."

"He knows now she will never marry him willingly. That is why he will not wait. He sent me here to fetch a priest to bless their marriage."

"Never!" Dylan lunged forward, but Griffydd held him back.

"Listen to me!" Bryce bellowed, ignoring the binding tearing into his wrists. "I am to return today, before the sun sets, with a priest. I was to tell you that Cynvelin regrets he cannot invite you to the feast. He also said it had been *caru yn y gwely.*"

At Bryce's attempt at the Welsh words, the baron jumped to his feet, an expression of such rage on his face, Bryce stumbled back, certain that he was about to die.

Dylan grabbed the hilt of his weapon, Griffydd stood motionless and Hu Morgan looked ill.

"What does that mean?" Fitzroy asked, his voice an oasis of calm in the tense room.

The baron looked at his friend and it was as if all the energy had been momentarily drained from him. "Courting on the bed. He's raped her."

At the confirmation of his fears, Bryce's hands curled into fists, impotent though they were behind his back. "I'll slit his throat!" he vowed. "Come! We have to go—now!"

"Without a plan?" Fitzroy said, the tranquility of his voice striking Bryce like a slap.

He stared at the older man, aghast. Did he feel nothing for Rhiannon's plight?

Then he got a good look at his fellow Norman's eyes.

Fitzroy would kill Cynvelin, too, given a chance, and not quickly, either.

Bryce fought to regain his composure, realizing that anger and hate would not help them outwit Cynvelin. He took a deep breath and once more addressed the baron. "I thought that if one of your men could dress as a priest, my lord, I would return with him. You and your men would have to follow under cover of the trees, for Cynvelin mustn't suspect anything. As soon as I could, I would get to your daughter and get her away from Cynvelin.

"Once she was with me, I would have my garrison open the gates of Annedd Bach to you. I would have tried to save her without your help, but my men would be no match for Cynvelin's guard. We will need your men to overpower them."

The baron regarded him steadily, his gaze never wavering. "You expect me to trust you with my daughter's life?"

"You must. I swear to you by our Savior and His Holy Mother, my lord, I will get her back to you."

The baron glanced at his eldest son. "Well, Griffydd?"

"I believe him, Father," Griffydd replied softly.

Fitzroy nodded. "I think his words have the ring of truth."

The baron turned to Hu Morgan on his left.

"Aye, my lord, I am agreeing with them," the Welshman said. "I, for one, can guess how easy it might be to convince a Norman that something is a strange and foreign practice. My own sweet wife thought the Welsh barbarians when we wed."

"And I, who know Cynvelin, know how capable he is of swaying a man with his honeyed tongue," the baron added.

"It's a trap of some kind, I tell you!" Dylan snarled. "Probably Cynvelin wants us to attack, then he will claim it is our fault if he hurts Rhiannon. For all we know, she could be dead already!"

"Shut your mouth, Dylan!" Griffydd snapped. "She's not dead, or he would not be wanting a priest."

"She wasn't dead when I left to come here," Bryce said. "I saw her in the window of the keep." He took a deep breath. "I'm sorry, Baron, but if I am not back before sunset, he might kill her. We mustn't waste any more time." He regarded the baron steadily, and intently. "I give you my word, on my honor as a Norman and the son of the Earl of Westborough, that tonight I will get your daughter out of Annedd Bach, if you will allow me that privilege."

"If I do not go with you, what will you do?" the baron asked.

"I would do my best to rescue her myself."

The baron nodded slowly. "Dylan, cut him free.

We will do as you say, Frechette. I put my daughter's life in your hands, and by God, you had better not fail me, or you will rue it.''

''My lord, if I fail, it will be because I am dead.''

Chapter Fourteen

Rhiannon sat on the floor, staring at the closed door, her makeshift weapon clutched in her hand. Every moment, she expected to hear Cynvelin's footsteps on the stairs.

Every sound made her jump with fear, thinking it was Cynvelin at the door, despair beginning to take the place of hope.

The afternoon had stretched in its interminable length ever since she had seen Bryce ride out the gate.

Where he had gone and why, she didn't know. Or when he would return. That he would, she did not doubt, at least not at first.

What if he did not return? What if Cynvelin had given him his freedom, and the only alternative to accepting the offer had been death? It could be that he had ridden away to preserve his life.

Bryce Frechette had forsaken his own family once; might he not abandon a woman who had no claim on him at all? There had been words of apology, a pledge of trust, a final wave—but what was that compared to a threat of death? Was there enough between them to warrant him risking his life for her?

She hoped...but she didn't know. She trusted, then that trust wavered like heat waves on a summer day.

And always, always, increasing her anxiety was the anticipation of a terrible fate at Cynvelin's hands.

Finally, as the sun shone low in the sky, when she was tired, hungry and full of despair, there came the sound of a key in the lock.

She got to her feet as quickly as she could, her body weak from lack of food and water. She used what little energy she had left to push upon the barricade with all her might.

"It's useless, Rhiannon," Cynvelin said from the other side, his voice easily carrying through the door. "I will come in there and you, my poor dear, cannot stop me."

Tears started in her eyes and she gave a great, choking sob, because she knew he was right.

At that same moment, he gave a mighty shove. The door opened and the furniture moved aside so that he could slide into the room.

She hurried to the far wall, snatching up her weapon as she went. Once there, she turned, holding the stake behind her back, and faced him defiantly. "Get out!"

"Ah, my darling!" Cynvelin cried as he straightened his slightly disheveled tunic, "I regret that I must refuse. I simply couldn't stay away any longer. I trust your solitary time has been spent in serious and productive musings. I hope you have concluded that you could do far worse than be my wife." He surveyed the tumbled-down barricade before he kicked the door shut with his foot. "There is quite a mess you've made."

He slowly advanced toward her. She lifted her hand, prepared to strike.

He looked at the wooden weapon and chuckled. "What's that? A toy?"

She shook her head, her expression grimly determined. "I'll use it if you come near me."

"Will you?" he asked calmly. He drew his sword and twisted his wrist so that the flat of the blade was parallel to the floor, the tip pointed at her. "I have a longer reach, my dear. I would put that down, if I were you, before you hurt yourself."

"No!"

He came closer, his blade moving inexorably toward her face. She tried to duck and move away, but she had not the experience of fighting he had, and he moved quickly, halting her when she felt the tip of his sword pressed against her back. She slowly turned to face him.

"Let go of your toy, Rhiannon," he ordered, still with that same calm voice, "or I might have to hurt you, and I really do not want to have to do that."

She didn't obey, even when he took a step closer and placed the end of his sword at her throat. "You are as foolhardy as your father, I fear."

He pushed the blade farther. She felt the stinging pain and the trickle of blood. "I said, let go of your toy!"

He would kill her if she didn't, so she finally submitted, the wooden weapon clattering onto the stone floor.

"That's better," he said, kicking it across the room before sheathing his sword.

Glaring at him, she put her hand to her neck to feel the warm trickle of blood.

"And yesterday you ruined a number of perfectly good undergarments to make a rope. How many?" He smiled slowly, his eyes gleaming in the waning light that shone in through the window. "All you had, perhaps? Do you have a shift on now, beneath that gown?"

Rhiannon pressed back against the wall and said nothing.

Cynvelin sauntered toward her. "Ah, well, what is a shift, more or less?" He reached out and took hold of her chin, hurting her, as she tried to turn her face away. "What am I to do with you?" he mused.

"You could let me go to my father," she managed to answer.

Cynvelin shook his head. "What, and take you away from Bryce Frechette? Oh, but he's gone, isn't he? He's abandoned you to me, my dear. Rode off and left you."

"He'll come back for me."

She saw the flash of surprise in his dark eyes. He let go of her chin, but his body continued to block her escape. "You sound very sure of that."

"I am," she answered.

He moved back, then leaned against the window-sill and watched her as a cat eyes a bird. "Even now, full of hate and looking daggers at me, you are still the most beautiful creature I have ever seen.''

She said nothing, trying not to look at the door that was not locked, lest she draw his attention to it.

''Intelligent, too,'' he continued admiringly. ''What a pair we will make. I knew that from the moment I saw you at Lord Melevoir's.

''And spirited. I must not be forgetting spirited.'' He rubbed his chin thoughtfully. ''As for Bryce, I suppose it is a pity he must die. What has passed between the two of you, I wonder?'' Hostility grew on his face. ''More than I knew, obviously.''

She thought of the one thing in Bryce's favor that might give Cynvelin pause. ''He's Baron De-Guerre's—''

Cynvelin suddenly lunged for her, grabbing her hard by the shoulders. ''I know who he is,'' he snarled. ''And I know how to make it seem as if he simply disappeared, like that shepherd and his family. Whatever else you think of me, Rhiannon, never imply that I am stupid.'' His grip loosened, and he ran his hands down her arms. She trembled with fear and loathing but never took her scornful gaze from his face.

''However, his disappearance may be delayed somewhat, since Frechette seems to have abandoned you and disobeyed me. I sent him for a priest to bless our union.''

''A priest? Better he should hear your confession.''

''For what? Wanting a wife and doing what I must to get her? Shall I confess that I have grown tired of waiting for my nuptial bliss? Surely he will understand that, for he is going to bless our marriage today."

"Today!" she gasped. "You gave my father your word! Does your word count for absolutely nothing, then?"

"You must not believe that," he said, lifting his hand, "or you would not dare to be so impertinent."

She waited for the blow, closing her eyes, but it didn't come. Instead, she felt his breath on her cheek. "Bryce was supposed to return with the priest to bless our union in the eyes of God." He shrugged his shoulders in a gesture of casual resignation. "However, he has not, so we will have to be wed without it. And he has not returned before sunset, as he was supposed to, so I gather he has left you to the better man, Rhiannon. The man who deserves you. The man who wants you. The man who can use you."

She forced herself to stare into Cynvelin's dark, evil eyes. "I will hate you till the day I die," she vowed between clenched teeth.

"Do you think I care?" he growled. Then, surprisingly, he stepped away, running a scornful gaze over her. "You should be grateful I would choose you to be my wife. Instead, you whine and beg to go home like a child, not a woman sought after."

"You don't love me and you never will, any more than I could ever love you after what you have done," Rhiannon answered. "You only want revenge against my father."

Cynvelin glared at her. "Love? What is that?" he

declared disdainfully. "It is a myth. Or perhaps a
story to amuse children. No one has ever loved me."

"Your mother—"

"My mother held me in front of her as a shield,"
he snarled, "so that I would take my father's blows,
not her. Love?" His heartless laugh filled the room.
"If that is love, I do not want or need it."

He put his hands on his hips. "No one ever pitied
or protected me, not even the supposed kind and generous Emryss DeLanyea. He always favored his sons
above all others, and never took the trouble to see
beyond a youth's harmless delinquencies to what
pain might lie beneath.

"So I," he continued, slapping his palm on his
chest, "became strong alone. Now I want a wife to
bear me sons, and I want to make Emryss DeLanyea
pay for what he did to me. That means I marry you,
Rhiannon, with benefit of clergy, or without."

Rhiannon desperately scanned the room, searching
for her sharpened piece of wood.

His voice grew cold again. "Selfishness is the way
of the world, my dear, and you had better learn that.

"Of course, it could be that your bastard father
has taken Bryce. It could even be that your darling
Bryce is dead. I can believe fiery-tempered Dylan
would kill him on sight."

Cynvelin walked toward her, still between her and
the door. His angry eyes glowed with hostility and
savage lust.

She could not see her weapon. All she would have
would be her hands and fingernails if he attacked her.

"Don't look so dismayed, my dear. You do not

see my eyes filling with tears at the possibility of Bryce Frechette's demise.''

"You gave your word you would not hurt me!"

"Alas, my dear," Cynvelin said, "that was only if your father did not interfere. If he did, the bargain is broken."

"Bargain?" she cried incredulously. "What bargain? You kidnapped me! What say did anyone but you have in this?"

Cynvelin halted a pace in front of her. "I wanted you to love me, Rhiannon, but if that is not to be, then I will make you suffer, as your father made me suffer."

"How did he make you suffer? He sent you away, that's all. He told me what you were like when you were in his company. He did what he thought necessary."

Cynvelin's nostrils flared. "So now I will do what I think necessary."

He grabbed her roughly. "You *are* a fool," he said scornfully, "if you think anything I do to you will make up for the way the baron treated me, or is the sum of the punishment I intend to mete out to him."

She flinched as he caressed her cheek. Then his arms snaked around her body and his mouth came crushing down on hers. Desperately she struggled, trying frantically to get away from him and his moist, oppressive lips.

His grip loosened for an instant and she thought she had her chance. She was wrong, for as she turned away, he grabbed the neck of her gown and pulled, tearing the fabric and exposing her bare back.

"Let me go!" she cried, stumbling away from him, clutching at her torn garment as she tried to run to the door.

His blow hit her hard across her shoulder and she fell to her knees. He came to stand over her, a triumphant smile on his face.

She peered up at him through her disheveled hair. "Now you are like your father," she said contemptuously.

Surprised, Cynvelin stepped back. Then understanding came to his eyes, and he smiled with genuine, disturbing happiness. "Yes, I am."

She scrambled to her feet and attempted to get past him. With a roar like a wild animal, he pulled her down hard, then climbed on top of her so that she lay prone on the stone floor beneath him. She tried to twist away, but he was too heavy.

"You are not getting away from me, Rhiannon," he snarled. "I have been tolerant too long. If you do not want to look at me, then I will have you this way."

As he tugged her skirt upward, she screamed a name, a plea, a hope of deliverance.

"Bryce!"

While they waited for the guards to open the gate of Annedd Bach, Bryce glanced first at the setting sun, then at Urien Fitzroy, now attired in a priest's robes with the hood pulled over his head.

Bryce felt a moment's doubt. As much as he was

pleased to have such a notable warrior at his side, it might have been better to have asked one of the genuine priests of St. David to come with them. Fitzroy was mounted on one of the priests' nags, but he sat on his horse like the experienced soldier he was. Madoc and the others might realize something was amiss.

When the gates swung open enough to let them enter, Bryce felt a surge of relief, for one of the lesser men of Cynvelin's guard stood inside. He gave Bryce a smirking smile and waved them in. Once past the gatehouse, Bryce and Fitzroy dismounted while the rest of the garrison entered.

Bryce went to the soldier at the gate, Fitzroy silently following. "Is Cynvelin in the hall?"

The fellow didn't respond, because he was giving Fitzroy a very long and quizzical look.

"Where is Lord Cynvelin?" Bryce demanded, drawing the man's attention.

The soldier shrugged.

Suddenly he heard a woman scream his name.

His gaze flashed to the keep from whence it came. The plan fled his mind.

He forgot about Fitzroy. He forgot about the garrison and the baron's men waiting in the woods outside Annedd Bach.

All he thought about was Rhiannon as he drew the sword the baron had given him and ran toward the keep.

Behind him, pandemonium erupted, but he scarcely heard the noise.

He barged into the keep, took the stairs two at a

time, and with his left hand pulled out the long dagger Fitzroy had provided. Once at the upper level, he kicked open the door of the bedchamber, shoving aside broken furniture and coming to a halt, staring in horror at the sight that met his eyes.

Rhiannon lay on the floor, her legs splayed, with Cynvelin on top of her.

She groaned and raised her tear-streaked, bruised face.

Not dead. Thank God, not dead.

Cynvelin scrambled to his feet, fumbling with the laces of his breeches, glancing at his sword belt lying on the floor close by.

"Beast!" Bryce snarled. He wanted nothing more than to attack, yet he was aware that Cynvelin might strike at Rhiannon first like the coward he was.

She reached out toward him beseechingly, her fingernails torn and bleeding from clawing at the floor, and she whispered his name.

Like a blessing of forgiveness.

Of love.

Resolve whipped through him, galvanizing his mind and heart and body into one determined being who must and would save the woman he loved.

Keeping his gaze on his abhorred enemy, his hot blood pounding in his veins, he took Rhiannon's outstretched hand and helped her to her feet. With her other hand she held together what remained of her dress.

"Go, my lady," he implored as he pushed her behind him, "and leave this carrion to me."

Suddenly Cynvelin grabbed for his sword belt,

pulling out his weapon and leaving the sheath behind.

"Go, my lady! Your father is outside the gates," Bryce cried as his enemy began to sway, hunched in a protective stance, prepared to strike, watching them with a mocking smile.

Rhiannon ran to the door, then turned on the threshold.

"Too late again, Frechette," Cynvelin chided. "Always too late."

"No," he heard her whisper behind him. "Not too late to save my honor, and my life."

At her words, Bryce drew himself up and regarded his enemy with proud scorn. "She is coming with me, Cynvelin, but first I am going to kill you for what you have done, and what you tried to do," he announced.

He glanced back at Rhiannon for the briefest of moments. "Go, now, my lady. Your father is at the gates—or perhaps already inside, to judge by the noise below."

Rhiannon had been too concerned with what was happening before her eyes to hear much else, but yes, she could hear the sounds of battle. The knowledge that her father was below tempted Rhiannon to flee the keep, and yet she would not go, not without Bryce at her side.

"That is why I went on your little errand," Bryce said to Cynvelin, "with another purpose quite my own."

She had not been wrong to trust him! He had gone to fetch her father and returned to rescue her.

"You're lying," Cynvelin declared. "He wouldn't risk her safety by disobeying my orders."

Clutching her torn bodice, Rhiannon watched the two men as they circled each other warily in the dim light. A glance at the window confirmed that soon it would be too dark to see.

"You think you can command a man like that?" Bryce retorted.

"I shall have to send condolences to the Baron DeGuerre and his charming wife, your sister, after I kill you," Cynvelin jeered.

"Isn't it a pity there will be no one who mourns your death," Bryce retorted.

Suddenly Cynvelin lunged. Rhiannon cried a warning even as Bryce twisted to avoid the blow. It was only a feint and Cynvelin kicked out, striking Bryce in the arm.

Rhiannon heard a sickening sound as the sword fell from Bryce's hand and skittered across the floor.

Bryce grimaced in pain but still held on to his long dagger as he regained his balance. "I might have known you would use your feet," he panted.

Cynvelin glanced at the horrified Rhiannon. "Staying to find out once and for all who is the better man, my dear?" He faced Bryce again. "Your arm is broken. Lay down your weapon. It is finished."

If only the sword had fallen closer to her! Rhiannon thought with dismay. But it was across the room.

Then she spotted her sharpened wooden stake, lying beneath part of the broken bed.

Bryce, too, looked her way. "Go, Rhiannon!"

He was in agony from his broken arm and could

feel the broken ends of bone rubbing together. Despite his pain, he had to keep Cynvelin's attention, because Rhiannon had not gone. She had dropped to her knees and was trying to get at something under the bed. His sword? No, it was on the other side of the room.

"I brought the baron with me," he said, "and he's not alone."

Cynvelin crouched again, ready to strike. "Do you think I'm afraid of him, or his sons or that bastard Dylan?"

"He's got Urien Fitzroy and Hu Morgan with him, too."

"Both?" Cynvelin gasped, his eyes narrowing. "You're a lying villain!"

"I'm looking at the lying villain," Bryce said, moving closer.

With his sword, Cynvelin had the advantage, but there were ways to parry the movement of the longer weapon with a dagger.

Suddenly Rhiannon got to her feet. Before Bryce could see what she held in her hand, she ran and struck at Cynvelin.

The Welshman shouted, spinning around as she jumped back. He lifted his sword to attack her.

In an instant Bryce had his broken arm around the man's throat, crying out in agony himself as he stabbed him. With a strangled cry, Cynvelin struggled in Bryce's grasp, trying to wrench himself free as Bryce jerked the dagger blade upward, past a piece of wood protruding from Cynvelin's side.

Then Bryce had to let go, for his arm felt as if it

were being torn in two. Cynvelin fell to his knees, his breathing hoarse as he dropped his sword and struggled uselessly, trying to reach the weapon in his back.

Rhiannon threw herself into Bryce's arms. He held tight to her with his good arm, never wanting to let her go.

Then he saw Cynvelin turning toward them, still on his knees. Fearing that his opponent was deadly yet and keeping his gaze on him, Bryce retreated toward the door, taking Rhiannon with him.

Blood seeped from Cynvelin's mouth as he tried to smile one more time. Then he fell forward, and died.

"We must not linger here," Bryce muttered. He grabbed a blanket from the floor and wrapped it about her. "Come."

She put her hand to his chest and he paused. "Listen!" she whispered.

There was no sound from the courtyard below.

Madoc and the men of Cynvelin's guard had put up a good fight, to no avail. The Welshmen of the garrison they had arrogantly dismissed as poor fighters and fools were better trained than they expected, and then there were the strangers, other soldiers not a one of them recognized.

"I'm getting out of this," Madoc panted to the injured Twedwr as they stood near the portcullis. "He don't pay good enough to die for."

Twedwr nodded and the two men ran to the gate, only to halt and stand openmouthed as a commanding figure strode toward them, his cloak swirling around his ankles, his bloody sword in his hand.

"I would be laying down my weapons, men, if I were in your boots," the stranger called out, his deep, commanding tones ringing against the stone walls.

And a scowling smile twisting his one-eyed visage.

"Baron DeLanyea!" Madoc gasped.

The name seemed to be whispered on the wind, and suddenly all was silent as the fighting ceased.

Madoc threw aside his sword. "Mercy, my lord!" he cried, kneeling. "Honorable soldiers we are, and willing to die for Wales!"

Twedwr followed his friend's lead, as did the rest of Cynvelin's guard, suddenly comprehending to whom these other soldiers must belong.

The baron cast a scornful look over Madoc and the rest of the guard. "A sad day for Wales it will be when we need men like you to defend it," he muttered, marching to the center of the courtyard. "Where is my daughter?" he called out.

"Father!"

The baron stared as Rhiannon, clutching a blanket around her, ran out of the building. With a gasp of jubilation and relief, he opened wide his arms and took his sobbing daughter into his embrace.

"Thank God," he whispered fervently. "Thank God!"

Chapter Fifteen

Bryce waited in the shadow of the keep's entrance, holding his broken arm, watching the reunion of Lady Rhiannon and her noble father.

Now that she was safe and Cynvelin dead, he felt...light. Or empty, all the joy and triumph suddenly overwhelmed by the realization of his culpability in her torment.

What did it matter if he had been lied to? He should have listened to her from the first. What was his potential knighthood compared to her distress?

Now, his part in her rescue seemed not nearly enough to compensate for all her suffering, and although she had looked at him as her savior, would that be enough to excuse everything that had gone before?

Griffydd, Fitzroy and Morgan went toward the baron, as did Dylan, still clutching his sword as if anticipating more fighting.

Bryce did not belong there, with them. He didn't belong anywhere.

"Where is Cynvelin?" the baron asked.

Bryce took a deep breath and left the shadows, marching toward the knot of men. And Rhiannon, who still embraced her father.

"Dead in the keep," Bryce replied flatly.

The baron nodded his acknowledgment. "Then let us leave this place."

"What of these others?" Dylan demanded, gesturing at Madoc and his fellows.

"Their fate will be decided later," he replied coldly. "For now, put them in their barracks and post a guard."

The baron looked lovingly at his daughter, who still held to him tightly. "Come, Rhiannon."

With his arm protectively around her, they walked slowly toward the gate.

Dylan sheathed his sword, albeit with a disappointed sigh, and joined Fitzroy and Morgan as they followed the baron.

Bryce stood motionless. She had not even looked at him.

He would not follow. He had no right to go with them. He had no right to expect her to think of him as anything but a man who had justly righted his own mistake.

She owed him nothing, not even a kind word.

"Your men are a credit to you."

Bryce started. He had not noticed Griffydd De-Lanyea, who had come to stand beside him. "The holy brothers will be able to tend to your wound. Leave one of your men in charge and come with us to the monastery."

Bryce knew he couldn't leave his arm untended, or it would never heal properly, and might worsen.

There was another, more powerful inducement to go to the monastery and one that he couldn't deny. He would be near Rhiannon at least a little while, before they parted ways forever.

Therefore, he nodded his acceptance and searched out Ermin, standing with the rest of the garrison. He gestured for the slender Welshman to come to him.

Ermin ran forward eagerly. "My lord?"

Bryce ignored the use of a title he didn't have. "I'm leaving you in command."

Ermin touched his forelock. "We'll keep those fellows as confined as novices in a convent, my lord! Off to the monastery, you, to see to your arm? Good is that. We'll get everything ready for your return."

Return? Bryce thought as he walked toward the gate with Griffydd. He would never come back, except to get his sword and what few belongings he had. He wanted nothing more to do with Annedd Bach, just as he feared Rhiannon would want nothing more to do with him.

The next afternoon, Bryce sat upon a stool in a tent pitched by the baron's men outside the monastery of St. David.

His arm had been set, with much cursing on Bryce's part and much thin-lipped disapproval on that of the infirmarer. Another holy brother who escorted him here said the tent belonged to the baron's son, Griffydd, but Bryce was to use it in his stead while the baron and his party remained at the monastery.

Apparently Griffydd DeLanyea emulated the Spartans, as far as luxuries went. The only furnishings in the tent were a cot and stool.

Bryce didn't mind the lack of trappings. He had no desire for material things, or honor, or titles. Not anymore. Not if he couldn't have Rhiannon's love.

He had not seen or heard from her since they had left Annedd Bach, which shouldn't surprise him.

A rather nervous novice suddenly stuck his head in the tent. "Excuse me, sir?"

"Yes?"

"The baron wishes to see you as soon as it is convenient."

"I might as well go now," Bryce replied, rising, for he certainly had nothing else to do except collect his belongings at Annedd Bach.

He followed the young man in the long, black robe toward the imposing walls of the monastery and through the gate. As he continued toward a large stone edifice, he scanned the yard, walks and garden for Rhiannon, but she was not there.

Soon they reached the common room, and the holy brother left him at the door, departing with obvious relief.

No doubt the sight of the imposing men sitting inside the room explained that, for Dylan DeLanyea, Fitzroy and Morgan sat on either side of the baron like a group of stern and noble judges.

"Frechette, welcome," the baron said as Bryce entered and approached.

"Baron." Bryce made his obeisance.

"We have a slight problem that requires your assistance," the baron began.

"As much as I would enjoy being of help to you, Baron, first I would like to know how Lady Rhiannon fares," Bryce said, thinking that a not unreasonable request, and he would be better able to think when he knew the answer.

The baron glanced at the men beside him as if he had expected Bryce to say something of that nature. "She is well, thanks to you."

"I did no more than any honorable man should, my lord, and unfortunately, at the start, very much less."

"She is disposed to forgive any part you played in that terrible business."

"She is a generous woman, my lord, and a credit to you."

"She seems to think you would be a credit to me."

Bryce's brow furrowed with puzzlement. "How so, my lord?"

"Well, Frechette, since I was Cynvelin's overlord, it falls to me to—"

"You couldn't be," Bryce interrupted, completely taken aback by his words. "Cynvelin would have said…"

He fell silent and reddened when he saw the baron's expression change, and not for the better.

"Forgive my interruption, my lord," Bryce said. "I should know that Cynvelin was less than forthcoming about many things."

"Indeed."

"That is why he came to Craig Fawr in the first place. That is why he was upset when I sent him away, for he knew he would get nothing more from me. I should have stripped him of his land and titles myself when I knew what he was, but I thought that would make him more dangerous, leaving him to roam about the countryside like a ravining wolf. It appears we all underestimated Cynvelin's capacity for evil."

"What of Cynvelin's men?" Bryce asked.

"We hanged the whole murdering lot of them this morning," Dylan announced.

Bryce regarded the baron's grim face. The older man sighed heavily. "Even without their leader, mad dogs cannot be left to roam free, as I have been made to learn."

"Yes, my lord," Bryce agreed. It seemed a harsh judgment, but he knew what kind of men Cynvelin's guards had been, and the baron was right. If he let them go, they would only rape and murder and steal again.

"Now let us speak of more pleasant matters. I wish to give you a reward for your assistance in the rescue of my daughter."

"You do not have to reward me, Baron," Bryce protested immediately. "Indeed, I do not deserve it."

A low, deep chuckle emanated from the baron's chest. "Your humility does you credit, Frechette. I was thinking a title and small estate, say, on the order of Annedd Bach, would be most appropriate, if you will swear fealty to me."

A thrill of excitement ran through Bryce, but one not nearly as great as it might have been, under almost any other circumstances.

"I can understand your hesitation, Frechette," the baron said. "You know little of me, and after making one mistake with such a serious business, you are not anxious to repeat it. I, too, would probably be wise to make my offer conditional until I know more of you.

"So what I propose is this. I shall leave Griffydd and Dylan in temporary charge of Annedd Bach, and you will journey with us to Craig Fawr. If by the end of the journey we are both pleased with the idea of an alliance, I shall knight you and bestow Annedd Bach upon you."

Bryce glanced at the others, who didn't appear at all surprised by the baron's words, so clearly he had already broached the plan with them. None of these men looked upset or angry, either, so they must approve of this arrangement—and him, too, perhaps.

"My lord, as grateful as I am for your offer of a knighthood and estate, I—" he began contritely.

"Frechette," the baron interrupted, his stern voice containing a hint of regret, "I trusted you when my daughter's life was in the balance. You made a mistake. I have made mistakes. So have all here. We will not dwell on them, but begin anew, from today."

"Aye. Dwelling on past mistakes is for wives to do," Morgan said with a straight face but merry eyes.

"As you're sure to find out eventually," Fitzroy agreed, one corner of his mouth lifting in what was almost a smile.

A knighthood and an estate…things Cynvelin had promised, too.

Bryce thought of his first days at Annedd Bach and all that had happened after. To be sure, as he had come to learn more of his men, he had grown to like it more, but the memories of Cynvelin would always be there. "My lord," he said slowly, "the knighthood I will consider accepting, but not Annedd Bach."

Baron DeLanyea looked rather taken aback. "You will *consider* accepting?" His brow lowered ominously. "I would know why my generosity is to be so summarily refused."

"I would like to try to forget what happened here," Bryce answered. And surely Rhiannon will feel the same, he added silently, with despair.

"I see," the baron replied, his gaze searching Bryce's face in such a way that the younger man felt the true reason must be as plain as if carved on his forehead. Understanding dawned on the baron's scarred visage.

Bryce blushed, yet said no more.

"I respect your feelings, yet I would caution you against making any impetuous decisions," the baron remarked.

"Aye," Morgan said gravely. "The baron never acts hastily, does he, men?"

Baron DeLanyea shot his companion a look. "I would not be criticizing if I were you, Hu," he muttered. Then he turned back to Bryce. "Do not give me a final answer now. Wait until we reach Craig Fawr."

"Very well, my lord," Bryce replied. Nevertheless, he was convinced that once he left Annedd Bach, he would never set foot there again.

Just as once he bade farewell to Rhiannon, he would never see her again, either.

He tried to put that distressing thought from his mind.

"So, Bryce Frechette, you will come with us to Craig Fawr." The baron spoke in such a way that this was more a command than a request. Then he grinned. "I'm sure your agreement to accompany us will please my daughter."

"It will?" Bryce cleared his throat, knowing he had sounded like an eager child, and yet he thrilled to hear those words. "I shall be pleased to go with you, Baron DeLanyea."

The baron suddenly looked more like a mischievous boy than a mighty warrior. "I am glad you agreed, or my daughter would be having my hide for boot leather."

Bryce returned his grin, delighted to know that Rhiannon cared what happened to him.

As she would for anyone who had helped her in such a situation.

If only he could speak with her!

The men rose.

"Since everything is settled here," Morgan declared, "it is time Fitzroy and I got home to our wives."

"This latest crop of lads I've got will have to be retrained if I linger here any longer," Fitzroy remarked. "Except for a certain young DeLanyea, they are nearly as clumsy and stupid as Morgan here was.''

"Liar!" Morgan cried. "And you never had the training of me."

"No, but I should have."

"Insulting me now, are you?" the baron demanded. "Well trained he is, and no mistake."

"If you are all going to start bickering," Dylan said, "I'm off to Annedd Bach."

The baron chuckled, and Bryce thought it would be a wonderful thing to have such camaraderie in his own life.

The baron and Morgan clasped hands. "Thank you for your help, Hu."

Morgan smiled, but there was a solemnity in his expression. "You know you have but to ask, and I will always come, Emryss."

The baron nodded, then turned to Fitzroy. "Thank you, too, Urien."

Fitzroy gave one brief nod of acknowledgment.

"Baron?" Bryce asked, trying not to sound too desperate, but fearful that if he did not ask now, he would lose the opportunity. "Will you allow me to speak with your daughter today?"

"I would allow it, Frechette," the baron replied kindly, "but I thought it best to wait for her to ask to speak with you."

"She has not?"

The baron smiled. "Don't be looking like that, Frechette," he said. "She will soon, I'm sure."

Bryce sighed with relief, then wondered if he should betray even that much of his feelings in front of the other men. He made what he hoped was a noncommittal grunt.

Dylan muttered something in Welsh that caused Morgan and the baron to smile, although the older man tried to look serious.

Fitzroy gave Bryce a sidelong glance, then said, "Sometimes we Normans have to stick together. Dylan, tell us what you said that was so amusing."

"He said Normans are fast to fight and slow in everything else," Morgan replied, winking at Fitzroy and Bryce.

"Normans are quick to take offense, and cautious when we should be," Fitzroy retorted.

"Now, now, boys!" the baron said placatingly, his words obviously intended to apply to all of them. "Leave Frechette to manage affairs of the heart in his own way. It is enough he will go north with us."

Bryce stared in wide-eyed wonderment at this apparent endorsement as the baron swept out of the room, followed by Morgan and Fitzroy. Dylan sauntered to the door, paused on the threshold and turned back to run a scrutinizing gaze over Bryce before he grinned. "Flies going to get in your mouth, Frechette," he said before continuing on his way.

The voices of the holy brothers raised in worship began to waft through the monastery, their chants like a soothing balm.

Except that Rhiannon could not be soothed. She paced the floor of her small cell in the guest quarters of the monastery impatiently, twisting the sleeve of her gown and chewing her lip. She knew her father had summoned Bryce Frechette to meet with him. She knew what her father was going to ask.

Unfortunately, she had been too unsure of what Bryce might answer to be a party to their meeting.

After what she had involved him in, a refusal would be a not-unexpected response. Her inappropriate behavior had caused Cynvelin to believe he could abduct her without serious repercussions, and because of that, Bryce Frechette had been party to an act that had now caused him great shame.

She knew how keenly that would disturb him, for he was an honorable man. She could believe he might refuse everything her father offered and leave.

Nor had he asked to see her since they had come to the monastery. Considering what she and Bryce had been through, he should know she would be happy to see him. Indeed, she would be more than happy.

Because she loved him.

After her rescue, when she had gone with her father to the monastery, it had occurred to her that perhaps her feelings for Bryce owed more to her situation and hope for his help than any deep emotion.

It had not taken much time to dispel that notion.

At first, at Lord Melevoir's, he had intrigued her with his combination of reticence and revelation.

Her admiration had grown as she saw what a good leader he was, justly respected by his men.

If they could forget Cynvelin and his evil scheme…if Bryce would come to her and give her cause to hope…if he would consider her for his wife…

The knock at her door made her jump and she hurried to open it, her heart seeming to beat in her throat.

Her father—not Bryce—stood on the threshold, a somewhat wary expression on his face.

"Is he coming?" she asked eagerly.

"What would you do if he refused?"

For the briefest of moments, she felt a pain so acute she thought she must be dying. Then she caught a certain look in her father's eye that replaced the pain with an almost equal thrill.

"He said he would!" she cried excitedly, embracing him. "Thank you! Thank you for asking him! You will not be disappointed!" she said, gazing earnestly at her father's face. "I assure you, he is a fine, trustworthy man!"

"He seems to be."

"He is among the best of men," Rhiannon declared.

Her father raised his eyebrow slightly. "Very sure of that you sound."

"I am. You will reward him, won't you?"

Her father smiled ruefully. "If he will take anything from me at all."

"He must! He deserves it."

"He is a proud man, Rhiannon, and sometimes proud men are not willing to be given things. Ask Fitzroy and Morgan if you doubt me."

"Bryce has earned any reward we could give him."

"I am thinking that there is only one reward that man wants," her father murmured.

"Then he must have it. Will you give it to him?"

Emryss DeLanyea did not reply, because he did not know what he would do if Bryce Frechette asked for the reward the baron suspected he wanted above all others. "You haven't asked to speak with him," he noted.

"No," she admitted. "I would not be so brazen."

"You think he should come to you first?"

"Don't you?"

"After what happened, it would take a bold, impatient man to demand to see a woman he helped abduct. An honorable man might be less assured of his welcome, and so wait for a summons."

Rhiannon stared at her father. "You think I should send for him?"

"I fear Bryce Frechette is so honorable and so unsure of his own worth, he won't do anything unless you first make certain he understands how you feel, if I am any judge of men."

Rhiannon looked at her father with somewhat amazed awareness.

"I should point out that if you prefer to wait some time yet, it will make for an awkward journey for the both of you."

"What should I do?"

Her father regarded her steadily. "Do you love this man?"

Although the bluntness of his question took her aback, she had no hesitation in answering. "Yes!"

"You think he loves you?"

"I...I don't know," she confessed. Then she lifted

her chin and straightened her shoulders. "I hope he does."

"You want him for your husband?"

"More than anything!" She eyed her father. "You would give your permission for us to marry if he asked, wouldn't you, Father?"

"I shouldn't admit it, but I would probably give you permission to marry a hunchbacked troll if that would make you happy. Fortunately, Bryce Frechette is not a hunchbacked troll."

Rhiannon busked him heartily on the cheek. "You are the best of fathers!"

"Well, my darling daughter," the baron said, smiling at her, "I think first you should find out if Bryce Frechette wants you for his wife."

"I will!" she cried, hurrying past her father. "At once!"

"Rhiannon! You should not—" he began, trying to tell her she should not be rushing off to Bryce Frechette. He was to wait for her summons.

But he was too late to stop his impetuous, spirited daughter.

By the time he got to the door, his daughter's skirt was already disappearing around the corner. He sighed softly. "What will your mother say?" he muttered wryly. "That you are your father's daughter, right enough."

Then he remembered his daughter's face when she spoke of Bryce Frechette, and smiled.

"Bryce?" Rhiannon whispered as she pulled back the tent flap and cautiously entered.

A hand reached out and tugged her farther inside. "Rhiannon!" Bryce said softly, grimacing at the pain in his broken arm the effort afforded him and fighting the urge to embrace her. "What are you doing here?"

She cocked her head to look up at him, blushing in a way that charmed him completely.

"Would you rather I went away?" she asked hesitantly. "I thought you might want to see me, but if you would rather not..."

"Of course I want to see you...if you want to see me, after what I did."

Her beautiful, luminous eyes widened. "You saved my honor and my life."

He stepped back, holding his arm, suddenly hopeful and yet still unsure. "My lady, as pleased as I am to see you—"

"Are you? Are you pleased?"

He had to smile. "Very much. Very, very much, my lady."

"Why?" she asked bluntly.

He swallowed hard, his longing and his doubt making it difficult for him to speak. "Because I was afraid you would never want to see me again, once you were safe."

"But I am safe because of you. Naturally I would want to see you, and thank you."

"Ah. To thank me," he said softly, turning away.

His manner emboldened her, and indeed, her delight made her mischievous. "My father said you are coming north with us. Is that so that you can collect your reward?"

"Perhaps," he muttered.

"Do you not think you deserve a reward?"

He faced her again, and she saw how serious he was. "No, I don't. I only corrected my mistake. One of many," he finished bitterly.

She could not help reaching out to stroke his stubbled cheek, rough beneath her fingertips. "If you leave us at Craig Fawr, where will you go?"

His strong hand covered hers. "I do not know, my lady. Maybe to my sister and her husband. Or north. Or back to Europe."

As he caressed her hand and held it to his cheek, as he looked at her with his intense, searching gaze, as she remembered so well his kiss that other time, it seemed as if everything—her heart, her breathing, the seasons—stopped.

"Please forgive me," he whispered. "I would have done better to listen to my own heart, not Cynvelin's fine words, for then I would have refused to have anything to do with a man who said he was marrying you."

She was sorry she had been so flippant. "Bryce, you saved me. But I did not come here to thank you, or see that you get a reward. I came..."

She hesitated, suddenly shy to put her feelings into words in the face of his intense gaze. But this was not the time to dissemble. "I came because I wanted to tell you how I feel about you. I admire you. I respect you." Her voice dropped to an intimate whisper. "I love you."

He stared at her. "What?"

"I love you," she repeated.

She turned her head and pressed a kiss to the rough palm of his hand, in gratitude and trust. She heard him suck in his breath and felt him move closer.

When he bent down and kissed her, tentatively and with gentleness, she did not withdraw. Indeed, overwhelmed with gratification that he had not left her to her fate at Cynvelin's hands, she responded with thankfulness and with joy.

And with fervent, passionate desire.

Bryce's embrace tightened, and it was as if his body kindled heat and hunger and longing within Rhiannon's.

When his tongue flicked against her lips, she instinctively opened her mouth. New sensations flooded through her as his tongue touched hers. She felt his fingers in her hair, stroking her, and pressed her hands against his muscular back.

He stopped all too soon. "You love me?"

"Yes. Do you—?"

He had his arm around her before she could finish. "I love you with all my heart, Rhiannon," he whispered huskily, his lips on her cheek.

She had never felt so happy in her whole life and embraced him, until his pained gasp reminded her of his arm. She shifted slightly. "I'm sorry."

He laughed softly. "I don't care if you break it again." He looked into her eyes. "I think I loved you from that first night in Lord Melevoir's castle, when you thought I was a thief. You were so foolishly fearless."

"And you were so rude! But I deserved it. I wish

someone had told me sooner how my behavior looked to others.''

"That was nothing compared to what I did.''

"What? What did you do? You were tricked by an evil man. So were we all. You came back to save me, when you could have ridden away. So let us forget that, and Cynvelin, too.'' She gazed up at him half shy, half bold. "Do you want to marry me?''

"Of course I do!'' He grew suddenly grave. "But I have nothing—''

"You will have a title and an estate.''

He frowned and moved away. "Annedd Bach. Even though your father offered it to me, I thought...'' He hesitated, searching for the words. "I would refuse it because of what happened there.''

Rhiannon went to him and ran her hand up his arm. "It is not the buildings that are evil. It was Cynvelin. I would be pleased to be the lady of Annedd Bach, if you are the lord.''

Bryce could ask for nothing more. Nevertheless, after all that had passed, he felt duty-bound to say, "Are you certain, Rhiannon? Could you be happy there?''

"Have you now grown circumspect, sir?'' she asked, a playful smile on her lips that gave him even better confirmation of her feelings. "Of course I could be happy there with you.''

Slowly, inwardly cursing his injury, for he wanted nothing more than to hug her tightly, he put his arm about her and drew her close again. Her arms went around his waist and she lifted her face, looking at him with love glowing in her vibrant green eyes.

He kissed her with all the pent-up passion he had been trying to subdue for so long. Joyfully he felt her relax in his arms, the sensation nearly as wonderful as the growing tension within his body. Her hands crept up his back to grab his shoulders, even as his unbandaged hand lowered to caress her buttocks. He couldn't help pressing her closer to him, to let her feel the arousal her kisses caused.

Her lips left his mouth, and he was bereft until he felt her breath warm against chest.

He swallowed hard and told himself it was a good thing she had stopped, so that he could regain his rapidly diminishing control. "We should cease before we go too far. We should wait for our wedding night."

"That is a Norman talking," she whispered. She pulled away to look up at him with a seductive smile, then moved her hand to boldly caress him. "We are not in England now, you see. You are in Wales, and here we have a custom."

"Another custom?" he replied as well as he could, for her continued movements were nearly driving him mad.

"Caru yn y gwely."

He had heard that before. "I would never dishonor you," he said, shocked by her implication.

She looked equally surprised. "How did you hear of it?"

"Cynvelin told me to say to your father that you and he—"

She cursed softly in Welsh. "He would." She gave him a disarming smile. "There is no dishonor in it if the woman agrees. Courting on the bed it is, and no shame to the Welsh.''

Bryce sighed with both relief and returning desire. Rhiannon whispered, ''Do you want to court me on the bed?''

For an answer, he sat on the cot and reached out to pull her down beside him. ''Is this what you mean?'' he asked softly, kissing her lightly.

She shook her head. ''No. This is sitting on the bed.'' She put her hands on his shoulders and slowly pushed him down. ''This is the beginning,'' she said gravely before kissing him feather-lightly on the chin, then each cheek.

''So far, it's very interesting,'' he whispered huskily, then his eyes widened and he nearly choked when she maneuvered her body over his. ''What...what are you doing?''

''Courting you,'' she replied, a mischievous twinkle in her merry eyes. She glanced at the side of the cot. ''I hope this doesn't tip.''

''Courting?'' he asked, his voice slightly strained. ''It seems rather more than that.''

''Would you like me to stop?''

''No...yes...shouldn't I be doing the courting?''

''Oh, but I am a bold creature with no shame, remember?'' Her hands began to caress his chest, then moved lower, as if on a treasure hunt.

''I hope you can forget I ever implied such a thing,'' he said, trying to maintain some semblance of control, wondering where this was leading and yet afraid to say too much in case she stopped. ''If this were anyone but you, I might think this was another trick." He gave her a sidelong look, even as his own hand began to make some tentative explorations of their own. "It isn't, is it?"

"I assure you, Bryce Frechette, this is a very time-honored custom."

He drew in his breath sharply.

She stopped and looked at him. "Am I hurting you?"

"Yes. But only my arm. What would your father say if he knew you were here with me?"

"He is more Welsh than Norman." Rhiannon shifted herself, so that she was sitting on his thighs, the sensation nearly driving him mad with need. "It is not marrying on the bed. Courting, is all. If you change your mind—"

He put his finger lightly over her lips. "There is a Frechette custom, my lady," he whispered.

"What is that?"

"Once we fall in love, we are in love forever."

"That is a DeLanyea custom, too," she replied softly.

"I love you," he said, and sighed as she insinuated her hand inside his tunic and stroked his rising and falling chest. "By heaven, yes," he murmured.

She smiled slowly. "A pity about your arm. You will have to stay lying down, I think."

"For what?"

"Are all Normans as daft as you?" she asked playfully. She proceeded to undo his breeches.

He gasped. Then she raised herself slightly, pulling her skirt and shift upward. "I have died and gone to heaven."

''No, Wales,'' she whispered, as she pushed his tunic up before pressing kisses to his chest.

He brushed his lips across hers. She sighed as he reached up and tried to undo the laces at the back of her gown with one hand.

With a sly and astonishingly seductive smile, she undid them herself, then slowly slipped her bodice lower.

When she bent over him, placing one hand on either side of his shoulders, his tongue flicked her nipples, one, then the other, the new sensation leaving her breathless as she arched against him.

''Gracious heavens, I want you,'' he whispered thickly.

Delighting in his love, she moved so that she felt his hardness beneath her throbbing body. ''Then have me.''

He was achingly aware of his own need, yet he would not hurry this.

He would make this for her gratification, to wipe away whatever stain Cynvelin had put upon her pleasure.

Or so he tried to do.

But she was too marvelous, too arousing in all she did, for him to maintain his self-control. And knowing that she wanted him—that was the greatest thing of all.

So it was that when she raised herself slightly over him, he could not wait. With a low growl, he hurriedly shoved her skirt upward.

A look of sudden panic in her eyes, she put her hand against his chest, and he halted, startled.

He thought of that horrible moment when he had first entered the bedchamber and seen Cynvelin atop her, his hands tangled in her skirt. Perhaps this was not the time, or the place, after all.

Then she smiled tremulously. "Let me."

With her gaze firmly on his face, she lifted her hips and reached down to guide him. "I want you, Bryce," she whispered, leaning over him, one hand ōn either side of his broad shoulders. "And glad I am that you will be the first. Look at me when you take me, and I will look at you. I will see only you, my dearest love."

Obeying her, he continued to look at her face as he slowly pushed in a little, then withdrew. She smiled as he repeated the motion, this time a little farther.

Her eyes closed for a brief instant, then opened. "Again, Bryce," she whispered fervently. "Do it again."

Keeping careful watch on her expression, trying his best to govern the powerful passion throbbing through him, he thrust upward again.

"Oh, Rhiannon," he murmured, biting his lip to try to dominate his desire.

She moved her hips, and he had to fight to keep his eyes open and not close them at the sheer ecstasy she made him feel, for he wasn't sure if she knew what she was doing, or was only trying to ease her position.

Then she did it again, and he realized she was meeting him, showing him her own need. He thrust again, finally fully enveloped by her, the sensation perfect and wonderful. He was caught in her body, transfixed by her intense and passion-filled eyes.

"Faster, Bryce," she whispered urgently, moving again.

He was only too eager to obey. He made love to her hungrily, each motion seeming to meld them more together as they continued to stare into each other's eyes.

Her mouth parted slightly as she began to pant, and he realized he was panting, too. Her lovely skin flushed pink, and her eyes darkened.

He tried to wait and prolong her pleasure. He told himself he would take all night, if need be.

But in another few moments, she arched, her eyes pressed shut as an almost savage cry burst from her lips. She clutched his shoulders and her knees gripped him. And he lost all constraint.

With a primitive growl, he closed his eyes and gave himself over to the exhilaration of release. "I love you," he gasped. "I love you!"

It took him a moment to realize she was saying the same thing. When he did, he started to laugh. She did, too, collapsing against his sweat-slicked chest.

"*Caru yn y gwely,* eh? My love, this is one Welsh custom I can appreciate," he said when he had caught his breath.

After a moment, Rhiannon raised her face and looked at him, her delightfully disheveled hair framing her face as she smiled happily. "I will have to teach you the others, Bryce."

"You have the rest of my life to do it in," he said,

gazing into her lovely eyes, content at last. Redeemed at last. Happy at last.

And she did.

* * * * *

Happy Birthday, Harlequin Historicals!

Now, after a decade of giving you the best in historical romance,
LET US TAKE YOU BACK...

to a time when damsels gave their warriors something to fight for...ladies wooed dashing dukes from behind their fans...and cowgirls lassoed the hearts of rugged ranchers!

With novels from such talented authors as

Suzanne Barclay	Margaret Moore
Cheryl Reavis	Ruth Langan
Deborah Simmons	Cheryl St.John
Susan Spencer Paul	Theresa Michaels
Merline Lovelace	Gayle Wilson

Available at your favorite retail outlet.

HARLEQUIN®
Makes any time special ™

Look us up on-line at: http://www.romance.net   HH10ANN

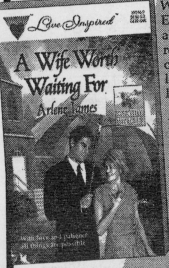

Heat up your summer this July with

Summer Lovers

This July, bestselling authors Barbara Delinsky,
Elizabeth Lowell and Anne Stuart present three
couples with pasts that threaten their future happiness.
Can they play with fire without being burned?

FIRST, BEST AND ONLY
by Barbara Delinsky

GRANITE MAN
by Elizabeth Lowell

CHAIN OF LOVE
by Anne Stuart

Available wherever Harlequin and Silhouette books
are sold.

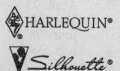

DEBBIE MACOMBER

invites you to the

HEART OF TEXAS

Join Debbie Macomber as she brings you the lives
and loves of the folks in the ranching community
of Promise, Texas.

If you loved Midnight Sons—don't miss
Heart of Texas! A brand-new six-book series
from Debbie Macomber.

Available in February 1998
at your favorite retail store.

Heart of Texas by Debbie Macomber

Lonesome Cowboy	February '98
Texas Two-Step	March '98
Caroline's Child	April '98
Dr. Texas	May '98
Nell's Cowboy	June '98
Lone Star Baby	July '98

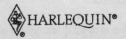

HARLEQUIN®

HPHRT1

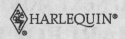

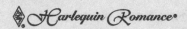

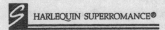